For

Heidi, T
Tom
with my love.

Acknowledgements

I owe a special thank you to my cousin Peter Swaine, who created such a beautiful painting for the cover of the book. I would also like to thank Brenda Hutchings who gave me huge support and encouragement from the beginning to the end; Peter and Kathy Hay for taking such an interest and for the great day out in Exminster; Sylvia Greinig, the present proprietor of Hampton House, for all her help and enthusiasm; Wendy Mewes for proving to me that there was a way forward and an achievable goal; Heidi Freer-Hay for being my first reader and for liking the book; and Harold Mewes for all his help, advice and hard work with the publication. I am indebted to Gill Hoffs, the author of "The Sinking of RMS Tayleur" published by Pen and Sword History in 2014, and H.F. Starkey, the author of "Iron Clipper - 'Tayleur', the White Star Line's First Titanic" published by Avid Publications in 1999. I recommend these to anyone who wants to read more about the wreck of the ship.

About the author:

Fiona Freer has two grown up children and a grandson, and lives with her husband in South Devon and Brittany. This novel is the result of five years of research.

INTRODUCTION

This novel is based on a true story. I spent the last eleven years of my career teaching in Hampton House, a fine Georgian mansion. I was keen to find out who had lived there in the past, and soon discovered that the house had been bought in 1851 by Charles Tayleur. We have forgotten him now, but he had once built locomotives with George and Robert Stephenson at his Vulcan Foundry in Warrington. Isambard Kingdom Brunel placed orders with Vulcan for engines for the Great Western Railway, and Tayleur's foundry at Bank Quay created a massive iron ship which was named RMS Tayleur in his honour. He became enormously rich, but died just a few weeks after the great ship tragically sank on its maiden voyage with huge loss of life.

When I began to research the family I was fascinated by the tumultuous story that emerged. Hampton House was inherited by William Houlbrooke Tayleur, who had recently divorced his wife Emma. William remarried, and it was when I detected some tension between his new wife and his three sons that I became even more interested in their lives. I hope I have treated the members of the family with sympathy and understanding, but I am aware that my treatment of Mary Ellen Tayleur could have been unjust. It is her misfortune that the historian who unearthed her story had an unkind stepmother of her own.

I found the family papers in the local record office and the documents were still tied with Victorian tape and grey with the dust from the clerks' coal fires. No-one had looked at them since the law firm deposited them there and I was shocked to see "IN LUNACY" stamped in red ink on most of them. William had not lived at Hampton House for long before suddenly and dramatically losing his sanity. I felt very sorry for him – even his children referred to him in all correspondence as "the lunatic".

I hope that any historian of the Tayleur family would recognise the facts in the book, but this is a novel and I have developed the characters in my own way and fictionalised events. I do not know if Mary Ellen ever met a group of smugglers in the cellar, but there was apparently a tunnel leading from the clifftop to the kitchen at Hampton which must have been built for smuggling operations. I have taken the liberty of changing some names and sending Charles up to Cambridge rather early. He later claimed in a letter that he had undergone a long sea voyage to New Zealand, and I have changed this into a European tour and sent Albert along with him.

Reading through the family papers I was struck by the fact that some members of the family were silent. Emma Tayleur died just three years after she had been sent back to her family in disgrace. And poor William himself, later hidden away as a shameful secret, was never heard either. I have attempted in this novel to give them all a voice again.

Fiona Freer
August 2015

The Tayleurs

Charles Tayleur (1785-1854) married Jane Hill (1782-1853)

Children of Charles and Jane:

William Houlbrooke (1803-1879) see below.

Mary (b.1804) married Richard Phibbs. Four children.

John (1806-1890) married Eliza Alderson.
One son - John Edward.

Charles (1810-c1854)

Henry Theophilus (1812-1866)

Sarah Jane (b. 1816) married Rev Oliver Omerod.
Eight children.

Edward (1820 - 1891) married Marianne Kenyon. No children.

William Houlbrooke
married 1. Emma Elizabeth Heathcote (1817-1852) Divorced 1851

2. Mary Ellen Knight (1817-1888)

Children of William and Emma:

Charles William (1836-1912) see below.

Cresswell John (b 1838) married Lucy Maria Stowell. No children.

Edward Heathcote (1845-1902) married Susan Grace. Five children.

Albert Gresley (1849-1880) married Ellen Pitfield.

Children of William and Mary Ellen:

Galfred (1854-1947) died unmarried.

Eveline (1855-c1883) married Arthur Sinclair Tower.

William (1856-1870) died of scarlet fever.

Charles William married 1. Mary Jane Preston (1837-1874)

2. Louisa Wolfe (d 1921)

Children of Charles and Mary Jane:

Alexander Charles (Alec) (1865-1935)
married Ethel Therese Brown. One son.

Ada Susannah (1866-1939) married Louis Lees. Three daughters.

Elizabeth Mary (b 1867) married James Frederick Baker.
Four children.

Katherine (1868-1953) married M.H. Graham. One daughter.

Noel (1874-1896) drowned at sea returning from South Africa.

Mary Ellen Tayleur
Hampton House - January 1858

My husband's madness was no creeping, insidious thing, advancing stealthily over years and allowing us to become accustomed to small changes. No – it was sudden, dramatic, violent – a hideous turn of fortune, a body blow that ended our mutual life, an eruption that froze us forever into the grotesque. The work of just a week, my husband turned from a genial host, efficient squire, friendly neighbour and forbearing father and became a lunatic. They have taken him away now, and I am alone with three young children and a handful of servants. He screamed when they manhandled him to the front door, and grasped the door frame in a desperate attempt to cling onto his home and his life. I hear those screeches still; their echoes seep from the walls.

It is just four short years since he inherited this mansion; such horrors were utterly unimaginable then.

I looked into every room that first morning, while my father-in-law still lay on the great mahogany bed in his nightgown and cap, a bandage wrapped round his chin, waiting for the undertakers to arrive. Death can ape the imbecile, but there was never anything slack-jawed about Charles Tayleur. I had spent much of the night sitting by his bed as he struggled to leave, or to stay, I could not be sure which. But now I could survey the property that was ours at last - the stable yard with two carriages, the farmery and apple orchard, the fields stretching right to the cliffs, more than twenty acres of pleasure grounds and parklands, and the great house itself, towering over the village of St. Marychurch. It is not an old house, having been built just forty years ago, but as handsome and elegant as any to be found around Torquay. Each room is of fine proportions and flooded with light from the large windows. The library is particularly impressive with a deep carved frieze of fruit and flowers extending right around the room, above the mahogany bookcases. I am no reader, but instantly imagined myself receiving callers there, and watching them gaze in admiration at such opulence. I would lose no time in purchasing the finest ornaments, clocks and paintings so as to make my husband's wealth and position quite clear.

I opened the tall cupboards in the kitchen and looked at all the glassware and the silver. There was a pretty yellow tea service and I told the maid to use it for the drawing room that afternoon, where my husband touched it fondly. "My mother's favourite," he explained. I refrained from remarking that he was fortunate indeed to have both parents living until he was beyond his fiftieth year, and good souls they were too. Indeed, they seemed to have been considerably better parents than he was himself. I had been living in Devon for over two years and to my knowledge his three sons had not visited during that time. My own mother died when I was small, and my father not long afterwards, but I was beyond waxing sentimental over old tea sets.

I knew of my father-in-law long before I first saw my husband. Quietly powerful and hugely rich, he is still famous for his work with the Stephensons and for his giant ship, which foundered. It was he who bought Hampton and set about re-building it more in keeping with the family's importance. He added the fine castellations around the roof and above the porch, even atop the pillars at the gateway so that entering the estate is almost as grand as sweeping into Hampton Court itself. He had the family crest carved above the door: a dexter arm in armour holding a sword out of a ducal coronet. He left his mark.

And we would leave ours. We would own Hampton, manage the estates, play our part in Torquay's fine society. But I was not to know that fate had already written a very different destiny for my husband.

I first met William Houlbrooke Tayleur eight years ago at the home of his sister in Rutland Gate; a house so stuccoed and porticoed that it reminded me of the icing on a wedding cake. Jane Phibbs is a most genteel lady whose husband works in the Queen's household, and our acquaintance was wholly approved of by my protective and discriminating uncle. I do not have friends in Wales. I imagine that people in our town believe me to be aloof and above the society on offer there. But Jane and I had a sweet friendship. We had met at a garden party during a previous season, my uncle having taken a house in Knightsbridge for a few weeks. I was a perfect companion for her during the long days when Mr Phibbs was away at the palace and the four children were being raised, educated and entertained by the nursery staff. We visited galleries, attended afternoon concerts, strolled in Hyde Park and embroidered screens with easy conviviality. I travelled to London often to stay with the family and on this particular visit in the spring of 1851 we were preparing, with some animation, to see the Great Exhibition. I remember that Mrs Phibbs was excited that night as the family dinner would include her eldest brother, who had business in London and would be staying for some time.

I walked into dinner on Mr Phibbs' arm, Jane's brother having told us not to wait for him. I had chosen to wear a soft blue muslin gown that showed just enough shoulder and had the new pretty lace sleeve caps which covered the parts of the arms one would rather not display at the age of thirty-four. At the door I stopped, and Richard Phibbs politely stopped with me as I gazed at what lay before us.

The dining room was in evening dress, its daytime self quite forgotten, the maroon walls, tropical plants and heavy drapes disappearing into the damask darkness around the side. The table looked like fairyland; candlelight from the simple glass candle stands glimmering on the waxed fruit, the gleaming cutlery, the crystal compotieres and the silver filigree on the decanters. The linen was creaseless and snowy white, the napkins folded into fans. The centrepiece was a tumbling mass of hothouse flowers with trailing tendrils of ivy.

"Jane, what a beautiful table," I said. "But I thought we were not expecting company this evening apart from your brother?"

"My dear Miss Knight," said Mr Phibbs, leading me to my place at the table next to him, "There is no company that my wife could possibly prefer; her brother is always our most longed for guest. I am certain we will find the fatted calf amongst the dishes before us, prepared in his honour and awaiting his arrival."

"What nonsense Richard," my friend exclaimed, "There is no meal my brother enjoys more than a well-boiled steak and kidney pudding, which I have ordered for tomorrow evening. Besides, calves are not a common feature in Rutland Gate, fatted or otherwise."

The soup and fish had been removed and the beef placed in front of my host, when the door opened and the butler came in, closely followed by Jane Phibbs' brother. This gentleman had clearly taken the time to change his clothes, brush his boots and remove all traces of a long road journey. I first noticed his spotless white gloves, the fashionable wide velvet lapels on his coat and the buttons of his waistcoat straining across rather a portly middle. His hair was dark and thick and had been combed to lie flat much against its inclination. His face was round and bore the pitted marks of some previous fiery condition of the skin, perhaps when he was a young man. He was smiling and holding out his hands to his sister.

"Mr William Houlbrooke Tayleur, madam," the butler announced.

Jane gave an exclamation of pleasure, left her seat and hurried over to him. "William, you look more like a great bear every time we see you!" She grasped his hands and surveyed him affectionately.

"And you, Sister, look ever more like a handsome Knightsbridge matron."

Jane turned to me. "William, this is my dear friend, Miss Mary Ellen Knight."

He bowed over my hand and assured me that he was delighted to make my acquaintance. I was wondering at his sister likening him to a bear. I had seen bears in a pit in Leeds and he seemed to lack completely their ambling air of bewilderment. Mr Tayleur was altogether more sharp of movement and full of lively spirit.

He grasped his brother-in-law's hand with real warmth as he made his way to his place next to Jane. "Phibbs! How's the palace?"

Mr Phibbs replied, "This one, or Buckingham?"

"This one seems sturdy enough; handsome by any

standards. How is the Queen? Prince Albert still complaining about the drains?"

"The drains are done Tayleur – completely overhauled. Absolute masterpiece of engineering. As for the Queen – the last time I dipped into the court circular she was busy and well. We rarely see her, but Prince Albert is always around. I will tell him that you kindly enquired after the plumbing."

Mr Tayleur looked over at me and smiled. "You have disappointed Miss Knight, I can see. She would like to think of you sitting regularly with Queen Victoria, sipping tea and eating lardy cake."

We all crumpled into laughter. "Lardy cake?" said Jane. "Really William, surely she nibbles on Highland shortbread, or perhaps delicate French fancies imported directly from Paris?"

"I think the Queen probably enjoys a muffin as much as the rest of us," her brother replied. "I can't imagine the Prince Consort having much truck with imported French fancies, can you Phibbs?"

Richard Phibbs looked up from carving the beef. "He's a good man, brilliant but steady. The establishment has never taken to him, even after all these years." Servants seemed to emerge from nowhere to place the plates in front of us and serve the oyster sauce and vegetables. Mr Phibbs commenced cutting the pheasants.

"The Queen may be rather plain but she's faithful to him. I envy him that," said Mr Tayleur. "A faithful wife is something to be prized."

His sister looked quite shocked. "William, I really cannot allow you to say such things in our home. You speak as if faithfulness is a virtue to which women find it difficult to aspire. This is an unjust indictment and quite untrue. Moreover, since you arrived our conversation at table has consisted of drains and the lack of wifely virtue. What will Miss Knight think of us?"

"Mere family sportiveness Jane; I'm sure Miss Knight will recognise that. If one cannot relax in the company of one's own family, what pleasure does life afford? All those unspeakable society dinners – local potentates stiff as boot brushes – mention a drain there and half the ladies will swoon away. But here, in the bosom of the family, we can all feel quite safe from any disapprobation."

"Whatever would Mother say if she could hear you?" They looked at each other with real delight and in Mr Tayleur's eye I caught the gleam of a naughty child.

"She would exclaim, 'Leave the table at once William!'" he laughed, "And her lace cap would be shaking so much with fury that the ribbons would be doing quite a dance. Then she would send bread and dripping up later – and Cook would make sure it was topped with plenty of brown beef jelly – and address me as 'you vulgar boy' at breakfast."

"You must have been quite a young rascal," said Mr Phibbs.

"Richard, he could be wild," said Jane. "When he was having one of his moments we were all an avid audience, believe me."

Mr Tayleur turned to me and helped me to a glass of claret. "And what about you Miss Knight, do you enjoy lively debates over dinner in the company of your own family?"

"Not at all," I said. "My parents are long dead and I have no brothers or sisters. My uncle often takes the opportunity to give me advice over dinner about how best to lead my life."

Jane's brother appeared to be delighted by this prospect. "Does he indeed Miss Knight? My dear Jane, pray extend an invitation to the gentleman this very evening! We could all take advice about how best to live our lives, could we not? Send the carriage out, we need a sage voice amongst us, some wise counsel with the cheese. Will Phibbs' coachman have to go far? Where is your home Miss Knight?"

"My uncle is in Wales at present, Mr Tayleur," I said, rather worried that he was as good as his word and would send for my uncle to come out in his nightgown.

"William, leave Miss Knight alone. Her uncle has his own carriage if he had the notion to go scampering about in the dark just to offer advice to an old fool like you!"

"You see Miss Knight, how I am regarded by my own family? At least when I am dining with the finest society in Surrey I am in no danger of being addressed by the hostess as …you old fool…" We all laughed. Mr Tayleur started to eat his pheasant. "Every time I dine on any game at all I find the shot in my portion," he explained conversationally. "It always happens. Aha – here it is – just as I predicted. It's a miracle I have never broken a tooth." And he carefully extracted a small ball, cooked black, from the meat on his plate. "I would hate to break a tooth. Makes eating so damned difficult. Carves up your tongue as well. Agony. I think I would rather shatter an arm than break a tooth."

"Miss Knight, I feel I should inform you that my son believes his uncle William always carries shot around in his waistcoat pocket so as to perform that trick on every occasion."

"No Jane, I assure you it is quite true. I always get the shot, every single time."

The roast meat plates were removed and jellies, creams, trifles and confections were brought to the table. Mr Tayleur poured Madeira wine into my glass and sat back in his chair to look straight at me. "What think you of trains Miss Knight? Have you had the opportunity to ride in one?"

"My uncle believes them to be dangerous, Mr Tayleur, and I doubt whether I will be allowed near to one until his confidence in them increases. But I am aware from Mrs Phibbs that your family is responsible for the growth of the phenomenon throughout the country."

Mr Tayleur laughed. "It is true that my father's foundry builds a great many of the locomotives in Britain at present. But as to danger, your uncle is perhaps wise to protect you from them as yet. The Rocket itself killed a member of parliament at the opening of the Liverpool Railway and not long ago my own brother took a fall from a footplate and injured himself quite seriously. But my father has recently built a number of locomotives to be sent to Russia. I like to think of one of them taking the Tsar himself on great journeys around his empire."

"From what I have heard of the Tsar," said Richard Phibbs, "He would have no need of a locomotive at all – he could pull the whole train round his dominions himself..."

"Richard, the idea!" said Jane. "Do stop teasing..."

We finished our meal in the warm glow of candlelight and friendship. I thought of the silent dinners at home with my uncle, where any sign of levity was frowned upon, and felt a dread of returning to the dour, grey house in Wales. I watched Mr Tayleur's hands as he poured liqueurs as he had, of course, removed his gloves on being seated at the table. His skin was quite dark and freckled, his fingers finely shaped and well kept. It was with some regret that I rose to follow Jane to the drawing room and left him.

Later I opened the shutter in my bedroom and pulled down the window sash. The curtain rippled in the evening breeze like bridal lace. Down below, carriage wheels rumbled over the cobbled road and the men's voices drifted up with the faintest scent of cigars. They were talking animatedly and laughing often, only becoming more languorous as I began to doze. William Houlbrooke Tayleur was large and loud, his vitality almost intimidatory, but his very presence had lit up the house.

In the morning Jane had made sure soused herrings were served for breakfast as her brother always expressed great partiality for these. Both Jane's husband and Mr Tayleur had risen early and already left for the city when I joined her in the dining room. I took some veal croquettes and sat down at the table which, without the magical candlelight and gleaming silver, was once more its ordinary self.

My friend rang for fresh, hot coffee and said, "Mary Ellen, please do not be alarmed by my brother's outspokenness and quite shocking subjects of conversation. I hope these did not prevent you enjoying yesterday evening's dinner."

I assured her that this was certainly not the case, and that I had found the evening quite charming and most amusing.

"I would like to help you to understand my brother a little more," she went on. "He has been made to suffer in recent years, and his life has been a sore trial. He was sadly and wickedly deceived by his wife and has been striving to obtain a divorce to put an end to his marriage. That is why he speaks so bitterly about feminine fidelity. The scandal was such that he was forced to leave his home in Lavender Hill and move some distance away, leaving that society altogether."

I was truly shocked to hear this. Divorce is a terrible thing, and only achievable at huge expense through an act of parliament. Mr Tayleur's wife must have committed a really heinous sin and wronged him deeply. I felt great pity for him.

"What has become of Mrs Tayleur? Where does she live now?" I asked, in total defiance of my breeding and upbringing which were telling me not to exhibit a vulgar curiosity but simply to await any further confidences should Jane choose to share them with me.

"Thank heavens she is no longer permitted to call herself Mrs Tayleur. William is finally free of her and she has had to go back to her former name, just as she has gone back to her former family. What they will choose to do with her I know not, though after the deep disgrace she has brought upon them all I would not be surprised if they have locked her away in a lunatic asylum!"

"Jane!" I blurted out in horror, "She was not mad was she?"

"Only mad with wickedness. No, it would have been quite impossible for him to divorce her if she had been insane. He would have had no choice but to lock her away at the top of his house while she raved and screamed within the hearing of any guests blessed with good ears."

"Please, this is too terrible," I protested. "I have never heard of anything so horrible. Surely this could never really happen?"

"Have you not read about such things? There is a novel, just recently published, about a husband who keeps his lunatic wife locked in the attics. She manages to escape at night and terrify the guests in their very rooms."

"No, I am afraid I have never been encouraged to

read novels; my uncle considers them to be quite harmful."

"Gracious Mary Ellen, I will lend some to you. Your uncle will never know, and you are quite safe from his disapproval while you are under our roof."

"But would I really wish to read about such a creature – a wife in an attic who ranted all day? I would never sleep soundly again. It is a dreadful idea; how could her husband, her family, possibly bear it? And why would Mrs Tayleur's family wish to treat her as a madwoman if she is not?"

"I am not certain that they have locked her away, but I do know that some young women who have disgraced their families and irrevocably lost their reputations are forced to live out the rest of their days in a madhouse. For what else is to be done with them?"

"And does Mr Tayleur have any children? Are they with their mother? What will happen to them?"

"He has three sons, but he is filled with horror at the thought of her having any influence over them whatsoever and he will never allow them to see her."

"So she has lost all her children," I said.

"Well, no," said Jane. I waited, but she was clearly unwilling to say any more. We sat silently and I thought about the misery that had filled poor Mr Tayleur's life. He did not seem at all the kind of man that any wife would wish to wrong. I imagined him sitting with his head in his hands when he first heard of her perfidy, or speaking softly to his little sons as he took them away from her forever – how had he explained matters to them? And most of all I wondered what Mrs Tayleur had actually done to bring such tragedy to the family and to cause her own ostracism forever.

During the next fortnight Mr Tayleur was much

occupied by business in the city, but it always seemed possible for him to return just before the tea trays were brought into the drawing room. I remember those summer afternoons clearly, the three of us sitting companionably together and Jane and her brother regaling old family tales amid much laughter. They told me about their father's new mansion in Torquay which has a good park and grounds that reach as far as the sea itself. Mr Tayleur had visited several times and looked at the many improvements that were being made to the house. He described the hall to me, with its beautiful mahogany staircase that sweeps up both sides to the landing above, under a high glass atrium through which the sun streams.

They told me about their father's business; the huge Vulcan foundry in Warrington run by their brother Edward, and Bank Quay on the River Mersey where there were plans to build a massive iron clipper – the first in the world to put to sea – which would bear their father's name. I understood that Brunel himself was a neighbour and had dined with their parents, along with placing orders for more than one engine for the Western Railway.

"Now tell us about your life in Wales," Mr Tayleur said, leaning forward towards me as if anticipating a saga of high adventure.

"There is little to tell," I said. "My uncle and I live quietly. Famous engineers do not come to dine, and the Prince Consort does not perch on the edge of a desk and seek our opinions. Sometimes I walk into the town and consider the new gloves and bonnets in the milliner's, and occasionally I arrange flowers in the church. That is all."

Mr Tayleur smiled slightly and raised his eyebrows. I wondered if I had disappointed him, and resolved to say as little as possible about myself. I felt it was my place to listen, nod and smile and show great interest in all he had to tell me. I knew I was fortunate to be acquainted with such a family and I badly wanted to remain close to them. I admired Mr Tayleur for his confident manner and the easy, friendly way with which he included me in any conversation. He was not quite handsome, but had a lively, playful air which made me warm to him increasingly. I enjoyed watching him – the way he would throw his head back and laugh when his sister amused him, his habit of running his hand through his hair so that his natural curls broke free from any oiling or combing, the deep brown of his eyes when he looked at me. And he seemed to enjoy sharing details of his life with me although he never mentioned his sons, and I never asked about them.

Our visit to the Great Exhibition of the Works of Industry of all Nations had to be carefully timed. Mr Tayleur had learned that the Russian exhibits had not yet arrived, being delayed by ice in the Baltic, and he very much wanted to show these to us. And yet we must not wait too long and risk attending when the ticket prices were dropped and the hoi poloi admitted. But when we finally walked across Hyde Park to the Crystal Palace and entered the great doorway, I felt that my life up until that moment had been a very poor affair indeed.

Mr Phibbs had decided that his eldest child, John, should accompany us as it would be an experience to widen the mind, and Jane felt that he would enjoy a certain exhibit of stuffed kittens in a variety of costumes that had been mentioned in the newspapers. Mr Tayleur had obtained a catalogue for the exhibition and had been studying this for some time. He was, of course, most desirous of heading straight to the steam machines in which he had a huge interest. "A brand new steam locomotive will be on display," he explained, "The Lord of the Isles – built for the Great Western Railway and weighing thirty one tons. We must also pay a visit to the huge hydraulic press built by my father's foundry at Bank Quay. It has won a prestigious exhibition certificate, which has been a source of huge delight to him." This would not have been my choice and I was feeling some trepidation about viewing these enormous and noisy objects, but Mr Tayleur's explanations and commentary, and in fact his presence and company, would be a very great pleasure in themselves.

Before we could find our way to the steam exhibits we had to walk down the central transept. Crystal Palace was a place of wonders; the setting for the kind of stories that a nanny would tell in the nursery firelight. The great domed roof soared up to the sky like a cathedral without stone, and sunshine poured in on every side, through each single pane of glass.

We passed through the great black gates, almost like the gates on a park but infinitely more intricate and splendid, the posts topped with displays of flowers and fruit, all made of iron. We were immediately assailed by a new world of colours. I felt that I had been half blind until that moment, unable to see what colours really were before. Huge flags of all the nations were hanging from the trellises above, as well as rich draperies and canopies of all kinds, and carpets and tapestries which were a mass of multi-coloured tones and hues. The columns that supported the structure were blue and gold and the trellis girders of the upper floor were bright red. Further down the walkway we could see enormous glass cases with red roofs, but before us was a towering pink, crystal fountain with cascades of water, and behind that were two tall elm trees, their topmost branches reaching up into the dome.

I was quite unable to speak, but this appeared to be a common sensation as the crowds of visitors were strangely quiet, gazing with wonder at the unimaginable sights. Vast pots and urns filled with exotic palms, ferns and broad-leaved plants were placed regularly along the wooden planking floor, and I ventured up to a palm and rubbed a leaf between my gloved fingers. "This makes me believe I am in quite a different country," I breathed. "I must be abroad, in a tropical land with a sandy beach nearby and no longer in Hyde Park in my best bonnet."

Mr Tayleur laughed. "As you know, my father has recently purchased several properties in Torquay, including Hampton House in St Marychurch. There the climate is so mild that tropical plants such as these are grown abundantly in gardens."

I was amazed. "Outside in the gardens? Not in a hot house or an orangerie?"

"Indeed Miss Knight, Torquay is full of palm trees; they line the roads and fill the parks. When my sister makes her next visit to our parents you must accompany her and look at palm trees to your heart's content. My father is not living in Hampton at present as the mansion is much disrupted by building works, but he has leased a fine villa – Oaklands – which is situated opposite the new Bishop's Palace. You would be very comfortable there. Although, I must confess, I would like you to see Hampton. I would enjoy hearing your impressions of it."

I assured him that such a visit would give me enormous pleasure, but I could not meet his eyes at that moment.

After walking for some time, past courts or pavilions filled with every kind of display, we located the steam machinery. There was a considerable amount of noise in this area as many of the machines were working, and there was much hissing, thumping and clattering. First we admired the massive hydraulic press, invented by George Stephenson and built by Charles Tayleur's company. Mr Tayleur informed us that each tube weighed over one thousand tons but it could be operated by just one man. He then led us up to "The Lord of the Isles" and let us take in its massive size and imagine the enormous power that lay within it. I found it surprisingly beautiful. It was deep, emerald green with red trims and the new metal gleamed and shone along the length of its perfect curve. It was quite spotless. The huge wheels had clearly been nowhere near any dust or mud, there were no scratches or dents and the whole engine had been polished until it reflected the crowds clustering close to it. It smelt faintly of oil, but apart from that it seemed to belong to quite another world.

Jane's son, who was not as tall as the great central wheel, asked if he could touch it.

"No," his father replied. "You will put a finger mark on it and then Mr Brunel will tell your mother to dust it."

Mr Tayleur was moving as close as he could to the giant locomotive, seemingly intent on examining it inch by inch, and I took the opportunity to look at him properly for the first time that morning. I hesitate to confess that there was much the same greediness in our observations – his for the gleaming engine and mine for...for what exactly? I have no brothers and no father, only an uncle who is more like a distant presence in his own parts of the house. I see gentlemen on the other side of the street, lifting their hats, or offering an arm to walk into dinner in the twilight. But here was a man who was close to me. I could smell the soap he had used and the starch in his shirt, and I could see the rough-cut bristles across which he had drawn his razor a few hours ago. He must have used rather less macassar oil today because his hair was already loosening in the heat and regaining its thick, natural curls. I thought to myself that here was a man whose life until now had been a well of tragedy and regret, cruel wrong-doing and deep bitterness. He was always most kindly attentive to me; he had even told me that he wished I would visit the family mansion that would one day be his. I dared to wonder if there could possibly be some small chance that his warmth was more than just good manners, and that perhaps he was beginning to notice me.

"Can you recognise the beauty of this locomotive Miss Knight?" he asked, turning abruptly to look at me. "Or do you still agree with your uncle that it must be shunned because of all the dangers with which it threatens our safety?"

I tried to gather myself together and frame a reasonable reply, but I had flustered myself with my thoughts and was unable to be calm. Besides, I could not help imagining this locomotive at night, screaming through dark cities, steaming in great gasps, fogs of black smoke pouring out as from a monster.

"It is quiet at present," I said, "and very shiny and still. But I cannot help imagining it full of coal with the furnace blasting. It would take on a life of its own and a terrible movement. It is a giant thing, Mr Tayleur, and I cannot feel anything but fear for it."

"Then it will be my ambition to change your opinion. When this engine joins the Great Western it will run right by the sea. You must allow me and my sister to accompany you on a gentle journey through to Torquay. We will cross great viaducts and travel through untamed countryside with incomparable views of the ocean. And you will tell me, Miss Knight, that you can find something of beauty in a train ride."

"It would be a very great pleasure to do that," I said. I looked across at my friend but she was busy showing her son the dials and levers at the back of the engine and she was unable to hear our exchange. "You are very kind, Mr Tayleur. I am sure that my views on the railway cannot really be of interest to you."

He looked at me and smiled. "Trains are the future and the future will come to meet us whether we are ready for it or not. I would hope that what lies ahead for you will be a great store of happiness, and travelling on a train could be just the beginning of that."

I wanted to tell him that I hoped his future would also be full of joy and that his terrible past would be quickly forgotten, but I found myself unable to speak. I just nodded and he seemed content with that. We stood for a moment longer in silence by the great engine, then he clasped his hands behind his back and walked over to his sister.

"You have all been very forbearing with me and my desire to subject you to steam engineering. I am most grateful for your patience, but now we must find exhibits that the rest of you will find fascinating. I know Phibbs was anxious to locate the alarm bed which tips up at the appointed hour and throws the sleeper onto the floor."

John immediately wanted to know if we would be able to see this working, and we set off to satisfy his curiosity.

"We must not linger amongst all the exhibits on the way," Mr Phibbs warned. "If we stood in front of every item for a full minute I am sure it would take an entire lifetime to get round the whole exhibition and we would never leave at all."

We passed clocks, watches and musical instruments, and priceless jewellery laid out on velvet drapes. Policemen stood about in case any visitors decided to smash the glass cases and John was thrilled to see the wooden batons tucked in their belts. The upstairs galleries were full of silks, shawls, laces and ribbons, as well as wax flowers, fine perfumes and crystal chandeliers. In one pavilion, huge panels of stained glass were arranged so that the light streamed through them. John remarked that it was as if we were standing in the centre of a rainbow, and his parents were greatly impressed by his observation and cleverness. I am not at all fond of children, but young John seemed to understand that he must remain silent unless he had some prodigiously intelligent remark to make that would charm the company and demonstrate to his parents that he is a marvel.

We all wondered at the electric telegraph, which was soon to be used to send messages through a cable right across to France, and an envelope machine which could cut, fold, gum and stack thousands of envelopes in one hour. Then Mr Phibbs suggested that I should now determine which pavilion we should all visit. I did not want to remain amongst the English exhibits. I had no interest in seeing the Bradford Court with its worsteds and woollens, or the tools and cutlery in the Sheffield display. I explained that I wished to view something from a foreign place and I would be particularly interested in Indian objects.

We set off again, and now the colours became even brighter. We passed the Chinese Court with its enormous hanging lanterns, bizarre pottery and strangely decorated screens. John was captivated by the camel saddle in the Turkish Court, where the carpets were so breathtaking that I really believed this was all an illusion which would suddenly disappear, leaving us standing in Hyde Park and wondering at nothing.

The Indian exhibits filled court after court, one of which was arranged like a sumptuous tent. The ceiling looked like acres of white silk gathered into a crimson centrepiece from which hung two giant, red tassels. Under this stood a magnificent throne, all made of intricately carved ivory, so tall that a flight of steps led up to the seat. Around the sides were huge, exotic fans. I wondered how you would have the strength to pick these up in order to fan yourself, but Mr Tayleur explained that servants would do this for you, all day if necessary. The hangings, clothes and carpets were covered in patterns and shapes beyond the realm of anything I could have imagined before. They looked as if they should be decorating the cloak worn by a sorcerer, or drawn upon Pandora's Box itself. Most wonderful of all was the stuffed elephant with a magnificent howdah on its back. This was all red and gold, and the rugs and robes that covered the animal itself were ornately patterned and edged with deep fringes. The howdah was a domed room with a large canopy to shelter the rider from the fierce Indian sun, and I stood in front of it in amazement, trying to imagine a life that would include riding through an Indian city in this fashion.

"The elephant is ours," Mr Phibbs remarked, "They borrowed it from the museum not two streets from here."

I was beginning to find the heat oppressive and I could feel moisture forming on my upper lip and I reached for a handkerchief. I had an unpleasant pricking sensation under my arms. Crystal Palace soaked up the sunshine like a gigantic hothouse, and the sumptuous materials and carpets made these courts feel airless and stifling. Fortunately Jane noticed my distress. "If we return to the central hall my dear," she said to her husband, "We could take a stroll under the lofty ceiling, and that should be more cooling than walking in here."

He agreed at once and they started to make their way towards the staircase. Mr Tayleur had been occupied examining the contents of a nearby glass case, and it took him a few moments to return to my side. "You are alone Miss Knight, and you look somewhat pale," he said with concern. "Come; sit here for a little while until you start to recover." He had found a chair, but it was positioned very close to the stuffed elephant which exuded an unpleasant odour and I rather doubted whether such a position would afford any relief. But if sitting there would result in us having some minutes alone, I was quite prepared to do it. He helped me to the chair and stood by very solicitously. "May I fetch a drink of water for you?" he asked.

"No, thank you but I will be quite well in just a moment. It is so hot in here; I could never manage if I had to live in a climate as warm as this."

"You would have to travel many thousands of miles to encounter a place with such temperatures, probably all the way to Africa itself. I cannot envisage you living in Africa, Miss Knight. Such a place would be altogether too wild and torrid for you."

"Mr Tayleur, are you by any chance taking the liberty of teasing me?"

"Indeed I am not, although the image of you living in a dried mud hut and cooking rice porridge over a fire under a sun as hot as an oven is one to relish." He smiled at this thought, then leaned close to me and took my fingers in his. "Miss Knight, allow me to say how very much I have enjoyed your company over the past few weeks. My sister has held the highest opinion of you ever since your first meeting, and I have come to share her great regard for you. I have been married, Miss Knight, but that marriage has thankfully been dissolved and I am now at liberty to marry again. I would be most grateful if you could consider becoming my wife. Your life would have every comfort, and even more so after my father's death when I come into my inheritance."

So he had been noticing me and the effort I had made washing my hair every night and tying it in rags for curls. He had noticed the pretty day dresses I had acquired during my stay and the neat new gloves. I had not annoyed him by speaking too loudly or too often or by saying anything unsuitable. I could, at last, move out of my uncle's house and become a wife. I suddenly remembered some items in the bottom of one of my drawers back in Wales. It had been the fashion when I was a girl to sew a trousseau and leave a space on the embroidered garments for the final initial of your name. When you eventually became engaged to be married you sewed in the first letter of your new name. I had twelve fine lawn handkerchiefs and a silk nightdress case embroidered with M and E, and now I would be able to add a final letter after all these years. The thought made me smile.

The heat seemed to be increasing and I dabbed my lips with my handkerchief. It seemed that my modesty had appealed to him and I decided that I should continue in much the same vein.

"Mr Tayleur, although I am deeply honoured and also flattered by your proposal, I am quite unable to understand it. Sir, I am not beautiful, nor am I quick-witted or well-read. I am at a loss as to how I could be deemed to be an ornament in your life or indeed any sort of asset."

"My dear Miss Knight, you do yourself much

injustice. If another person had said those things about you I would find it necessary to take them to task. I find your calm, quiet manner most attractive and I believe you would be a companionable wife and a charming hostess. You listen with patience and quite without judgement to my ramblings and expositions. I know that we could discover a peaceful life together. I am not searching for great beauty – it is a dangerous thing. Beautiful women expect to have their own way in all things, even when that involves crime and betrayal." He shook his head as if to dispel forever that dark part of his life and I knew that I wanted him to be able to look forward with hope to a new, perfect beginning. He bent closer to me and took my hand. "Sweet Mary Ellen, you are the wife that I need now. Say you will always be with me and that we will have the rest of our lives together."

I smiled at him. "Yes William," I said. "We will be together always." He did not mention his sons, and neither did I.

We walked back to the main hall in order to find my friend and her family. I put my hand on Mr Tayleur's arm rather timidly, but he smiled at me and drew my arm through his. When we encountered Jane and her husband they looked at us rather quizzically, but chose not to remark on our new intimacy. We were all becoming tired by this time, and the sun was dropping lower behind the glass palace. We made our way back to the pink crystal fountain and the elm trees, and then out through the black gates and the huge glass entrance itself. As we waited for our carriage John was chattering about all the wonders we had seen, but I was standing quietly and trying to imagine how life could ever be quite the same again.

I returned to my uncle's drab, grey house in Wales just one week later, and broke the news of my engagement. It was raining, as it usually was, and a dismal mist hung about the garden. My uncle had come to sit with me in the drawing room, which had a musty, neglected feel as it had been unoccupied for so long. I poured tea into his cup and then had to return the pot to the tray quite hastily as my hand was shaking. "I am engaged to be married," I told him. He waited silently to hear more, his face set like stone. "During my visit, Mrs Phibbs' brother asked me to be his wife and I agreed."

"And which brother might that be?" he asked.

"William Houlbrooke Tayleur," I replied, and as I said his name I wondered anew how such a man could possibly want to marry me. I thought of the day in the Indian court and the feel of his arm under my hand, and the proprietary kiss he had brushed onto my cheek before he helped me into the carriage when I left London. But my uncle's face was flushing red, and it was immediately clear to me that his response was one of horror.

"By all the lights of heaven, Mary Ellen, why do you wish to drag us into this arrangement?"

My hands began to shake even more and I pushed them down the sides of my chair to keep them from my uncle's sight. "I cannot understand why you consider it to be unsuitable," I argued. "You were pleased enough to encourage my friendship with Jane Phibbs. Her husband has a most eminent position. Their home is a watchword for refinement and class."

"His sister perhaps, but you would not be joining the Phibbs family. That is not the name you would bear. You would be marrying into a family irrevocably tainted by scandal and divorce. Scandal and divorce Mary Ellen – what would your father say about such a match? With what neglect would he charge me for allowing you to sink into a mire such as this? I do not need to remind you that on your marriage a settlement of twenty thousand pounds will be made to your husband. That constitutes your father's entire fortune. His life's work, to go to such a creature."

My uncle's face had never looked so grotesque. His beaked nose reminded me of a vulture, the lines around his mouth had deepened since our conversation began and seemed now to have dark depths, and a blue vein was throbbing near the wart on his temple. I felt desperate to end my time within his house.

"Uncle James, you are quite forgetting that the Tayleur name is in fact synonymous with wealth, power and influence. Is not his father a great man? A lion in industry as well as a man of considerable property? William is his heir. William will inherit his estates and his businesses."

"A lion in industry? What nonsense! His foundry builds locomotives you foolish girl; he is not a silk magnate or the owner of half the world's diamond mines, or responsible for supplying cotton cloth throughout the Empire. And another son has the main interest in the business, not the reprobate who is after marriage to you. From what I hear, Charles Tayleur is very even handed with regards to his children and he has settled large fortunes on his daughters."

"But William is his eldest son – the majority of the properties will belong to him, along with all the rents and incomes…"

My uncle stood up impatiently and paced towards the window. "I don't care if he will own Buckingham Palace and half of London with it! His marriage ended scandalously and no quantity of fancy houses will commit that indigestible fact to oblivion."

"Uncle, he put his wife aside because of her wrongdoing; he was not at fault..."

"Dear God, Mary Ellen, you are bleating like an ignorant servant. Open your eyes and recognise the truth. What can be said about the moral tone of his household if his own wife was behaving in a way I find myself quite unable to discuss with you? You will be forced into a life on the edge of sin if you marry this man."

"How can it be anything to do with me, Uncle James? She has gone. That part of his life is quite over..."

He walked over to my chair then, and placed his hand on the back of it, as if to pull me towards his way of thinking. "But her children have not gone. You will be required to gather them into your home and care for them. They will become your family – the offspring of such a woman!"

"They will be away at school so I will rarely have to see them. And when they do visit their father, I intend to treat them firmly and teach them proper moral values."

"And what of the son he refuses to acknowledge? How long will it be before he turns up at your door?"

I was taken by surprise. What had my uncle heard? I knew nothing of a son disowned. This must be a wild story generated by the scandal, a wicked rumour, a salacious exaggeration created by gossips. "I am surprised at you Uncle! You warned me never to listen to tittle-tattle or repeat it, and here you are using an unkind, baseless story as a cornerstone for your argument! Shame on you!" My uncle merely raised his eyebrows. "I am of age. I can marry William Tayleur if I wish, even without your blessing and approval. I have waited many years for a match as prestigious as this and I cannot let it go. I am no longer a girl and I must thank you for your kind advice, but assure you that I will marry him whatever you feel. He is kind and rich and this has to be, without any doubt, the very best path for me to travel."

My uncle covered his eyes with his hand. "You will regret this," he said.

Betsey Rose
York Place - May 1852

She died asking for her boys. Not little Albert – seeing him just made her cry and it had done for weeks – but the older ones. They never came here. The master would tell her that a visit was being arranged, that their father had agreed they would come soon, but it was always a lie. She hadn't seen them for more than two years.

She hadn't seen them, in fact, since she arrived here late one night with her hair all over the place. There was just her in the carriage, her and the baby, not even a nurse with them. The baby was only a couple of weeks old. They hustled her upstairs and there wasn't much talking. After that Mr Heathcote left for up country and he hasn't often been back. There has just been her, always upstairs, and baby Albert, and a few of us down here to look after them.

At first she would sit by the window gazing into the street, staring at each person who passed. If the bell rang she would start up, then beg me to tell her who had come to the door. I don't know who she was expecting, but no-one came. She would listen for the post as well but she had to give that up because she never received any letters. In the end she just sat, looking at nothing, and tears would suddenly start to roll down her face out of nowhere.

I felt sorry for her, though I knew there must have been wrong-doing somewhere along the line. The master told us to call her Mrs Heathcote, but we all knew she was his sister. He came back on one occasion and closeted himself upstairs with her. When he left he told us that she must not go out for a while, though she never went anywhere to speak of, and asked us to make sure she didn't catch sight of a newspaper. Well after he'd gone we bought one, just to see what all the fuss was about. Eddie the footman could read and he went through it, column by column, until he found it.

"This looks about right," he said. "There's a headline about the son of an iron founder divorcing his wife because of her adulterous behaviour." Then he read it aloud carefully, looking up now and again to make sure we were following. "Mr William Houlbrooke Tayleur, whose father owns the Vulcan Foundry in Warrington and until recently worked with the Stephensons on the manufacture of steam locomotives, has been forced into seeking a divorce because his wife Emma, after sixteen years of marriage, has started a criminal relationship with another man. The man has not been named, but he is thought to be a member of parliament. Mrs Tayleur has lately given birth to a son which Mr Tayleur has stated is not his child."

There was worse to come. A couple of days later Eddie brought home a different newspaper and that one told a lot more of the story. "The gentleman accused of criminal relations with Mrs Tayleur is Lord Arthur Lennox, son of the Duke of Richmond and a married man. His Lordship called at the Tayleurs' house while the master was in Torquay, but was sent away by the maid. He returned and somehow gained admittance, and made his way straight up to Mrs Tayleur's bedroom. When the monthly nurse entered the room with medicine in the middle of the night she discovered Mrs Tayleur and his Lordship in the bed together, and both were naked."

I suppose we were all shocked, though we must have guessed half of it. We sat there in the kitchen without saying anything for quite a while and then I decided to take her some tea and check that she was bearing up. She was a harmless little thing. I could imagine her being a bit dizzy; the type to get into a scrape like this if truth be told.

She was crying went I went up, half-lying on her bed and using several handkerchiefs. She sat up when I entered the room, looked mighty glad of the company. "Do you never wish you were married Betsey?" she asked me.

"In my line of work there's little chance of meeting anyone, madam, and followers aren't encouraged even if I did. I've got plenty to keep me occupied without a husband to look after into the bargain."

"Marriage can be very hard," she went on, as I poured her tea for her and stirred in her sugar. "My husband had a vile temper. It was like a storm brewing and he would shout and be furious about the most unlikely things – a noise he didn't like or a meal cooked badly, or one of the boys answering stupidly. Then he would often be away from home for weeks on end. When he came back it would be alright again for a while. He could be kind, even loving, but I never really knew where I was." She sipped her tea. "It is all over now for I no longer have a husband. He has ended our marriage and cast me off, but there was a time when he did love me Betsey. There really was a time when we were happy."

Not long after that she went out walking on her own. The weather was bad and she didn't have any stout shoes to wear – she only had her soft slippers and it was very wet. My belief is that she walked towards the Houses of Parliament and hung around outside on the street for a good while. She must have been hoping to catch sight of her lover, or even talk to him. She was well-wrapped up in a cloak so no-one would spot her but she still caught cold, probably because her feet got so wet.

"I went down to the Thames, Betsey," she told me after I had wrapped her in a blanket and had beef tea brought up, "And I stood on the bank for an age, watching the black water and willing myself to walk into it. I even ventured down the steps until it was clutching at my clothes and I was gagging with the smell, but I couldn't bear to go further. How can they do it, those poor women who end their lives there? How can they wade in until their skirts take in the water and become a dead weight – the dead weight of death? How can they open their mouths and swallow all the stinking filth and let it cover their hair that they have spent a lifetime brushing? A hundred strokes every morning and a hundred strokes each night only to end floating in night soil and butchers' waste? I did mean to do it. I did mean to become one of the pitiful "Found Drowned" that are listed in The Times. As I was walking towards the river I kept wondering what my husband would feel when he read my name there, whether he would be sorry and wish we could go back to better times. Whether he would regret sending me away so cruelly. And Arthur, who could have saved me, would he think about the happiness we found together and wish that he had given me a home and looked after me?"

"Now, now madam," I protested, putting my hand on her arm in an attempt to steady her, for she was rocking in agitation and distress. "How could you think of doing yourself harm? You've got the master to take care of you now, how would he feel if you had done away with yourself? And little Albert; you can't want to leave him all alone, to be sure?"

"My brother would be relieved, Betsey. That's why he leaves me in London – well away from his acquaintances. London is the very place for lost women. I can be forgotten here, invisible amongst thousands of others. No-one needs to see me or listen to what I have to say. I could walk out onto the streets and disappear forever and just become one of the fallen women that everyone believes me to be..." And she covered her face with her hands and broke into desperate sobs.

There was no comforting her from then on. She would sometimes sing "Charlie is my Darling" while swaying round the room in dance-like steps, or croon lullabies endlessly as if rocking a baby to sleep. I asked her if she would like me to bring little Albert to her, but she just stared at me, her eyes as empty as her arms.

The first seizure took us all by surprise, none of us having witnessed such a thing before. She was sitting by her dressing glass and I was putting up her hair. She had the dreamy look she often wore – it made me think she was visiting happy times in the life she had before – when her eyes suddenly rolled back and she fell onto the floor. Her whole body went stiff and stretched like a corpse and she started to jerk and shake so that the china on the wash stand jumped and rattled. I screamed for help and Eddie came running, but all we could do was grasp her arms and legs and try to hold her still so she didn't damage herself. Her face was fearful – her mouth all drawn into a line and her jaw rigid.

Eddie was terrified. "Lord, Betsey, what on earth's wrong with her?"

"These are convulsions Eddie, she's having convulsions. Here, help me lift her onto the bed then you must go for the doctor right away."

She slept for hours afterwards and the doctor gave me a tincture to prepare for her every morning and evening. He asked me if she had recently been feverish and I told him all about the walk to the river and her meaning to do away with herself. "She is suffering from an inflamed brain," he said. "You must keep her warm and calm. Where is her husband?"

"Mr Heathcote is in Warrington," I replied, thinking it best not to go into details.

"Then I think he should be sent for at once; her condition is critical. She may have other seizures and each one is severely injurious to her health. Make sure she is watched at all times."

We sent for the master but he sent back to say that he was much taken up with business at present, but would come when he could. I sat with her then, night and day, and she passed into terrible fevers when she did not know where she was or what was happening to her, and then into sleeps so deep that I was not sure she would ever wake again.

Some mornings were better and we would stack the pillows so she could sit up straight and I would brush her hair. Some days she even sat in her chair by the window while I aired her bed and changed the sheets.

"I wish my sons would come; do they know that I

am ill Betsey? Has my brother told them and made arrangements for them to visit? They must have grown considerably since I last saw them. Who is ordering their new clothes now? Edward's boots especially must not be allowed to get too small. I was always so careful about their boots.

You would like my boys, Betsey. You would admire Charlie – so tall and handsome with his dark, curly hair. Cresswell and Edward have thinner faces and no curls, but they are all handsome and clever. What is happening about Edward's school? He is just of an age to go away for the first time and nobody has informed me. And Charlie will be sixteen now. He will need proper collars for the holidays. I do not even know which public school my husband has decided on for Cresswell. Has he been sent to Eton with Charlie? Why have I been told nothing? I am their mother Betsey; I need to know about them. I need to see them again."

"Oh, you will see them soon, madam, I'm sure. Do not upset yourself, they will all be fine boys and getting on well."

Suddenly her face lit up and she sat forward in the chair. "Of course! Why did I not think about this before? Betsey, I need writing paper if you please, and pens and ink! I will write to Charlie myself instead of waiting for my brother to send to my husband."

Well I had to fetch them for her and she was all fired up. She scratched away for some time and when she had folded the letter and pressed the sealing wax she seemed calmer than I had ever seen her. I put the letter out for the master but I don't know if it ever reached her son. I would wager a guinea that it didn't.

The following evening it was warm and I had the window open. The days were lighter for longer and she was sitting up in bed with the breeze stirring her hair.

I was sewing a new nightdress for her as she had no longer any use for day clothes. "Betsey," she said, "You are so kind to me. Are you not shocked by me? Do you not feel tainted by having to wait on me?"

"You've never done no harm to me, madam," I said.

"But you must know that I harmed my husband?"

"It seems to me that he was the one who did the harming."

"No Betsey, I did a shameful thing. I loved another man." She waited for me to answer this. Perhaps she wanted me to hold up my hands in horror, but I just sat quietly and kept on with my stitching. "William was always so impatient with me. He made me feel like a silly girl most of the time, while he was a serious business man with important connections. He stood for parliament one year, when I was at home waiting for Cresswell to be born. They were dangerous times, the Orangemen were trying to take the seats in Liverpool and there were riots and violence. I can imagine William holding his own at the hustings, but to no avail. The Orangeman won with a large majority. But that was my husband – brave and strong and powerful. I was just a wife who liked to sing and dance and make the home pretty and I irritated him. The children irritated him as well and he was often away. He would stay with his relatives. Then I met Arthur at a neighbour's supper party and I soon realised that he treated me much better than my own husband did. He would ask me questions and really listened to my answers as if they were of great importance and were worth considering. He would look into my eyes and make me laugh and paid attention to me as no-one had since my own father died. I grew to love him Betsey, and as I realised that I also realised that I wanted him in a way I had never wanted my husband, not even in our early married life. Many men have mistresses, and I am convinced that my husband had several, but my shame was that I was a married woman, and becoming Arthur's mistress would cause a dreadful scandal and ruin all of us. I thought he would help me when William discarded me but I never heard a word from him, not one single word. I had thought that he loved me Betsey, but in the end I was loved by no-one at all."

"Indeed you were, madam; you were loved by your boys and I'm sure they think of you every day of their lives. And little Albert adores you and always will. You must stop fretting now, what's passed is passed and you must forget about it all now."

But that was her last rational evening. She got feverish again soon after and she would toss and turn in the bed, her hair all wild and hot and sweat forming on her flushed face. She called for her mother, and although she must have been half way through her thirties I swear she looked like a girl with her thin cheeks and over bright eyes. She started a low muttering and I caught the name William over and over again, followed by more crying and thrashing about the bed. After three days of fever she went quieter and her eyes seemed to see nothing. She died early in the morning, just as the sun rose and the birds started to sing, and at the last she held out her hand and said, "Charlie…"

Charles William Tayleur
Eton College - June 1852

They treat us like small children and keep us in complete ignorance; nobody ever tells us anything. My mother's brother has written to tell me that she has died. How could she die? She was still young and never ill. But there will be no explanation and I will just have to hope that one day I will be able to piece together some sort of truth about it all. My father has said nothing about her death.

I found out what happened when Albert was born by putting together what my brother Edward saw – he was not away at school being only six years old – what servants said later and what they told me here, some of it while I was pinned face down on the dormitory floor with several boys from my form and older sitting on my back and forcing me to listen. How did they know about it? It seems they picked up all the details from overheard conversations in their homes, gossip and half-truths. It makes me rage to think about all those people pursing up their lips and rubbing their hands over our troubles.

"What has your mama been up to, Tayluuur?" they taunted me. "Lifted her skirts for a Lord no less!"

"Lordy, Lordy, Tayluuur! Your mama's a trollop!" I leapt for that boy's face but got caned for my trouble.

My mother was tried and condemned by spiteful servants, vicious neighbours and old men sitting in the House of Lords who had never met her. She had no chance to answer their charges, she had no voice, no-one listened. Is that justice? If I had been able to stand up for her before a court the first thing I would have done would be to destroy the credibility of those terrible witnesses. That would have been done easily enough.

Apparently she had become friendly with a gentleman. He was married with three children, as well as being prominent in society. He had been in the army and is now a member of parliament. I don't know how they met, but at every social event they would make their way towards each other and remain together, talking closely, laughing, exchanging secrets. People noticed. They must have watched my mother, waited for her to gravitate towards him, then nudged and smirked and laughed at her.

Perhaps she was lonely. My father was often away and she liked company, enjoyed people who made her laugh. I think she needed to feel loved by some-one and my father no longer seemed to care about her.

He started to visit the house, always when my father was not at home. Edward saw him quite often. He told me that he was tall with sandy whiskers and pale, gingery hair. The neighbours must have watched him coming and going because someone alerted my father. Edward said that he shouted and raged at our mother and insisted that she must not see the gentleman again.

"You cannot forbid me to have friends," she had shouted at him, "What am I expected to do with myself? You go away for weeks at a time and I just wither away here. I don't have a life: I'm always waiting, waiting for you to come back or waiting for you to disappear again. I'm still young but sometimes I feel I lead a widow's life and I'm not ready for that yet. You make me feel as if I am in a cage."

Edward said she cried while our father banged

doors and raged about improper behaviour and bringing disgrace. But the young man stopped coming to the house.

I know she continued to see him because she met him once when she was out walking with Edward. They pretended to be surprised to see each other, then took Edward into a tea shop and sat at a secluded table at the back. Edward noticed that the young man called my mother "Emma" and she in turn addressed him as "Arthur". They touched hands as they helped my brother to butter and poured milk for him, and talked quietly with their heads close together.

Not long after that my youngest brother, Albert, was born. My father only stayed for two or three days then travelled to Torquay to visit my grandparents. He has never been able to bear the disruption of having a baby in the house – he always hated the crying and people walking round the house through the night. He used to say that the house had a particular smell after a birth and that it made him ill.

About a week or so after he had gone Lord Arthur Lennox turned up at the door. The nurse told him that my mother was still in her room and could not possibly receive callers. He went away, but he must have returned later and gained entrance to the house somehow. Perhaps he persuaded a housemaid by pretending to be the doctor, I don't know, but he actually made his way up to my mother's bedroom. I have tormented myself over the reason for his visit. Did he have a wish to see my mother's new baby? If he did then there is only one possible explanation for such a desire. Or did he simply want to see my mother again despite all the risks involved, and took the opportunity afforded by my father's absence?

The nurse's tale is that she took it upon herself to carry a medicine dose into my mother's bedroom in the middle of the night. If she had been a witness under oath in a court of law I would ask her why exactly she did this. Had my mother suddenly been taken ill and asked for medicine? Was she sick or in pain? Was it routine procedure to wake a sleeping patient to administer medicine with no particular purpose? This nurse was not even a member of our household – she was a monthly nurse, employed for a few weeks to care for my mother and the new baby. She hardly knew my mother. She stated that she entered the bedroom carrying a candle, which she held aloft to give herself light by which to pour a draught of medicine into a glass at the table. In so doing she saw that my mother was not alone in the bed. Lord Arthur Lennox was lying next to her.

Her next action was to leave the room and call another servant. This was Ann Ash who was a maid and slept in the attic. Despite the lateness of the hour, Ann Ash was not asleep in her room but was waiting outside my mother's apartment, fully dressed.

I would have asked her why she was thus engaged. Were both servants simply determined to see for themselves what was happening in my mother's room? Were they using my mother as entertainment so that they could delight their low-born counterparts for years to come with these salacious details?

It never seems to have occurred to any of the people who have since condemned my mother that these women could simply have been lying. Did they have some kind of grudge against her? Servants are perpetually harbouring one grudge or another. Did the monthly nurse take a dislike to her and decide on a course that would ruin her? Did they want to bring attention to themselves, increase their own importance, have a bit of sport? No-one ever asked my mother if this tale was true, or gave her any hearing if she claimed it was not. It is more than possible that Lord Arthur Lennox never visited our home that evening and that if he did, he never returned a second time nor made his way upstairs. I cannot ask my mother for the truth; it is too late now to give her a voice.

When my father returned from Torquay these servants were waiting for him at the door, agog with their lurid account of the sandy haired visitor and his overnight stay in my mother's bed. Edward remembers my mother waiting in her room, shaking with fear, and my father taking the stairs two at a time still in his riding boots. His face was dark with fury and his eyes were bulging but he said nothing, just dragged a portmanteau from the closet and started to rip my mother's clothes from drawers and strew them across the floor.

"For God's sake William..." my mother said trying to catch his arm, but he shook her off violently.

"Don't touch me or speak to me. You are nothing to do with me or my family. You will leave this house immediately and never come near me again. And you will take your bastard child with you!"

"But where will I go? My place is with you, I am your wife, I beg you not to send me away..."

"My wife? My wife? You would have done better to remember that when you were besporting yourself with lovers, madam. You are no wife of mine – you had best look to them to give you a name from now on, you no longer have any right to mine."

Edward told me that our mother was kneeling on the floor by this time, trying to catch hold of her husband's legs. "William this isn't true...please..."

But my father was having none of it. He stormed out of the room to order the carriage. He wasn't there when she left and it was the servants who had to pull

Edward out of her arms and use force to get her into the carriage. She was screaming. They passed the baby in to her and a few bags of possessions, but it was very little when I think of her grand dresses and all her trinkets. My brother could hardly recount this incident to me and I rocked him in my arms while he sobbed and described the carriage pulling away, my mother trying to climb out but being hindered by her skirts and having to hold the wailing child.

I do not know where she went. I returned home for the Christmas holiday and tried to ask my father about her whereabouts and when we would see her again. He lapsed into a terrible rage as soon as I spoke, forbade me to mention her name ever again, told me that she was dead to him and left the room, throwing over a small table as he went.

I sat with my two brothers in the nursery and we shared our bewilderment and grief. Edward was overwhelmed with relief to have us both back from school at last and to have company and a means of voicing his fears. I had earlier spoken to the housekeeper about my concern for my brother and she told me that he has been subject to night terrors, waking frequently and calling piteously for his mother. He is reluctant to eat or enjoy any activities and has started to wet his bed before the morning. Cresswell had suffered less than I at school. Being younger, his classmates had not yet the knowledge necessary to understand what my mother and Lord Arthur Lennox were purported to have done together, unlike the boys around me who understand only too well.

I did not know how best to help my brothers and I was also tormented by the fate of the baby. I had never seen him, being at school when he was born, but he is our brother even if my father is correct in doubting his parentage. Edward asked about him frequently and I felt that it was necessary for my brother to see both our mother and Albert in order to quieten his fears and his terrible sense of loss. But facing my father with these concerns was a terrifying prospect.

I began by writing to my uncle Charles Heathcote, who lives in Warrington and also has a house in York Place in London. He wrote back informing me that he had no knowledge of my mother's whereabouts. This worried me greatly – if they had not sought refuge with my mother's own family then I could not imagine where they would have gone. My father's relatives were also unable to help me; it began to seem that she had never existed. But then, of course, it transpired that they did know and they planned to keep us in complete ignorance until my uncle Charles was forced to inform me that she had died. He told me that it was a sudden death and that she had not suffered. I had a thousand questions, but I wrote to him to ask about my brother Albert. What would now happen to him? My uncle replied that he was not yet certain what would become of Albert.

How do you offer sufficient comfort to two stricken brothers? We are all apart and will not be together until the commencement of the summer holiday. I have sent letters to both Edward and Cresswell, exhorting them to be brave and to look forward to the time, in eight short weeks, when we can be together again. I have told Edward that I will take him fishing and swimming in the lake. Maybe we will even go boating. But how can I possibly hope to ease a pain like this with a few outings? At least Edward can weep. It does not do to weep here.

I remember that my mother had a pair of small gold scissors in the shape of a stork, the long beak forming the blades. She kept these in her workbox and I loved to play with them. This workbox was an object of fascination with its little drawers and compartments full of mystifying treasures: hooks and spools, tapes and ribbons, buttons and finger guards, even a wooden toadstool. I would form the buttons into ranks on the carpet, army facing army, while my mother chose rosettes to be the generals and made standards from darning needles and scraps of silk.

She was very beautiful. All children believe their mother to be beautiful but mine really was. She was always laughing – she found life happy although she must have had difficulties. Unlike many mothers she delighted in our company, perhaps because my father was so often away.

In the glass cabinet in the drawing room was a tiny porcelain tea service, carefully preserved from her childhood and destined for my sister, who was never born. She would unlock the cabinet and hand us the cups and saucers, jugs and teapot, and the little plates with their blue flower design. Cresswell and I would choose officers from amongst our wooden soldiers and these would be provided with afternoon tea with every observance of elegant propriety. She loved to dance and would suddenly kick off her slippers and whirl around the drawing room, teaching us steps that would be needed when we entered society. She was always patient with our fumbling attempts which usually ended with gales of laughter and my brother and I in a tangled heap on the floor.

From before that time I remember a blue woollen wrapper that held the smell of her and how I loved to press it to my face. She called us Charlie and Cress and would sing "Charlie is my Darling" while I was sitting on her knee. I remember her cutting my nails with her golden bird scissors. I often had sore little tags of skin next to my nails and she would nip these off and rub salve into the soreness. We called them "wicked stepmothers".

We believed that her childhood had been full of terrible incidents. In defiance of fashion she would not allow a picture or looking glass to be hung above the mantelpiece, nor would she have any ornaments directly above the fire. She explained that sparks could easily fly onto nightgowns or dresses and set the wearers alight. She had a fear of uncooked fish and fishbones. Whenever fish arrived at the table she would prod it suspiciously with her fork and enquire of my father, "Are you sure it is cooked?" while she raked through it for bones. Cresswell and I could only think that acquaintances in her early life had suffered agonising deaths in pillars of flames after approaching fireside ornaments, or choked helplessly with fishbones caught in their throats, or writhed in extreme pain after eating a piece of plaice that was not quite cooked through. She told us about trips when she was a child to the sweet shop at the end of the road which was owned by two sisters who both had beards. For many years we would covertly examine the faces of female sweet sellers for any evidence of whiskers.

I know that I am fortunate because I had all the years with her until I went away to school; poor Edward had only five or six years, and Albert – what did he have? I know now that when your mother dies you lose the one person who deeply loved you and would always continue to do so whatever came to pass. And I know that one day I must find Albert and return him to us, to be part of us again.

Mary Ellen Tayleur
Hampton House - January 1858

Looking back I can see that no sooner had we found happiness in each other than we sailed blindly into horrifying storms, with more than one shipwreck. We had believed fate to be feeling benevolent when the first wife died, rendering William a widower and offering more respectability to our union. My uncle however was still implacably opposed to our marriage and I moved to Teignmouth to stay with relatives of William's, enabling us to see each other regularly and in good company, William having taken up residence in Oaklands, close to his father at Hampton. But William's mother began to fail, taking to her bed in much pain, and on October 3rd 1853 she died, the day before the launch into the Mersey of the Tayleur, the huge iron clipper named in his father's honour. We were told later that there were gravestones amongst the cargo – perhaps passengers feared the unavailability of suitable stone to mark their final resting places in Australia, or it could be that they planned to start a business in that line. But a ship launched upon a death with a hold full of tombstones could be said to be doomed from the outset.

We married quietly and in mourning on December 7th in the parish church of East Teignmouth and I moved into Oaklands at last. There were no bridal visits and I was much alone, William spending most of his time sitting with his father whose tragic loneliness was a piteous spectacle. The ship was an enormous comfort to him and he loved nothing better than reading reports of its fitting out in Liverpool. The newspapers carried descriptions of its towering size and potential for speed, the massive cargo holds and the light, airy accommodation for even the steerage passengers – quite different from the cramped, stinking spaces usually allotted to emigrants who paid the cheapest passage. It was recognized as being the strongest, safest, largest and fastest merchant ship ever built. And this paragon of sail had as its figurehead, not a mermaid or a maiden with long, flowing locks, but a full length carving of Charles Tayleur himself, dressed in a dark frock coat. He told us that this made him feel as if a part of him was sailing to Australia, breasting the waves of the warm southern oceans and facing towards a new world. The naming of the ship and all the accolades it was attracting were the greatest recognition of his achievements. This great ship was the pinnacle of his career.

At midday on Thursday January 19th 1854 the Tayleur left Liverpool for Melbourne, chock full of gold prospectors and their families looking forward to fresh lives and unimaginable good fortune in a new country. My father-in-law was not in sufficiently good health to make the journey to watch it set sail, but my brother-in-law Edward sent dispatches describing the happy occasion: the cheering of the passengers thronging about the decks and the crowds of spectators who shouted farewells and waved handkerchiefs. Apparently many sailors from other vessels in the port climbed high in the rigging of their own ships in order to watch the Tayleur slide past and marvel from above at its great size. Charles Tayleur read these letters again and again and clipped all descriptions of the event out of the newspapers. He also treasured a communication from the manager at Bank Quay which confirmed that an Emigration Commissioner had inspected the ship and declared he had "never seen any ship better fitted". He kept a globe by his chair and frequently traced the route the ship would sail, imagining no doubt his own effigy encountering exotic sights and vistas that few men could ever claim to have seen.

The weather was bitter cold that winter and I well remember one Monday evening. William had left his father in more heartened spirits and returned to Oaklands. We were sitting close to the drawing room fire and had just ordered more hot tea, when a servant came into the room looking rather flustered.

"There's a man come down from Hampton," he said, "He says the master is needed urgently."

William went straight to his horse, much agitated, and rode out into the freezing dark.

The following morning I had heard no news of what ailed my father-in-law and so I took it upon myself to order the carriage and be driven up the road to Hampton, so that I could ascertain for myself what was happening and what help my husband may require. A maid let me in after some ringing at the door, and my husband came down the stairs to greet me. He had, I remember, rather an impatient air on seeing me.

"What is the matter Mary Ellen?" he asked. "I cannot come back to Oaklands at present – my father needs me here. Forgive me, but I have no time for your concerns."

I pulled my cloak from my shoulders and lifted my chin with some defiance. "I have not come here seeking assistance for any concerns of mine," I replied. "I came to be of service to your father."

William seemed to soften somewhat on hearing this,

and showed me into the drawing room. "My father is keeping to his room," he explained. "He has been badly shocked and upset by two messages he received yesterday evening, each one brought up from the telegraph office."

"Good God!" I exclaimed, "What has happened?"

"The manager at Bank Quay wired to say that the Tayleur is believed to be wrecked with the loss of many lives."

I put my hand over my mouth, reeling with horror. "But that is impossible," I gasped. "The ship was built with watertight compartments – it is the safest ship in the world..."

"That is what makes all this so unbelievable," William said. "But a few hours later a further wire arrived, this from Edward, stating that the ship had been driven onto rocks off Lambay Island in a storm. He wrote that hundreds had perished, but there were some survivors being succoured by coastguards until they could be transported to Dublin. I have already ridden to Torquay to telegraph both my brother and Mr Heathcote requesting further details as soon as they learn anything." He handed me the messages so that I could see for myself, and my father-in-law came down to the drawing room to receive me.

He stooped over as though he had actually taken a mortal blow to the body, and his skin was grey and lined. Since I had last seen him just a few days previously he seemed to have increased in age by a great number of years. But he was as kindly and courteous as always, ordering refreshments for me, making sure that I was sitting near the fire but protected well by the screen. I poured tea for him but noticed that his hands were shaking badly when he reached for the saucer.

The Morning Post was brought in and he fell on it

anxiously, turning the pages with such haste that my husband took it from him and examined it in a more careful manner. There was merely a paragraph that day, containing the facts as we already knew them but also stating that there was a good chance the ship could yet be saved. The Irish papers had more and Edward telegraphed in the afternoon that hundreds of bodies were still in the sea around the wreck and would be unrecoverable until the storm dropped. "One man has survived by climbing up the rigging, some of which remained above the water," William read to us, "But he was left clinging onto the freezing ropes for fourteen hours before the sea had calmed sufficiently to allow rescuers to reach him. The exact numbers of survivors are not known, but most are now in Dublin. There are very few women or children amongst them, as most have perished." At that, my father-in-law placed his hand across his face and wept.

I sent for my maid and some clothes and moved into the room that had belonged to William's mother and is mine to this day. Although I occupied myself by ordering tempting, nourishing meals for Charles Tayleur, and sometimes sitting with him in a dutiful manner, I still found time to get to know the house that would be mine before too long. I soon felt strongly that the mansion was waiting, holding its breath in anticipation. I knew that I was the right person to embellish it and ensure that it could hold its own amongst the fine villas of Torquay.

My father-in-law had not been long in residence, and his ailing wife had little opportunity to organise the selection of wallpapers and curtains. I was glad; no doubt she would have favoured the hopelessly old-fashioned style prevalent when she was a young wife. Some of the rooms had received attention during the recent alterations and smelt of new plaster and distemper, while others were untouched and retained the drapes and wallcoverings of previous residents. I knew I could make this imposing building into my own territory and create rooms that were as impressive as the exterior. I would make sure it would become one of the most elegant residences in Torquay, fit to receive the best in society and a true reflection of my husband's wealth. I felt impatient to begin.

In the meantime, Charles Tayleur became thinner, greyer and more bent, and I often kept him company while he read the terrible newspapers. William was furious about these. "Keep those damned papers away from my father!" he raged at the servants, but Mr Tayleur fretted terribly if he was denied them, imagining every kind of horrible circumstance that was being kept from him. It was better in the end to let him read them.

They made desperate reading. The writers employed pain-laden phrases and during the week following the wreck, newspapers all over the country from the Dundee, Perth and Cupar Advertiser to the Royal Cornwall Gazette sought to tantalize and horrify their readers with ever more lurid details about the loss of the Tayleur. There were survivors' tales of escaping from the struggling ship by climbing across ropes and spars to the merciless cliffs. Petrified women attempted this but most were too weak to maintain their grip and fell to their deaths in the black, churning water below, some even pushed by others behind them. Other passengers tried to jump overboard and swim, only to be taken up by the fiercesome waves and thrown onto the rocks, many having their heads smashed open and their bones broken. An elderly gentleman from foreign parts saw a baby lying on the deck, both its parents having met their deaths, and he carried it by clamping his teeth on its dress as he climbed across the rope. It was now known as the "Ocean Child" and was attracting much interest and pity.

My father-in-law was not alone in finding these accounts deeply distressing. I can still see with vivid clarity both the images that those reports produced in my mind, and the line sketches that appeared in the newspapers to add a more dreadful reality to their outpourings. The terrible events of that tragic Saturday tormented me through many sleepless nights, until I fancied I could hear the hopeless screams of the shipwrecked in my own bedroom. As soon as I retired at the end of each evening dark, frightening thoughts crowded into my mind. Hundreds of ordinary, innocent souls had suffered unimaginable horrors that day. In that God forsaken place there had been no help for these desperate people. Not a living soul knew what they were going through. They must have peered up through the mist, longing and praying to see rescuers climbing down towards them, but there was no-one.

Survivors' stories continued to be printed, each one adding more horrifying details. The storm had raged relentlessly, vast waves lifting the ship like a broken toy and hurling those clinging to the ropes into the surging water. Heavy trunks, sea chests and large pieces of timber from the wreck floated dangerously in the sea between the ship and the cliff, smashing with great violence into anyone trying to reach the rocks. Men carried their wives or children on their backs and tried to climb, swim or jump to safety, but few succeeded. The pitiless water engulfed the deck over and over again, tearing passengers from any place to which they were clinging, and drowning them before they even met the sea. Nearly every woman died, and there had been at least a hundred on board.

Only three children were saved, from all those families. It was no place for the weak.

Once on the shore however, those who did survive were faced with a sheer cliff face and had no hope of rescue unless they could climb it. They spoke of the storm still battering them as they climbed, the freezing gales trying to pluck them from the rock face and their grief and fear for relatives they could not find.

The papers often differed wildly, particularly in the numbers they quoted as having lived or drowned. The crew were dastardly in one account, saving themselves first and then escaping to safety without a single thought for the poor, desperate passengers, still in hopeless peril. But then the crew were stalwart and courageous in another report, throwing ropes to people in the sea, pulling them to safety, helping them to scale the cliff. The ship itself was still in good condition, being iron and not wood, and the underwriters were planning to raise it as soon as the weather improved sufficiently. But then, in another paper, the wreck was broken up, sunk in deep water, the masts, rigging and spars all carried away by the storm. Charles Tayleur suffered as much from these discrepancies and from the lack of true facts as he did from the nightmares he experienced, night after night, about drowning, broken children, and a yawning black sea waiting as he fell towards it.

The survivors' stories were soon replaced with speculation about the cause of the shipwreck, and indeed my father-in-law had already been overtaken by dread about the apportionment of blame. After only two days the newspapers were reporting concern about the rigging being faulty – the ropes were too new to run through the blocks causing catastrophic delays when manoeuvring the sails. The compasses on board were all deviating due to the iron hull, the crew were unable to sail the ship and could not understand English or carry out orders and the captain could not control them.

It seemed that the appetite of the English people for this horrible story was insatiable, and newspapers continued to print the tales of anybody who had been remotely connected with my family's ship. William regularly saw the Bristol Mercury and the Exeter Flying Post, but his brother sent daily packets of The Illustrated London News, The Leeds Times, The Glasgow Herald, The Stamford Mercury – any paper in fact that contained an account of the wreck. And the stories grew more harrowing and horrifying by the day. Being aware of the suffering that these accounts were causing both his father and myself, William gave instructions that the newspapers were to be kept locked in his study. He was clearly angry when he discovered me with a copy of the Morning Post in my hands after he had issued this directive.

"My dear," he said, with strained patience, "I believe I made it clear that the newspapers were no longer suitable for any eyes but my own."

"You did, my love," I replied rather tremulously, "But I need to look for something hopeful in these accounts. It helps me to know that some passengers did survive and did manage to find their loved ones alive. I know they were only emigrants and for the most part poor and shiftless, but the fact that women and their children died in such numbers has saddened me dreadfully."

"Mary Ellen," he replied testily, "you must realise that newspapers are not to be trusted. They are more than capable of taking a morsel of truth and distorting it beyond all recognition. They care about nothing but the number of copies they sell, and the more salacious the content, the more greedily their readers will purchase them. Why do people want to read this torrid detritus? Not from any pity for the victims I can assure you. These are the people who read novels and penny dreadfuls, and they may as well be reading those for all the truth that these contain."

With that he took the newspaper out of my hand and carried it off. I saw no more accounts of the shipwreck until after my husband had been taken away. It took several days for me to overcome my reluctance and enter his study; it had always been the place where he made himself remote and inaccessible. It was exactly as he had left it – a newspaper was lying on the table, a pile of unopened letters were waiting on the desk, the lid was off the inkstand and a pen was jutting out of it. Several documents were strewn over the floor where he had thrown them while in the first grip of madness. The lingering smell of cigars and hair oil brought back a confusion of different memories, but I forced myself to sit at his desk and examine the contents of the drawers, and I also unlocked the large grey safe in the cupboard at the back of the room. I came across a yellowing letter addressed to my stepson Charles. I was about to throw it away in the basket but noticed that the seal was unbroken and put it back in the safe to deal with it later. I saw no reason to send it on. In the safe I found the newspapers that William's brother had sent to him and all the papers he had obtained for himself; in fact every account of the wreck and its aftermath. Free from his prohibitions I sat in his own chair and read the reports that had been kept from me. The tragedy struck me afresh, all those years later, when the drowned had rotted in their graves and the previously avid readers had forgotten it all.

Worst of all were the descriptions of rescuers

climbing down to the wreck in the days after the calamity, and finding a huge number of bodies caught on the rocks. Most of these were naked because their clothes had been torn off by the violence of the sea and the gales. Worse still, some bodies were without heads and many were horribly mutilated. It was enough to offend every Christian sensibility, and I must admit to being as shocked and appalled as my husband had expected I would be.

At the time my husband told his father that the story was no longer newsworthy, and all the newspapers remained safely locked away. I do not know how Charles Tayleur came across one. Perhaps he stopped a servant who was carrying one to my husband, but somehow he managed to obtain a copy of the Stamford Mercury which contained a particularly fulsome and grisly report of the scene of the wreck after the storm.

We entered the drawing room to discover him with the paper on his knee, but he was slumped forward and seemed to be in the grip of a violent seizure. On rushing to his aid we found his face drawn downwards in an awful grimace and his eyes staring quite without sight. I held him around his shoulders and stammered, "Papa, Papa..?" while my husband ran to the door and shouted for assistance. Page came in quickly, left again to fetch the footman, then we managed somehow, together, to carry him up to his bed. He seemed to be trying to talk to me, but could only make groaning sounds and these ceased when he lay down in his room and quickly became insensible.

While he lingered upstairs the debate in the newspapers raged on. What had caused this incomparable ship to be wrecked in such a manner and who was to blame?

"The captain, John Noble, survived," my husband

remarked one morning. "While not actually going down with the ship, he waited until the last moment to launch himself into the sea, where he was savaged by the stormy waters before being pulled out by two young men on the rocks. As he gripped the cliff face a huge swell washed his two rescuers into the water and they drowned. He is now facing many questions about the loss of his ship, and possible prosecution for manslaughter." I was silent; I knew that the investigations into the tragedy were playing on William's mind. John Noble may not be the only person held to account.

Most damaging to my family were reports that the masts were too far aft, the rudder was quite the wrong size for such a giant ship and rendered it impossible to steer, and the designs had been changed at the last minute. A Board of Trade inquiry was held just a few days after the ship was wrecked, and the coroner's inquest a few days after that. William gave strict instructions to his brother in Warrington that no representative from Bank Quay Foundry must be sent to the inquest. It was vital, he reasoned, that the company should keep a distance from any inquiries. Their presence could indicate blame, guilt and responsibility.

I found my mind dwelling on the question of blame, and became very troubled by this. If the family's foundry was held to account for the loss of RMS Tayleur, this could surely affect my father-in-law's fortune and our future security. These concerns exercised my mind to such an extent that I became determined to broach the subject with William, and ask him if our lives would be changed by the shipwreck. I waited until we were taking afternoon tea together in the drawing room, and explained my fears as I offered him a plate of scones.

"You must not trouble yourself with this my dear," he said, taking a scone and buttering it. "You forget that you are still a new bride. Your presence here at Hampton has been a great comfort to my poor father, and your time would now be best employed in taking over the management of this house. I do not foresee that we will leave the mansion now, and in all probability you will soon be mistress here. Perhaps you could ask to look over the linen and the silver, and go through the kitchen books."

I felt some impatience with this. "I fear I would be unable to concentrate on the kitchen books until you have given me some reassurance that your family's fortunes will not founder with the ship."

William seemed to realise then just how troubled I had been, and he put down his plate and took my hands. "You have been making yourself quite sick with fretting over this lamentable business, and I am sorry. I will explain as much as I can. There have now been four inquiries into the loss of the ship and not one of them has attributed any blame at all to Bank Quay. The owners have been criticized for not holding sea trials, even though that is far from normal practice. Noble was found at fault because he failed to return to port when he discovered that the compasses were not reading true, and for not taking depth soundings to ascertain his true position. But his courage during the day of the wreck stood him in good stead with the jury and he has now had his master's certificate renewed. A report on the condition of the ship clearly showed that there were no design faults with the vessel, and therefore the foundry was in no way responsible for its loss. Does this set your mind at rest my dear?"

I admitted that it did indeed, and also remarked that his father would feel great relief when he was well enough to learn these facts. But sadly that time never came. Charles Tayleur recovered sufficiently to be fed slops from a cup, and to turn his poor distorted face towards the window, but he never spoke again and seemed hardly aware of our presence in his room. He died eight weeks after the tragedy, the last victim of that terrible shipwreck.

The enormous amount of business involved in becoming squire certainly helped my husband to overcome the grief he suffered on losing his father, and the discomfort he had felt when the ship was lost. He was much occupied in his study, and I used my time to become familiar with the linen and the silver and inspect the kitchen books as he had suggested. I impressed upon the cook and the maids that I had my own way of doing things, and this must become their way from now on. I often walked around the drawing room and the library and gazed at the furniture and the precious objects. I had never dreamt that one day I would own so much.

I was very curious about the size of our property, and followed William into his study to find out. "How far do our lands extend?" I asked him. "Of what exactly does the estate comprise? Of what am I mistress?"

In order to satisfy my curiosity William took a large map out of the safe cupboard and unrolled it across the table. "The house is here," he said, tracing with his finger, "And these are the gardens, lawns and orchards. This path leads out to the pleasure grounds; we will ride that way tomorrow."

"And what are these names?"

"They are the fields: Old Woods is laid to pasture, as is Rake Hill and Middle and Higher Oddicombe. These fields here are sown with barley and wheat. And we have two plantations – one fir and one hard wood."

I studied the map closely, paying particular attention to the outer extremities of our land. "Look William, this field – Clay Park – leads right to the cliffs. Do these form part of our estate? Is this beach below our very own?"

"The cliffs do indeed belong to us, but the beach is the property of Torquay Council. Few people use it as it is very difficult to reach. I believe previous owners of this house fashioned a pathway down the cliff so that they could take their families to visit the beach freely. There are stifling and rigorous bye-laws governing the use of several other Torquay beaches, but they have left this one alone because you can really only reach it by boat. It means we could walk on it together; most of the other beaches are designated solely for ladies or for men."

"So there is much sea bathing here?"

"Indeed there is. See, these beaches nearer to town are for the ladies and these three are just for men."

"What about these small coves here?"

"There are no regulations about those as they are rather steep and rocky and consequently not favoured for bathing."

"Look William, this name is very strange. Why would they call this inlet Brandy Cove? What an odd name for a seaside place. How droll."

My husband glanced away from the map and studied me for a moment. "I believe it is due to the colour of the sea when the sky is of a particular complexion," he said.

"A sea that is the colour of brandy?" I queried. "I have never heard of such a thing!"

"My love, you are forgetting that many of the cliffs here are of a deep red hue. When the sky is dark, the moon reflects the red cliffs and the sea does indeed take on a brandy like appearance."

Old tales and legends began to stir in my memory. I remembered hearing stories about the daring doings of smugglers around the coast of Devon, and I had read a poem with my governess about ponies trotting through the dark, and the importance of turning your face away lest you should catch sight of their villainous faces.

"Could the name be anything to do with smugglers using that cove to land their contraband?" I asked.

William was taken by surprise. "What do you know of smuggling?" he replied. "I would have thought it was hardly a fit subject for your uncle's conversations."

"Surely everyone has heard stories about smugglers in Devon? Their exploits are well known. Are we living in an area where such activities take place? Could we be in any danger from these desperate criminals?"

"Calm yourself my dear. I can assure you that you are several years too late for encountering any of these 'desperate criminals' as you call them. The government has lowered the duty on imported goods – it is no longer the excruciating levy it once was - and now there are coastguards set up around here it would not be worth the risk to attempt to bring in a ship. You have reached Devon long after the smugglers have all gone."

"But the name of the cove makes it clear that smugglers did indeed operate in these parts William. I would like to see it very much indeed."

"I fear Brandy Cove is much too dangerous to attempt a visit. The path is treacherous and the cove itself little more than shale. I will take you to the beach at the foot of our own cliff Mary Ellen; we can ride in that direction when we have inspected the pleasure grounds. Would you like to do that?"

"Very much, although I am far from being an expert horsewoman. My opportunities for riding have been few and far between."

"Then it is time you got more used to the saddle my dear. I will send the men this afternoon to clear the path down the cliff and make sure that it is safe."

We rode out the next morning to survey our estate, although I was feeling somewhat insecure on horseback. My husband was a wonderful rider and he walked his horse close to mine as I was apprehensive that my mount may suddenly take fright and bolt away at a high gallop. We passed the farm where Mr Edwards, the tenant farmer, provides so much food for the mansion that I wonder at him being able to make a worthwhile living for himself. We discovered the pleasure grounds to be sadly overgrown and found ourselves making animated plans for their revival as we skirted the fir plantation and headed for the cliff. We even increased our speed and fairly tore across the last field, my husband keeping his horse neck and neck with mine so that I should be completely safe, and both of us laughing aloud to feel the wind against our faces and the beating of hooves upon our very own land.

The view from the top of the cliff was breathtaking and I gazed out across the sea, which was calm and blue. We tethered the horses to a tree and set off down the tortuous path, William sometimes holding my elbow or my hand, or gripping my arm tightly as we made our way downwards. The path was quite firm and even wide in places, built around the contours of the slope and making good use of gentler and more even areas. Planking had been used to shore up steps and the route had clearly been used often.

"Surely your father did not venture on expeditions to the shore," I remarked. "Why is this path so well-used? Did he send servants down to the sands for any purpose?"

My husband replied without turning round, "No, I told you yesterday that I would send men to clear the way for us and to make it safe. They cut away the undergrowth and the overhanging branches so that you could descend in comfort."

I frowned. There was nothing newly cut about this vegetation. The path had been beaten down by many feet over a great number of years, and was obviously a thoroughfare in regular use to the present day. "Would other people make use of this path?" I asked.

William stopped and looked at me rather impatiently. "My dear Mary Ellen, this is our private land. Who do you imagine would be climbing up and down the cliff here? Perhaps hordes of day trippers streaming in this direction for a spot of sea bathing? If the path is being used as you seem to think, it must be either local fishermen or boys from the village. Please do not concern yourself my dear, try to enjoy our expedition without filling your head with visions of trespassers."

I was not at all convinced but I was not prepared to risk my husband's temper, and I lifted my skirts once more and set my face towards the sea.

The way down the cliff was a forest of sycamores with an occasional ash tree or lonely pine and I noted that there was not a single palm tree in sight, despite all the extravagant claims of William and his sister. Tight ropes of ivy throttled most of the trunks and the trees appeared to be straining upwards, struggling for sunlight. The ground was thickly covered in scurvy grass with large, leathery leaves like lily pads, and as I looked down the cliff from a dog-leg bend in the path we seemed to be walking into a soft, green tunnel. It was not until we were about half way down that I became aware of the sighing and whispering that was the noise of the sea, and caught glimpses of it gleaming between the trees.

By the time we reached the beach itself we were both panting with exertion and feeling hot. William threw off his coat and stock and loosened his shirt at the neck.

"Goodness me," I exclaimed, "I have never seen you look quite so dishevelled!"

"Have you not?" he asked, and I flushed red as I remembered the nights we now shared inside the crimson drapes of my four poster bed. "Come, Mary Ellen," he went on; "You must walk on the sand and dip your toes into the sea!" And he helped me to perch on a low rock while he unlaced my boots, reached his hands under my petticoats, unclipped my suspenders and drew down my stockings.

"William!" I gasped in horror, "What if somebody should see us?"

"Who, pray, could possibly happen upon us here? There is no way down to this beach save by our own private path, and the only people who ever come here are passing fishermen. If a fishing boat hoves into sight I will help you back into your stockings with the greatest possible speed. But the fishermen will have no idea who we are – we could be Victoria and Albert for all they know."

He took my hand and led me down to the sea, which looked like frills of lace laid across the sand. I held my skirts up high and stepped into the water. The cold made me gasp, but it was glorious to feel the sea bed sinking under my feet as I walked, and the water lapping round my ankles. I looked back at our cliff; its grizzled, grey limestone contrasting sharply with the rust red of the promontory looming at its side. Between the trees, roots straggled down the cliff face like rope ladders and it struck me suddenly that, with the onset of winter once again, all the rich greenery of the sycamores would disappear, leaving just stark bare branches and the suffocating ivy.

Two or three weeks after that morning I suffered the most terrifying event of my life, although it was nothing compared with what was lying in wait for all of us in just a few short years.

Something woke me in the night. I lay with my eyes open, suddenly alert and anxious, although I could hear nothing. The great house lay silent, like a sleeping beast. William had not come to my room, which was unusual, and I supposed that he was still still drinking brandy by the study fire. I did not know what had woken me, but I was aware of a strange feeling in the dark air – something like danger or fear or tortured nerves. I shivered, and forced myself to think that the house is surely too young to harbour a ghost. I lit the candle on my night stand and swung my feet onto the rug. The cold immediately sliced into me and I reached for my warm wrap, then lifted the candle to the clock face. It was two in the morning. I went over to the window, pulled up the bar and opened one slat of the shutter. There was no moonlight, but the garden seemed still and empty and there was nothing untoward outside my window. My heart was still beating with deep, racing thumps and I decided to go in search of my husband and confide my fears and ask him to ascertain whether there was any threat to our safety.

I didn't trouble myself with the gas, but simply carried the candle out onto the landing. William's bedroom was empty, so I set off down the stairs. The candle threw huge shadows against the towering walls and I felt a clutch of fear. I had never seen the house like this before; it was always busy with servants' footsteps, muffled voices, the crackling of fires, doors opening and shutting, kitchen sounds. Now I could hear nothing but my own ragged breathing.

I reached the bottom stair at last and opened the door to the study. It was dark and empty, but the fire was still glowing in the grate and the room felt warm. There was only one place my husband could be – he must have gone down to the butler's pantry to procure another bottle of port or brandy. Perhaps he was engaged there in discussion with Page. I crossed the hall and opened the heavy door into the servants' part of the house. When it had swung shut behind me I heard a deep rumbling noise. It sounded like thunder, but this had not been in the air outside, it had come from below my feet, in the earth. It was a truly terrifying sound and brought to mind the accounts I had read of earthquakes, although surely these were a scourge of far off foreign lands? My mind was racing in an attempt to find some reasonable explanation. I had heard stories of mine workings collapsing underground, causing the buildings above to crumble in minutes. I was now desperate to find somebody and walked quickly through to Page's lair. Neither William nor the butler was in there, but I could see a light coming from the kitchen.

I hurried down the passage and through the kitchen door. The gas was lit and I blew out my candle, then gazed round the room in surprise and horror. The table was covered with cider jars, bread loaves that had been torn into chunks, a cheese cut roughly and a cold joint. There were crumbs everywhere. I was most particular about the way in which the kitchen must be left at night – the slightest morsel of food left out would attract mice and cockroaches – and I half expected to see fat black rats already crawling amongst the mess. How could our cook have left all this? And then I realised that she must be unaware of the liberties that had been taken within her domain; this must be the doing of others. Someone else had been in our house.

Suddenly I heard voices and realised that there were people in the cellar. So that was it! Perhaps our footman had brought his rascally friends into the house and they were even now making free with the master's wine. I gathered up my skirts and started to make my way down the stone steps. This was not easy. The steps were steep and very narrow and each one appeared to be a different height from the one before. Twice I almost stumbled but managed to regain my balance, even though my legs were shaking so hard that it was almost impossible to place my feet with any surety.

The cellar was well lit with candles and I saw the man immediately. He was roughly dressed in a ragged black coat and had a black hat pulled low over his forehead. I had never set eyes on him before and I screamed loudly. Then I looked feverishly to see if he was carrying a knife or a pistol, expecting that my life was about to end then and there.

But he looked back at me with real fear, grabbing his hat from his head and shuffling his feet awkwardly. "How dare you invade my house?" I shrieked at him. "What have you stolen from us, you ruffian?"

The man was silent. At that moment the terrible rumbling could be heard again, but much louder, and seeming to come from just a few feet away. It went on for some moments, getting louder all the while, and I looked round wildly to try to discover what could possibly be the cause. It was now clear to me that there must be a problem with the foundations and the entire mansion was about to collapse around us. I shut my eyes and started to pray.

Suddenly a low door opened in the cellar wall and Page stepped out, bent double to allow his tall frame through the small opening. I was vastly relieved to see him.

"Page – thank God!" I exclaimed. "There is something terribly wrong – a dreadful noise is coming from underneath the house and I believe we could all be in great danger, and if that was not bad enough I have found this thief here in our cellar. Please convey him to a room that can be locked and then in the morning we can alert the authorities and he can be brought to justice."

The ruffian and the butler exchanged glances, and then Page pulled the door closed behind him.

"Now Mrs Tayleur, there is no cause for alarm. This is no ruffian, but Sam Settleby from Petitor Farm. Do you not recognise him, madam? He is often here with deliveries."

"No I do not recognise him," I replied impatiently. "I do not concern myself with farmhands bringing deliveries. Surely he is not bringing goods at this time of night?"

"Well, the farm is very busy at present, madam," Page replied. "They have just started the sowing and there is much to be done through the day. Is that not so, Sam?"

Sam Settleby nodded with some violence, and twisted his hat round in his hands.

"Perhaps this is the first moment he had free, madam."

I stared at Page in frank disbelief, and noticed that he was not wearing his uniform but some black clothes of a decidedly scruffy nature. The thundering, rumbling sounds had recommenced, and I looked to see if the walls were shaking. They were not, and both Page and his accomplice appeared to be quite unconcerned about the noise. They seemed much more worried about my presence in the cellar, witnessing their roguery.

"I do not believe you Page," I said. "In fact I think you are up to no good and that you are in league with this ruffian to cheat your master and make off with his valuable wine and spirits."

Page looked horrified. "Oh no, madam, I can assure you that you are totally mistaken."

"Well, we will see how you explain all this to the master in the morning," I retorted.

Page looked very uncomfortable, but at that moment there was a loud knocking on the other side of the door in the wall.

A voice sounded through the stone, "More tubs here! For God's sake open the door!"

Page turned to me, "Mrs Tayleur, I think you should go back to your bedroom and try to get some sleep. I will deal with everything here and in the morning we can both talk to the master about it. I beg you to leave it to me and go upstairs now."

"I have absolutely no intention of going back to bed and leaving you down here to steal my husband's goods! You will go to prison for this. You will certainly never work again – I will make sure you leave our employ in disgrace and without references!"

Something heavy was now banging against the low door, and the farmhand went over and pulled it. It was pushed from behind, and a stout barrel was rolled through onto the stone flags. It was quickly followed by two more. Page turned his attention from me and began to roll the barrels over to the wall of the cellar, where Sam helped him to lift the ends and stand them against the wall. The thundering had commenced again and there were suddenly many voices. Three men climbed through the low door, pushing more barrels in front of them. They looked very surprised to see me, and stopped in their tracks.

Page took control of the situation and proceeded to introduce me for all the world as if we were in the drawing room upstairs. "Mrs Tayleur, this is Harry Mills from the marble works and Robert Smith, a fisherman from the village. I presume you know Mr Pomeroy who works in the post office?" I was lost for words. I did indeed know Mr Pomeroy and was used to seeing him on the other side of the counter, weighing parcels and searching for villagers' letters on the wooden shelves behind. I was dumbfounded to find him in my cellar in the dead of night, wearing shabby garments and apparently rolling barrels through a tunnel. I pulled my wrap tightly around me.

All three men dragged their hats from their heads and nodded to me. Then Mr Pomeroy came over and shook my hand. "How good of you to come and meet us, Mrs Tayleur," he said.

"We will have to see what my husband says about all this," I replied.

Two more barrels thundered into the cellar, followed by our footman. One of the gardeners followed behind him with yet more. The cellar was noisy and crowded by this time, and the servants seemed anxious to disappear into the shadows around the walls rather than face me. Page was at the door now, helping to bring the barrels through and lending a hand to the crouching men as they came out and stretched upright with relief. The others were deftly righting the barrels and storing them neatly.

More barrels rumbled in, and I heard Page say, "The mistress is here, sir."

"The devil she is!" came the reply, and my husband

emerged from the tunnel. His dark coat was shiny with cobwebs and his hair looked wild and windblown. His necktie had disappeared, his shirt was open at the collar, his face was smudged with dirt and the legs of his breeches appeared to be wet. His eyes were alight with excitement and he looked as if he had been having a very merry time indeed.

"Up and refresh yourselves!" he commanded, waving the men towards the steps to the kitchen. "By God you deserve it! What a fine night, eh Page?"

"A fine night indeed sir," the butler replied, ushering the motley group up the stairs and turning to cast one look in my direction.

William and I were left alone in the cellar with the candles guttering and fifty barrels stacked round the walls.

"What are you doing?" I asked him. "Why on earth has half the village been congregated in our cellar? Page told me this was a delivery from the farm – is that really the case? Why on earth would Mr Pomeroy from the post office be assisting with that? What is inside the barrels William?"

William looked mightily pleased with himself. "These are kegs of brandy Mary Ellen, just landed on Oddicombe beach from a boat that lately left Roscoff."

"Why have they been delivered during the night?" I said, and then I gasped and put my hand over my mouth. "Of course! I see it all now – these kegs have been smuggled from France and you have paid no duty on them! You told me that smuggling no longer takes place here! You said it was not worth the risks!"

"I am always glad to receive intelligence concerning an advantageous undertaking," he replied. "There are still occasional landings here at Marychurch and it is always worth participating."

"You are no better than a common criminal." I

exclaimed. "Whatever would my uncle say? He warned me, he begged me not to marry you. But even he never suspected you to be capable of this."

At that, William threw his head back and roared with laughter. "It will give me great pleasure to invite your uncle here for a visit and pour this very brandy into his glass, then ask him what he thinks of it," he retorted.

I took my breakfast in my room the next morning although I had not slept late. I felt furious with everybody around me – furious that I had been so alarmed and frightened, furious that my husband kept such secrets from me yet shared them with servants, furious that I had been forced to meet with lowly persons while wearing night attire. It was a scandalous circumstance that must never be repeated. When I had recovered my temper somewhat, I descended to the study to tackle my husband.

He was busy at his desk with piles of ledgers, but looked up in a friendly enough way when I entered the room.

"Are you feeling better my dear?" he asked.

"If by that you mean that I am no longer afraid the house will fall down around our ears, or that we will all be murdered by the cut-throats I discovered in the cellar, then I am feeling reassured about that. But I demand and deserve an explanation of your behaviour last night. How can you – a gentleman and squire – partake in a criminal activity with lowly, common persons as your accomplices? I am at a loss to understand you. Are you not ashamed of yourself? I am expecting the Excise officers to arrive at any moment and take you away in chains."

William sighed and took off the glasses he used when he was reading. "I will do my best to explain matters to you Mary Ellen, but I do not hold out a great deal of hope that you will understand. Please sit down in the soft chair and stop towering over me like an avenging angel."

I tutted my disapproval but sat down on the chair as he requested.

"Like you, I heard tales of smugglers when I was a child and loved the cunning they employed to outwit the Excise men. The danger and adventure were hugely attractive to young boys. My brothers and I used to read the stories of Jack Rattenbury and his exploits in this very district, and wish we could be riding with him, and throwing ourselves into ditches at his command. When my father bought the freehold of this mansion he was told of a tunnel that went from the top of the cliff to the cellar here, and discovered that previous occupants of the house had been much involved in smuggling, even in recent times. He immediately wrote to tell me of this, knowing I would be keenly interested."

"But surely they were gentlemen?" I asked, quite shocked by his revelation.

"Of course they were gentlemen. The gentry all over this area have long obtained their fine brandies by this means." He stopped and smiled broadly. "I could tell you of a certain squire with a manor near Dartmouth who kept his illicit kegs hidden in his carriage. The weight of these became so onerous that the wheel axles splintered and he had to prop up the conveyance with bricks!"

"Are you not afraid of discovery? There were several ruffians down there last night, any of whom could inform the authorities about your involvement."

"Why are you referring to them as ruffians? They were our own servants and trusty men from our village. Not one of them would ever pass information to the Excise. The people of Marychurch have been bringing smuggled goods ashore for at least three generations. Oddicombe is an ideal landing spot and everyone takes part. There are several cottages around here with hiding places built into the walls or under the hearth stones and the locals are well used to tipping kegs or parcels into certain hollow trees. You can only be arrested if you are caught actually carrying the goods, and women cannot legally be searched at all. There is a hawker in the village who is well known for carrying pigskins full of spirits under her petticoats."

"You seem to view this as a sport rather than an act of theft," I remarked with disapproval.

"There is some truth in that. But Devon smugglers have never had a reputation for violence, merely cleverness. It is different in other places; I believe smuggling in Kent often resulted in the deaths of both smugglers and Excise officers."

"I presume last night was not the first occasion you acted as part of a smuggling gang?"

"You are correct. When my father informed me about the tunnel under his new property I was keen to investigate, and made certain enquiries on my first visit to Torquay. Page was only too happy to impart information as he had used the tunnel on several occasions. He told me that the tub men would light matches at the top of the cliff in order to call the boat in. They would then descend using the path we walked down, and wade out to meet the Frenchmen who rowed the tubs towards the beach. They could rope two tubs across their shoulders to carry them up the cliff, then those assigned to the mansion would be counted and rolled through the tunnel. I was immediately anxious to take part, and Page sent me news of boats leaving Roscoff, giving me time to travel down to my father."

"But I thought you despised the French? You often tell me about your boyhood fascination with Waterloo and the French wars, and how your mother would threaten that Bonaparte would get you if you would not go to sleep at night. You believed the French to be devils..."

"I was a boy then, and unable to appreciate the quality of the brandy the French can produce. I don't mind meeting them across the bows of a rowing boat in total darkness. There is no call to be convivial with them."

"None of this strikes me as being particularly clever," I said disparagingly.

"My dear, you should hear the story of Resurrection Jackman from Brixham. The revenue men had been suspicious of him for years, but never managed to catch him with any contraband. After learning about a particularly large consignment of goods that had been spirited away into the alleyways of Brixham, they turned up at his cottage. They were disconcerted to find the house full of grieving women – his wife, daughters and sisters were all there, wearing black and sobbing splendidly into their handkerchiefs, for Jackman had died a few days before. His coffin was on show in the downstairs room, though it was already closed, and what a size it was! Jackman must have been a giant of a man! The officers were suspicious, so the widow told them the funeral procession would take place the following night and the coffin would be taken to Totnes where her husband was to be buried. They turned up, but had difficulty following the procession in the dark as it is a hell of a road. Suddenly they caught sight of a spectral grey horse coming towards them, and mounted on the horse was a large man whose chalk white face was glowering at them through the black night. It was Jackman's ghost! They turned their horses round and galloped away in terror, but Jackman was no more dead than you and I, and his coffin was full of smuggled goods. Is that not a splendid story Mary Ellen, and Brixham itself just a few miles up the coast from here!"

William was well-pleased with his tales and his own part in these local shenanigans, but I felt that the best thing to do was to pretend none of it had ever happened. I was cool towards Page from that time on, and always sent my maid to the post office on my behalf, but did not mention the matter to my husband again.

During that summer my stepsons came to stay at Hampton for the first time. They did not make a good impression, being tall, gawky and rather tongue-tied. It had been many months since they had seen their father as they had been spending school holidays with William's brother John at Shevington Hall, while we established our new home and our life together.

"I have been organising the nursery," I told my husband before they arrived.

He glanced up from the newspaper. "Is there any need for that? Charles is eighteen and Cresswell is sixteen; I had not supposed that they would be using the nursery. The elder boys will certainly dine down with us, but I suppose Edward could dine there alone if you wish him to do so."

"I would have thought that the dining room food would be far too rich for a child as young as Edward. Surely it would be more wholesome for him to eat plainer food upstairs."

"As you wish," said my husband, and he shook out the newspaper before applying himself to its pages once more.

Their arrival was awkward. We went out to meet the carriage as it crunched up the drive and turned in front of the house. The coachman pulled open the door and the eldest jumped down. He is the only one of the brothers who has a real look of my husband about him – he has the same thick, dark curly hair and fuller face, whereas the others have the fairer hair and long thin face of their grandfather. He stepped up to William immediately and they shook hands in a fumbling way.

"Charles," said my husband, "This is your new mama," and he held out his hand and drew me towards the boy.

"I am very pleased to meet you Mrs Tayleur," Charles said quietly, and he bowed over my hand. When he straightened up he did not meet my eyes.

"You will address my wife as Mama," William said, and anger was clearly discernible in his tone. Charles said nothing, but by then the two younger boys had scrambled out and were standing shyly with their hands inside their sleeves. Their father turned to them and said firmly, "Cresswell, Edward, come and greet your new mama." I held out my hand and they took it in turn, mumbling that they were pleased to make my acquaintance. We were all relieved when the housemaid came out to show them to their rooms.

They remained occupied upstairs until it was time to dine. I had given instructions for their rooms to be well removed from the main landing and we were thankfully not disturbed by their chattering and noise while we dressed. Edward remained upstairs to partake of boiled mutton and rice pudding while the rest of us sat around the mahogany table which was set out with tureens of watercress soup, sweetbreads and kidneys, braised fillet of beef and a dish of stuffed tomatoes. I presume the boys were well used to dining with their uncle for there was nothing amiss with their manners, apart from their reluctance to make any kind of conversation. I had expected that my husband would ask them about their schools and how well they were doing with their lessons, but he did not. When we had all eaten ice cream and sipped at glasses of Madeira wine, I noticed the boys looking at me expectantly. The eldest was narrowing his eyes and I realised that they were waiting for me to withdraw and drink tea elsewhere so that they could be alone with their father.

"No doubt you are accustomed to your aunt taking tea in her drawing room," I said. "But we do not adopt that custom here if there are no other ladies present. I much prefer to remain with your father while he enjoys his port, rather than sit alone in separate rooms for the next part of the evening." And with that I rang the bell for Page and requested both tea and coffee to be served in the dining room as usual. The boys exchanged a glance then asked to be allowed to retire, pleading tiredness after their long journey.

The next morning the younger boys seemed quite happy to be exploring the gardens and the stable yard, although there was no horse of a suitable size for Edward to ride. Cresswell came downstairs in riding attire after lunch and cantered off to find the pleasure grounds, while Edward occupied himself with the dogs. Charles however, seemed desirous of spending time alone with his father and I did my best to prevent this. I did not want him to worry my husband needlessly. William had plenty of cares and concerns with the estate to manage, and I had recently acquainted him with the news that we would soon be starting a family of our own.

"Are you no longer in the habit of riding out, sir?" Charles had asked earlier, when his father showed no intention of walking to the stables.

"Your mama is unable to ride at present," William replied, "And I prefer to keep to the house in the morning, and enjoy her company in the drawing room."

When my husband later withdrew to his study Charles followed him, and I found both of them standing, some distance apart, by the window.

"My brothers have been discussing the house at Lavender Hill," Charles was saying, "And we were wondering where some of the old things have gone. I cannot see anything here that we used to have at home. Where, for instance, is the great clock that stood half way up the stairs? I remember lying in bed and listening to it chiming the hour when I was very small."

"Most of the furniture was rented with the house," William replied, looking out of the window at Fore Street. A dray cart was standing outside The Dolphin and barrels were being rolled across the cobbles. I had to draw nearer in order to hear their exchange.

"What became of the contents of the nursery? I particularly wanted to find the wooden soldiers and some of the books. There are many of the play things that I would like to see again."

"The toys in a better condition have been brought here and put in the nursery for the use of other children."

"And those that were not in such good condition? What has happened to those?" William was silent. I was feeling increasingly impatient, and wondering why a grown man of eighteen would wish to find children's stories and battered toys. Charles continued, "I was also hoping to find, sir, some personal treasures from Lavender Hill that belonged to my mother and were very dear to her."

At that point I could contain myself no longer and I hurried over to the window. "I would prefer it if your days at Lavender Hill were not mentioned in my home,"

I said. "That time is in the past. It brought considerable grief to your father and I will not allow that sad period to intrude in any way into the happy home we have here. Please do not bring up these painful subjects again."

"Forgive me," my stepson said, and bowed briefly. "It was not my intention, Mrs Tayleur, to cause you any distress. I was simply hoping for a private discussion with my father."

"Dammit Charles," William barked, "You will call my wife 'Mama'!" Charles was already striding across the room and pulling the door open. "Come back here immediately and address her in the proper manner!" But we could hear Charles taking the stairs two at a time and then a door slamming at the back of the house. William was flushed a dark red with anger. "My dear Mary Ellen, I cannot apologise enough for my son's crass behaviour. He was sorely indulged when he was a small child and, as you can see, the result is a wilful disposition and a spoilt character."

I cupped my husband's face in my hands and smoothed the heat away with my fingers. "You must not concern yourself my love," I reassured him. "When our own children are born we will know how to raise them to be modest and full of respect."

William looked thoughtful. "Emma was always a damned fool over those boys. She was forever reading with them or playing some absurd game. I told her I was paying the nurse's salary for no purpose because she left the servants with nothing to do. I worried my sons would grow up with womanish ideas and I was heartily glad when it was time for them to go away to school."

"It is an acknowledged fact that mothers who interfere overmuch in the nursery produce wild and unruly children. Perhaps your first wife suffered from impaired judgement in more than one area of her life."

"That is enough, Mary Ellen. You have just told Charles that you will not countenance the Lavender Hill years being mentioned in our home. You are correct in this and the past must be left to lie in silence now. We will none of us speak of this again." And he took his newspaper from the desk and left the room. When I enquired from Page as to the whereabouts of my husband, he informed me that the master was in the library and that the door was firmly shut.

William later rode out towards Torquay and I was left to take luncheon with my stepsons. It was a quiet meal. The younger boys seem uncertain as to how to address me and call me "Ma'am"; the term being perhaps half way towards fulfilling their father's wishes. Charles still called me "Mrs Tayleur", with icy politeness, and I cannot hope that he will ever call me anything else. We were served with lamb's fry and new potatoes and when we made a start on the gooseberry pudding I felt it was time for conversation of some kind. "How do our meals here compare with those at school?" I asked. "Our cook is called Eliza Tozer – is she better than the cooks in the school kitchens?"

"They are much the same," Edward replied. "We have a lot of boiled mutton there also." The other boys said nothing.

"And when will you all be going back to school? Surely you must be looking forward to returning to your friends and your studies?"

"We will return at the start of the Michaelmas term, ma'am," said Cresswell. "But Charles has left school now. He goes up to Trinity in Cambridge after the summer."

"I was not aware of that," I said, somewhat taken aback. "What do you intend to do there Charles? What exactly is the purpose of attending a Cambridge college for several years?"

"I will train to be a barrister Mrs Tayleur."

"But the cost of getting you admitted to the Bar will be considerable. Why are you so set on this course? What did your father have to say about it?"

"He felt that a career as a barrister would be fitting, ma'am."

"What on earth led you to fix on the law as a profession?"

"I wish to speak for those who have no voice," said Charles. "I will defend those to whom no-one has listened. I want to defeat injustice and achieve a fair hearing for the people in our society who are deeply wronged and disadvantaged."

I felt exasperated. "For heaven's sake Charles! In what way have you ever experienced any form of injustice in your privileged life?"

"You are correct Mrs Tayleur; it is not due to any injustice that I myself have suffered. I wish to be a voice for the poor and the dispossessed."

"Working for the poor?" I exclaimed. "A slum attorney! The last job God made!"

But the insufferable boy would not take correction and continued to argue with me, against every convention of courtesy. "It is not only the poor, ma'am, who have no means of being heard. Women who are divorced by their husbands lose everything – their homes, their children and all claim on any family fortune, even though they may have contributed to this with their marriage portion. I would do my utmost to work towards some entitlement for them."

I stood up then, and found it difficult to control my voice and the shaking of my hands. "I do not think that this is a suitable subject for discussion in front of the children. Nor do I believe that you have acquainted your father fully with these preposterous ideas. He will be horrified. I would appreciate it if the three of you would leave the room now; I feel very disquieted by all you have told me."

They scrambled to their feet and made their way to the door. Edward and Cresswell kept their heads lowered and avoided glancing at anyone, but Charles had defiance written all over him.

I shut myself in the upstairs drawing room and paced the carpet, quite tormented by the stupid boy's utterances. At first I could not wait for William's return so that I could acquaint him with Charles's wild statements and arrogant discourtesy. It was not only the expense involved that had upset me, or even the idea of having dealings with the very lowest forms of human kind, but the boy's claims about divorced women, which must be a direct reference to his wretched mother. But then, despite my fury, I remembered that I had not wanted my husband to be troubled by these children and their concerns. I decided that, as their new mother, I should be the person to rectify the matter.

I began that very afternoon, on finding Charles examining the volumes in the library. I sat down in the carved walnut reading chair as it helped me to keep my back rod straight, rather than sinking onto the morocco settee. "First of all Charles, I would like to establish just how long you and your brothers will be staying here?"

He looked up, surprised. "We believed that we would be here until the commencement of the new term, ma'am. Where else would we go?"

"I think you were spending your holidays with your uncle at Shevington Hall?"

"Well yes, but that was only because our father was getting the mansion prepared. This is our home now."

"No Charles; this is my home, not yours."

He seemed much taken aback. "Mrs Tayleur, I am not sure that I understand you. Surely our home is with our father and he is now living here."

"Charles, you are a young man nearly nineteen years of age. Is it not time you found a means of supporting yourself and establishing a home of your own? Your father will have a new family to provide for very shortly. He has done right by you and now owes you no more."

"Madam, I am the son of a gentleman; what would you have me do? Sell potatoes from a barrow? Hawk round doors peddling clothes pegs and pins? I am aghast that you could imagine some such employment would be more suitable than a university."

Despite my rising anger I endeavoured to maintain a patient, level tone, as if explaining something simple to a child. "Both your father and your grandfather employed themselves wisely from a very early age, making their own way in the world and their own fortunes. Neither of them went up to Cambridge or lived as parasites on the fortunes of others. The cost of having you admitted to the Bar will be almost as great as buying you a commission!"

Charles was visibly choked by this. "Perhaps that is your answer, madam! Buy me a commission and send me to the Crimea and pray that I never come back alive! Then I will no longer be a parasite!"

"You would never make a soldier, Charles. You don't have the backbone for it. A grown man who whines about the whereabouts of toys and story books would not be capable of leading others and facing an enemy. You do not have the courage."

He jumped up from the chair then, and rushed out of the room, a habit he seems to have acquired. I was just thankful he refrained from slamming the door on his way.

Our next opportunity for a tête-à-tête did not occur for several days; the boys kept to their rooms while in the house, and spent a great deal of time riding and rambling in the grounds. They were all surly and silent at table, but William did not remark upon this, or indeed seem to notice it at all. About two weeks after their arrival I came upon Charles in the billiard room. I had heard the clack of a cue hitting ivory, and the thump of a ball landing in a pocket and supposed it to be my husband playing, but when I entered the room it was Charles I discovered, bending alone over the table. He stood up as soon as he was aware of me, and bowed his head slightly.

"So this is how you are spending your time," I remarked, and my disapproval must have been discernible.

"I am merely occupying a spare few minutes here Mrs Tayleur, I hope that is acceptable. My father has promised us a trip to Exeter as my brothers and I need to visit a tailor before the new term commences. He is seeing about the carriage and then we are joining him."

"Exeter?" I said. "He never spoke of Exeter to me. It is not long since we went there; I am sure there can be no real need to go again so soon."

"As I said, ma'am, my brothers and I need to order clothes for the new term."

"Do none of your clothes fit you now? What is wrong with those you wore during the last term? This will be a costly exercise and I am far from being convinced that it is actually necessary."

Charles flushed with anger and his voice shook slightly as he replied. "My brothers have grown Mrs Tayleur, and it is indeed necessary that they are fitted out afresh for the new school year. Furthermore, as you are aware, I am no longer attending school and the clothes I own at present will not be appropriate to wear in Cambridge. I am sure my father would not wish his sons to look like scarecrows and attract the scorn and mirth of others."

"Is there no tailor to be had in Torquay? A local man would be much more reasonable and would not necessitate continual trips all the way to Exeter for fittings. I will speak to your father. I am amazed that he thought to organize all this without recourse to me. It is most unlike him."

"Perhaps, ma'am, he considered that gentlemen's tailoring requirements would not be of interest to you. Also, I believe that my brothers would greatly enjoy a drive with their father; they have hardly spent time with him during their visit."

"Your father has other matters to occupy him now Charles. He has a new family to think about. I understand that Cresswell and Edward must complete their schooling, but as I have explained to you before, you should be making an effort to find a worthwhile direction for your life. I have been considering this carefully and I believe that a career abroad would suit you. There are wonderful opportunities all over the empire for young men of your age – you could do very well for yourself. There is nothing to keep you here; you have no family and no responsibilities. I will ask my uncle to make enquiries on your behalf; perhaps a post in India or Malaya will become available."

That shocked him. I do not honestly think that he had ever contemplated making his own way. He just expected William to support him while he idled away his time at billiard tables and Cambridge drinking clubs. "I could not leave my brothers Mrs Tayleur. You state that I have no family here but I have three young brothers to look out for. I cannot simply leave them."

I felt myself flush with a sudden heat and a buried dread began to surface. My uncle had told me there was an unacknowledged son, and Jane had hinted at it, but I had refused, from the very beginning, to face this. "Three brothers? Three brothers? Whatever do you mean? I cannot understand you Charles. Cresswell and Edward are under the care of your father and myself; they have no need of you."

Charles was clearly deeply disturbed by our conversation and was attempting to conceal this from me by busying himself with chalk and the billiard cue. This hid the workings of his face but I could see that his entire body was shaking. I pushed home my advantage. "May I enquire as to whether you have heard from your uncle lately? I am sure he would like to see you all at Shevington before you return to your educational establishments. We should make arrangements for a journey there before any more time is lost."

He wheeled round to face me, his cheeks red with temper. "Madam, my young brothers have only just been reunited with our father after a lengthy separation, would you deny them some time with him? This is a very large house, is there not room for us here? Do you resent our presence in our own family home?"

"As I have already explained to you Charles, this is my home and not yours. Your father will soon have a new family."

"You are forgetting, ma'am, that one day this entire estate will belong to me, regardless of how many children you provide for my father."

"And what makes you so very sure of that?" I enquired softly.

"Madam, I am my father's eldest son. My father owns this estate, and others, as tenant for life. On his death I will become tenant for life in my turn, before handing the estates on to my eldest son."

"Charles, your father is free to dispose of his assets as he sees fit. He could write a will which leaves all his estates to my son and not to you."

"Forgive me, but I believe that is not possible. The disposal of the family property is governed by my grandfather's will. He purchased the freehold of all the estates and laid down that the eldest son must inherit these. Your son will be unable to do so."

The wretched boy really is insufferable. He speaks to me as if I know nothing and he has the whole world of knowledge at his disposal. I could feel my teeth grinding together and a flush of rage creeping up from my neck. "Oh, hark at the young barrister! Your grandfather is dead and gone – how can his opinions dictate what happens in the future? No-one cares what he wished for in the past. Your father will make up his own mind."

Charles appeared to be unable to speak at this point, and seemed to be struggling to maintain his composure and his temper. I moved closer to him and put my hand on his arm. "Tell me Charles, do you know whether your mother brought a significant fortune to her marriage with your father?"

He did not shake my arm away, but merely bowed his head and murmured, "I have never been told. My mother was one of ten children so I would imagine that her marriage portion could only be small."

I drew back and straightened up so as to appear as tall as I possibly could. "Well I must inform you that I brought a fortune of twenty thousand pounds to my marriage. That money is now irretrievably part of the estate. Can you imagine that I would want my fortune to be inherited by you? Surely you must understand that I would fight for the rights of my own son? As long as there is breath in my body I will work to ensure that my child inherits Hampton and all that goes with it. Whatever your grandfather's will specifies, my son will not be the product of a worthless union besmirched by impurity and betrayal. It is altogether more fitting that he will be your father's heir."

Charles smashed the cue heavily onto the green baize table and rushed from the room. I smoothed down the front of my skirt and smiled. I will not be defeated by an arrogant young upstart.

Charles William Tayleur
Trinity College - Michaelmas Term 1854

Our first visit to Hampton House was bloody. My stepmother has a spaniel face with protuberant eyes and a pug nose, her hair is the exact shade of the fingers of those who smoke a great deal of tobacco and her skin is like uncooked pastry. She is rigid with respectability and Christian correctness and it was very clear from the moment we drew up at the front door that she had no wish for us to be there. Our father seems greater in size but somehow diminished in his person. He is fearful of causing any upset to his new wife, yet I can remember him being fearful of nothing before. It is a long time since we were in his company and both our grandparents have died since we last met, but he did not feel the need to discuss anything with us. It was enough that we were to be provided with meals, beds to sleep in and grounds to roam in.

The mansion is certainly imposing, with fine mouldings above the windows and a handsome porch added by my grandfather. Edward immediately admired the castellations and asked if he could go onto the roof and watch for enemies from behind them. Once inside the house is even grander, and the staircase is particularly impressive, rising from the centre of the hall and then splitting to curve round both sides of the huge stairwell, under the great glass roof. But my father's new wife has fussy taste. The rooms are smothered by dark, heavy drapes and cluttered with expensive ornaments. The mansion almost seems to be uncomfortable, like a person who has been dressed unwillingly in someone else's clothes – a duchess tricked out like a tart.

Our rooms were not on the main landing, but right at the end of the corridor and approaching those used by the servants. Edward had been banished to the nursery like a baby, and even had to eat his meals there with no company at all. He soon took to calling our stepmother "Mouldy Mary". When I asked him how he had come up with this name, he explained that she came from a place called Mold in Wales. There is a painting of this dismal, God-forsaken spot hanging in the hall; a gift from our father so that she does not miss her home too sorely. I notice that she has not bought a picture of Liverpool docks for him in case he still suffers for want of that view.

We quickly discovered that Mouldy Mary would go to any lengths to prevent us spending time with our father. The drawing room is a large, handsome apartment and if we were conversing with him at some distance from her, she would take a hasty leave from whoever she was sitting with and fly across the room, positively scampering in her anxiety to hear every part of our conversation. "What are you all discussing?" she would demand, grasping his arm proprietarily. She would not rest until he had acquainted her with every comment we had made, every question we had asked and every answer he had given.

She was dismissive of my brothers but seemed to find my ideas and opinions particularly aggravating. "Mouldy Mary's kicking up the dust again," Cresswell would observe when my remarks at the table had caused her to leave the room in a temper, and she could be heard shouting and growling at the servants. "You make her mad as Bedlam Charlie – you ought to be careful." And Cresswell was right. Mary Ellen made it very clear to me that she would have me disinherited and take my birthright for her own child.

But she had already robbed us of much more. By her refusal to allow any reference to be made to our happy home at Lavender Hill or any mention of my mother's name, the spiriting away of all our childhood playthings and any possessions from that time of our lives, she made us feel that it had not been real. It was lost to us, and all we had left was a home that was not our home and a father who was no longer able to be our father. We clung together in our rooms at the far end of the corridor, reminiscing about the life we lived when we had a mother and howling with laughter at Cresswell's mocking impersonations of Mary Ellen.

"What about a ride today boys? Land's End is in that direction – don't trouble yourselves to stop at the edge… Nothing to play with Edward? Take some of Eliza's nice knives up to the nursery with you…" He caught her simpering expressions perfectly, complete with the hard dislike which crossed her face whenever she looked in our direction. Somehow, when she had made a sharp, painful comment over dinner, it eased the hurt to gather together afterwards and repeat her conversation using as much comedy as possible. We became adept at capturing the high, genteel, complaining tone of her slightly Welsh voice, and the downward pull of her facial muscles which were beginning to show signs of heavy jowls to come.

The end came quite suddenly on the morning following the argument with my stepmother in the billiard room. I was very anxious indeed to speak to my father alone and I watched her movements closely until she withdrew to her bedchamber and locked the door. I knocked hastily on the door of his study and found him seated at his desk, much engrossed in his papers. I shut the door behind me. "What do you want, Charles?" he asked, his eyes still roving over the writing in front of him.

"Father – I must talk to you."

"What about?" he said, looking up and raising his eyebrows.

Where should I begin? With the legal situation regarding his will and my inheritance? With his feelings towards my plans to study at Cambridge and become a barrister? With his wife's ambivalent attitude towards us and her desire for us to leave Hampton as soon as possible? I just did not know and I was only too aware that my time was limited. No doubt my stepmother was availing herself of her chamber pot, and as soon as she had completed her private ablutions she would be hastening down the stairs to investigate the closed study door.

"There are many things I want to ask you..." I began.

"Then get on with it," he said impatiently.

"Father, I feel we must leave Hampton shortly to visit our uncle at Shevington." He did not show any surprise on hearing this so I can only presume that Mary Ellen had already persuaded him of the importance of such a visit. "Before we go, I need to ask you..."

At that moment I heard the key turning in my stepmother's door and the rustling of skirts hurrying down the stairs. I became flustered. How could I best use the few seconds left to me?

"I need to ask you about my brother. Please tell me where he is living and who is caring for him. I would make the journey to see him if I knew his whereabouts."

My father looked confused for a moment and then the door opened sharply and my stepmother whirled into the room.

"Now, what is all this about?" she asked, with a false smile and an attempt at pleasantness. She walked quickly over to my father and patted him on the head, much as you would a small child or a dog. Did he have any idea how foolish that made him look? Did he appreciate the indignity of such a ridiculous caress?

"Well Father?" I continued defiantly, "My brother – please divulge his whereabouts."

"Charles, what nonsense is this?" my stepmother interceded. "Your brothers are both upstairs, idling their time away doing goodness knows what."

"No, not them – I wish to know where Albert is living so that I can go and see him."

A glint of something very dark and dangerous appeared behind my stepmother's eyes. "Who is Albert?" she asked. "How can he possibly be your brother?"

"Madam, this is between my father and myself.

Please allow him to answer my question."

Mary Ellen spluttered, "How dare you speak to me like that! Remember your Bible Charles – honour your father and mother that your days may be long..."

"You are not my mother. It is not your privilege to correct my behaviour."

"If your own mother had attended more to such correction you may not be the rude oaf that you have become."

"Charles!" my father roared over her, "For God's sake hold your tongue. If you can't speak to my wife in the proper manner then don't speak at all. Get out of the room."

"I will indeed leave once you have given me the information I have asked for. Where is Albert living?"

"William my love, who is Albert?"

My father jumped to his feet. "He is the whore's child! He is nothing to me and no part of this family. This is a decent house and if Charles dares to bring up this subject again God help me I will hold his head under a tap and wash out his mouth with carbolic!"

"My mother was not a whore and you know that!" I shouted.

"Charles," my stepmother cried, "Don't upset your father – look at his colour..."

His face had indeed taken on a livid hue, but he came towards me from behind the desk and made a move to catch hold of my arms. I grabbed at his collar, his hair; I cared not what, and shook him with all my strength. "She was a good woman and a good mother, despite all you say to deny that."

He took hold of me and lifted my feet clear of the ground, then elbowed the door open and shoved me through with such force that my head smashed into the stair banister. I was aware only of the study door slamming shut behind me and my own blood streaming into my eyes and forming a pool on the floor. I tried to get up but was overcome with giddiness and nausea. Page was running towards me but whether through concern for my welfare or a desire to sponge the blood from the good Brussels carpet I have no idea. I pulled myself up by grasping the banister and pushed the butler out of the way. The hall seemed to heave and spin around me. Somehow I staggered up the stairs and reached my room and immediately started to throw some clothes into a bag. Downstairs there was the clattering of a housemaid's box as the damage to the carpet was speedily addressed.

My brothers came running into my room. "What's the commotion Charles?" Cresswell asked. "What have you done now? My God! Who has wounded you?"

I put my hand up to my forehead and discovered that blood was still oozing from a deep gash over my eye. I started to rummage for a handkerchief but seemed to be leaving a mess of blood amongst the linen in my drawer.

"For God's sake, let us do that," Cresswell said impatiently. "Ned – use the water from the washstand and his flannel, anything will do just to staunch the flow..." They forced me to sit down on the bed and, between them, managed to reduce the bleeding and make my countenance more respectable. While they worked I regaled the whole episode. There was no call for comedy this time. I explained that I would leave for Shevington immediately and stay with our uncle until the commencement of term. My brothers insisted on accompanying me, but I explained that they would not be allowed to do this, and our uncle could send for them very shortly. He would make the necessary arrangements for new clothes, allowances for next term and for all our travel needs. Edward was particularly distressed about me leaving and clung to me in tears, but I promised that we would soon be together once more and in happier circumstances.

I had a little money, and grabbing this up with my bag and hat, I ran down the stairs and out of the back door. I left Hampton through the kitchen yard, unwilling to have anyone witness my departure. As I flung myself across the road I turned back for one last look at the mansion. The windows were gleaming in the morning sunshine, but inside they were obscured by the heavy curtains and blinds. I do not understand my stepmother's need to keep the windows covered in this way, even in the middle of the day, rendering all the rooms dark and dismal. Perhaps it is to protect her precious crimson brocade from fading, or to keep her hideous face in the shadows. If I do one day become the master of Hampton, and this looks ever more unlikely, I will throw the curtains back and fill the rooms with light. Intense dislike of her rose up in my throat, and her red hair and spaniel face floated before my eyes. I quickly turned away from the house. I do not know if I will ever see it again.

I knew from one of our few dinner conversations that the railway station was not situated in the middle of the town. My father had described the town council's prejudiced view about the derogatory effects of a station in the town centre, and the great inconvenience of goods vans shunting about in front of the new wave of high class holiday makers now flooding into Torquay. So instead of turning left to head into town, I started towards Plainmoor as this lay in the direction of Barton Hill, where I believed the station to be. I walked quickly with my head down, avoiding curious glances from passers-by who may wonder at the angry cut over my eye and the tormented twist of my features.

As I tramped the dusty pavements a burning sense

of injustice assailed me. I had done nothing to make Mary Ellen dislike me, save being the son of my mother. It was quite permissible for her to make terrible statements about my parents' marriage, my mother's virtue and my own character, but wrong for me even to express any opinions or to have my own ideas about a career. She had ranted at me and insulted me, while I must stand as silent and stupid as a post for fear of seeming discourteous. I had committed no fault, yet I was to lose my place as the eldest son and my hopes of inheriting my father's estates and my grandfather's legacy. How could one woman bring all this to pass? I then considered the changes in my father and the unhappiness of my young brothers and found myself grinding my teeth with impotent rage.

I stopped outside The Fortune of War and entered the bar, so as to ascertain the most direct route to the station. The bartender showed no surprise on beholding my bruised face and angry expression – I probably looked no different from his usual customers – and cheerfully pointed out the way.

It took me short of two hours to reach my destination and I was still in time to catch the afternoon train to Paddington. We have often travelled on trains, due to my grandfather's occupation and the whole family's interest in locomotives. I have never before had to purchase a seat in a second class carriage, but the small amount of money I had brought with me would not run to first class travel.

Once the train was moving I could close my eyes at last, make some attempt to calm my anguished feelings and ragged breathing and plan the journey to my uncle's house. It crossed my mind that just a few years ago I would have had a much more arduous task before me, being forced to undertake the trip by stage coach. Our grandfather had once greatly entertained us with the tale of such a coach rumbling along Devon roads in the darkness, while the driver became concerned about a large dog that seemed to be bothering one of the lead horses. The horse was troubled and afraid and the driver had the devil of a job keeping the coach on the road. When at last they reached the next coaching inn and drew up under the lights in the yard, he saw with horror that the dog was in fact a large white lioness, which had cruelly mauled the horse and caused much terror amongst the whole team. We were left with a tirade of questions for my grandfather to answer – where did the lioness come from? How did the brave driver persuade it to leave the yard quietly without eating any of the passengers? Why was it white? And most importantly of all – was this a true story? My grandfather would simply smile and assure us that he knew it to be true as he had read it in a newspaper.

But I had no lions to fear as the train steamed along by the sea – through Dawlish and Teignmouth towards Exeter. The rhythm of the wheels clicking on the line, the hissing and chugging of the engine and the smell of oil and smoke all brought back poignant memories of the train journeys we had undertaken together as a family. We would all, my mother included, crowd against the windows to watch out for bends in the line when it was possible to see the other part of the train and wave to the passengers there who were leaning out and looking at us. My brothers and I loved to walk down the carriage, hanging onto seats to enable us to stay upright, until we came to the end of the train. There we would gaze out of the back window at the line itself, flashing by underneath us with a speed that defied nature. We never forgot that our own grandfather had been a major force in the development of this modern wonder.

Although I had set out with the intention of travelling straight to Shevington Hall and procuring the sympathy and assistance of my uncle, a different scheme began to form in my mind as I watched the countryside fly past the window. I had travelled through London before, though never alone, and I was familiar with the route I would need to take to reach Lavender Hill, where all our previous journeys had ended. I felt a great need to see my home again; although what I would do there I had no idea. I could then complete the trip to my uncle's house without a great deal of time being lost.

It was evening by the time I reached Paddington Station, and I enquired of a porter where I could catch an omnibus to take me into the city. He directed me to a nearby public house, The Yorkshire Stingo, from where the omnibus picked up passengers for London. I made sure to climb upstairs on this conveyance, my mother having always had a fear of infections lurking in the straw on the floor inside.

On alighting in the city I realised how hungry I had become, and set off to find a place where I could eat before looking for lodgings. The gas lights were hissing and several ragged children were still out on the streets in the dark, gazing wistfully into shop windows. Some were drawing near to a vendor who was selling hot potatoes from a brazier, probably for the warmth. I looked at them. Most had bare feet, but one boy was wearing a large pair of shoes tied on round his ankle which flapped as he walked – clearly the soles had been cut off. Even from where I was standing I was aware of the smell emanating from their clothes; it appeared to be a mixture of dead mice, blocked drains and strong cheese. They had probably lost their parents and had no-one who cared whether they were alive or dead. My grandfather was a famous engineer who worked with Brunel and George Stephenson, my father was a wealthy merchant and even my own allowance would support several simple families, but I was as motherless as they were.

In this frame of mind I entered a chop house in order to buy a meal. I had never eaten in such an establishment before and I was struck by the smell of frying fat and the lack of light. Both my table and chair felt greasy and the waitress who attended to me was wearing a filthy apron. The other diners were all men, mostly alone and intent on their food. My chop, when it came, was served with a fair amount of gravy and nothing else and the fine side dishes I was accustomed to felt far away indeed. The fat down the edge was yellow and crusty, as an old whore's garter might look, but I was hungry and it tasted well enough. At least it was one dinner where I was expected neither to make courteous remarks to Mary Ellen nor listen to her barbed replies.

There was no shortage of hotels in the city and I soon found one that I could afford. The room I was shown into was small and bare but not unlike the accommodation I had enjoyed at school during my final two years there, when I was allotted my own room instead of sleeping in the dormitory. I got very little sleep – carts, carriages and cabs were continually passing under my window; no doubt the early morning traders and deliveries beginning before the evening revellers had finally retired. Once I thought I heard a scream and several times there was an outbreak of shouting and indeterminate cries. As I lay on the hard, narrow bed I wondered if my father was thinking about my whereabouts. Had he sent an urgent message to my uncle asking to be informed when I arrived? Was he worrying about how I was spending the night? But in my heart I knew that he would be encased inside my stepmother's crimson brocade bed and sparing no thought for me at all.

The following morning I took a cab out to Wandsworth and then walked to Lavender Hill, drinking in all the familiar sights as I did so. I passed the sweet shop with the same bottles of toffees and sherbet lemons behind the thick glass panes; the milliner's where my mother bought her gloves and the bakery where you could buy perfect, tiny loaves, still warm, which we would cradle in the palms of our hands on frosty mornings. I looked into the park where we were often taken for walks and where we had all sailed toy boats on the lake. And then I walked up the drive to my old home, a place I had left without ever dreaming that I would only return like this.

The first thing that struck me was the smell of wild garlic which had always grown in the woods at the side of the drive. My brothers and I often played games in these woods, bruising the garlic as we ran around, and the pungent smell took me back instantly until I could almost hear Edward's complaining voice asking us not to go too far ahead and leave him behind. Perhaps that smell will always have the same effect on me, even when I'm an old man and the games themselves have been long forgotten.

The drawing room was situated at the front of the house and, like that at Hampton, had tall windows that reached to the ground. I stepped up to these and peered inside. As my father had explained that he rented the furniture along with the house, I suppose I was expecting to find the room much as we had left it. Perhaps my mother's tea sets and dishes would yet be displayed on the lace covered shelves of the china cabinet, the fire screens with their embroidered cottages and hollyhocks would still be in their place next to the fire, the green and white striped sofas would look as if my mother had only just straightened them after rescuing Edward's marbles from down the back. But I was wrong; the room was unrecognisable. It had been a light, pretty room and it was now transformed into an apartment much more fitting to Mary Ellen's taste than my mother's. Every available space was filled with occasional tables, all heavily draped with dark cloths and covered with clocks, marble statuary and framed pictures. Several glass domes stood about, harbouring displays of dried flowers and stuffed birds. The seats were all buttoned and stuffed to such an extent that they looked unforgiving and uncomfortable. The only part of the room that must have been the same was the fireplace, but this was so bedecked with a thick, stiff pelmet and a clutter of ornaments that I could not make out any part I recognised. Hanging above it was a large, ornate mirror, so clearly the current tenants share none of my mother's caution where fire is concerned. Of these tenants there was no sign – the fire was not burning as it was summer and it was still much too early in the day for the gas to be lit.

I followed the path towards the rear of the house and came into the kitchen yard. I was about to look into the windows there when a man emerged from the back door and said, "Are you looking for someone, sir?" He was still in shirtsleeves having clearly not taken the time to pull on his coat, and an apron was tied over his clothing. He looked as if he may well have been blacking boots.

"Yes... that is to say... I was wondering if the Tayleur family are still living here. I had heard that they may have moved away, but as I was passing I thought I would come and enquire."

The manservant scratched his head. "The Tayleurs

you say, sir? Now that is going back awhile. They must have left here a good three years ago, perhaps even more. I've been working here the last two years and they'd been long gone when I arrived."

"Did any of the staff here work for the family?" I asked.

"No sir; the mistress hired all fresh. No one was here then."

"Do you happen to know why the family left?"

He looked at me, clearly wondering just what connection I had with the previous tenants and why I had wandered into the kitchen yard to discover information pertaining to them. "Well now, there were a lot of stories going round the neighbourhood at the time, sir. I believe there was rather a scandal. Mrs Tayleur was entertaining a young gentleman here while her husband was away. Mr Tayleur sent her back to her family along with a baby she'd had that he was having nothing to do with." He watched me closely to judge what effect his revelations were having upon me. I endeavoured to hear him out without moving a single muscle on my face. "Then Mr Tayleur left here quite soon after. I suppose the place held unhappy memories for him sir, and he wouldn't have liked to think of that young gentleman visiting here and seeing his wife."

"Did you know any of the family?" I asked, as coolly as I could.

"I couldn't say that I knew them sir, but I did used to see Mrs Tayleur out and about on the high street. She was often with her young boys I seem to recall."

"What was she like?"

"She always looked full of spirit sir, and very lively and smiling. She was a nice looking lady and lovely with those boys of hers. I wouldn't like to think that anything bad happened to her – I hope she managed alright in the end."

I looked down at that and swallowed.

"Would you care to come inside, sir, and have some refreshments?" he asked while I was recovering myself. "I'm sure the master and mistress would be glad to see you and they may even know more than I do about the Tayleurs. I'll just step inside and tell them that a young gentleman is here making enquiries."

"That is very kind of you but I have no intention of troubling your master and mistress. You have been most helpful – thank you. I am grateful for the time you have given me but I must now resume my journey; the afternoon is wearing on. Good day to you."

I waited until he had re-entered the house before making my way out towards the kitchen gardens. Swallows were circling as if gathering together ready to start on the long journey south, and leaves were already falling and cluttering the ground, announcing the end of summer.

In the walled garden I could not be seen from the house, and I wandered between the rows of cabbages, the canes of bean plants, the straggling peas and the marrows on neat heaps. Against the wall were spades, hoes, rakes and several old watering cans and sieves. Presumably they were the same tools that the gardeners used when we lived here; surely newly appointed gardeners were not expected to bring their own tools with them? I doubted whether my father had come out to the kitchen garden to retrieve old implements while the carriage was waiting to drive him away. I came across a rubbish heap in the corner and idly turned it over with my foot. There seemed to be a quantity of broken harness and several pieces of cracked pottery of a design I did not recognise. I found a shoe and examined it carefully, but it was not of a size that any of us could have worn. Now I knelt down and started to dig into the heap with my hands, pulling aside a squashed, rusty cake tin and part of a white wash bowl. There was some paper, probably too bloodied by the meat inside to be any use for other purposes, and a smashed mirror which looked as if it had adorned a servant's bedroom. I began to dig more fervently. I was not even sure what I was looking for; perhaps I just wanted to find some sign that we had once lived there, proof that we had been a family, a clue that we belonged in the past of that house and had not been obliterated by what came next, washed away by the breaking scandal and my father's new marriage so that it seemed we had never been there at all.

Then I saw the glint of something shiny. I burrowed amongst some scraps of old leather until my fingers closed over a small cut glass bottle. I pulled it out and rubbed off some of the soil and dirt caught in the fine grooves of the pattern. It was a perfume bottle and I recognised it. It was the very perfume bottle that had always stood on my mother's dressing table. I eased out the stopper, put the bottle to my nose and drew in a breath. Despite the bottle being empty, despite it having lain at the bottom of this rubbish heap for God knows how long, despite my mother having died several years before, I drew in the smell of her. It was unmistakeable. It was the scent that always hung about her dresses, it was the scent I associated with being held close and treasured, it was the same scent that would linger in a room and whisper that she had passed through just moments before. I replaced the stopper and squeezed the little bottle tightly. And then, sitting on a rubbish heap with the evening drawing in and the summer ending, I wept at last.

Charles William Tayleur
Trinity College Cambridge – September 1854

My stepmother has been delivered of a son. My father has given him our oldest family name; he is to be called Galfred. The news caused me to think of Hampton with its rolling parklands and clear view of the sea. It seems it will be a stolen prize, treasure denied to me.

Trinity College Cambridge – November 1855

My stepmother has been delivered of a daughter – Eveline.

Trinity College Cambridge – December 1856

My stepmother has been delivered of another son. He has been given my father's name – William.

Mary Ellen Tayleur
Hampton House - January 1858

My husband had always been rather short of patience, as I witnessed on the one occasion he shared something of his business dealings with me. A few months after the birth of our youngest child he burst into the drawing room, arresting my attention from my letters, and demanded, "Pray tell me my dear, what is the first thought that comes into your mind on hearing the word Peru?"

I looked at him steadily and tried to conceal my confusion, as Peru summoned no thoughts to my mind whatsoever.

"Come Mary Ellen – quick, quick. The value of this lies in expressing your immediate association of ideas...Peru, if you please."

I cast my mind back to the desultory lessons with Miss Huckleback, who did indeed occasionally draw my attention to the yellowing globe. I'm sure I could, if pressed, have found Peru upon its surface but I was completely at a loss now, having to match any facts or thoughts to its name.

"Could they, do they perhaps grow bananas there?"

He smacked his fist onto the side table so hard that the ormolu clock jumped. "Bananas? For heaven's sake Mary Ellen! Bananas indeed! No – surely you think of darkness? You have heard the epithet "darkest Peru" have you not? Eh? You must associate Peru with darkness surely?"

I could not help noticing that a dark hue was in fact

traversing his face at that moment, and he seemed to be having considerable difficulty keeping his temper.

"Why of course William, I was just about to mention that." He looked disbelieving, and barely concealed a snort of contempt. "Is Peru of particular interest this morning?"

"It most certainly is Mary Ellen, because your husband has gone some way towards relieving that darkness and providing light for the poor beleaguered inhabitants of that nation! What do you think of that?"

I could make nothing of this at all, and started to feel nervous in front of my husband's excited and furious questioning.

"You must explain to me my dear William, and then I will understand just what you have done."

"I have bought shares in the Lima Gas Company! Invested the twenty thousand pounds you brought to our marriage in lighting up the streets of that far flung city and beyond! Imagine the work there now – the Peruvian workmen setting up miles upon miles of street lighting, the laying of gas pipes, the lamp lighters tramping along the roads and putting up their ladders, the crimes that will no longer be committed, the feeling of safety among the good people of Lima – all because of my investment and your dowry. We have given those people a gift of light, and all you could imagine was bananas. How narrow your vision is Mary Ellen. But I must not blame you for the shortcomings of the education you received." And he whirled out of the room and slammed the door so hard that a piece of the wooden panelling fell off.

I sat quite still at my desk with one hand on my breast, under which my heart was thumping and knocking with some violence. One ridiculous memory had come into my mind. Many years previously my uncle and I had stayed in a hotel and from my bedroom window I looked directly down upon the street. There was a lamppost on the other side of the road and several children had tied skipping ropes to this and were dancing round it as if it was a maypole. They were singing a song I was unfamiliar with but it sounded catchy and tuneful and the girls were clearly having a happy time. I leaned out of my window and watched them, and wished that I could dance around a lamppost and pretend that it was a maypole, and have friends who would sing with me as if it was spring. I had been on the outside looking in, and that was still the case.

Shortly after this tetchy exchange I noticed that my husband was finding it difficult to look me in the eye; in fact he never made eye contact with anyone at all. He started to move restlessly around the house, perpetually running up and down the stairs and frequently going outside, although he had no reason for doing so, and did nothing when he was out there.

And with that began the week of horror. I found William in the peachery one night after dark, frantically measuring the temperature and shouting that it was too cold and that the peaches would die. I tried to explain to him that it was winter and there were no peaches, but he pulled his arm away from my grasp and went back to feeling the pipes. "That damned gardener, letting it get so cold in here. Why isn't he doing his job properly? Why is it so cold? Surely he understands that peaches need warmth? Where the devil is he? Why am I paying him when he can't do his damned job? Go and fetch him – bring him here to explain himself!"

Somehow I persuaded William that it was late in the evening and the gardener would be asleep but we would see to the peaches in the morning, and I got him back into the house. After I had gone to bed he came into my room and woke me to tell me he was worried about Cresswell. My husband never showed much concern for his older children, and certainly never shared any worries about them with me, so this took me by surprise.

"He is not playing enough cricket – I should have sent him to Eton like Charles. Wrong choice of school. Rugby is a bloody stupid game. He needs to learn all the tactics and strategies of cricket. Teaches you to concentrate and have patience, gives you a good eye... I don't know what Cresswell is learning at that school; his letters read as if they were written by a half-wit."

"Surely schoolboys do not play cricket during the winter?"

William glared at me. "Waterloo was won on the playing fields of Eton," he said. "Although he was a real duffer while he was there, by all accounts."

I pursed my lips. This was, at last, a rational statement that I could agree with. My stepson Charles had been at Eton and I was sure it had all been an expensive waste of time. I felt a small stab of triumph to hear William describe him in such terms. "Charles was coddled and indulged when he was a child and his character was permanently impaired," I said. "In my opinion he should be sent overseas to pursue a career that will correct his many faults and give him some back-bone."

"In your opinion? I hear a great deal about your opinions, madam, and often desire that you were capable of keeping them to yourself." William was looking dangerous now. His cheeks were suffused with a dark purple and his bloodshot eyes were narrowed with dislike as he turned in my direction. "Not Charles, you stupid woman; the Duke of Wellington, the hero of Waterloo. Up guards and at 'em!" And with that, he suddenly grabbed one of my tall toilette china candlesticks from the dressing table and proceeded to thrust it repeatedly into my bed curtains, grunting and growling all the while. "This is how we did it," he remarked, "We knocked the stuffing out of Boney like this. I was there – I saw it all."

"Don't be silly William; you were only twelve years old when the battle was fought. You could not possibly have been there."

"If Fat George could claim that he was there, then we all can – every servant and shopkeeper - all charging at the French in our butchers' aprons with our meat cleavers and bags of potatoes. A nation of shopkeepers indeed. A nation of shopkeepers we may be, but we pulverised you. Stand together! Hold firm – shoulder to shoulder! Keep the squares strong!"

He began to sing in a booming voice,

"Boney was a warrior,

Away, ay-yah!

A warrior and a terrier,

Jean Francois!

Boney went to Waterloo,

Away, ay-yah!

There he got his overthrow!

Jean Francois!"

He walked over to the door and drew himself up very straight, then spoke in a cross, high-pitched tone, "Get to bed William! Go to bed quietly or Boney will get you! He gets all the bad boys. He's coming up the stairs for you William – listen." He put his finger up to his lips, "Shh." A look of real fear passed across his face and he seemed to be listening intently for the sound of Napoleon's boots mounting the staircase, then fell suddenly back on the bed and exclaimed, "By God, I think I've lost my leg sir!" He dropped the candlestick and it broke, felt both legs tentatively as if making sure that they were still attached to his body, then slumped forwards and put his hands over his face, groaning. "Next to a battle lost, the greatest misery is a battle gained."

I sat next to him and touched his arm tentatively. "All this was a very long time ago," I said. "You must not upset yourself over something that happened forty-three years ago. It is all in the past and you can forget it now."

"Forget the past?" he said. "There is no chance of that; it is all creeping up on me. It gets nearer every moment and hangs over my shoulder like a black, clawed thing."

I poured some water from the jug into a tumbler and handed it to him. He seemed strangely quiet now and so I stood up, moved carefully over to the bell pull and rang for help. When my maid came in I asked her to fetch Page so that we could assist my husband to his room.

We were making stumbling progress across the landing when Galfred appeared from the nursery corridor. He was wearing his long, white nightgown and staring at us. "Mama?" he asked in a perplexed little voice.

William stopped when he heard this sound and turned to look at the child. "What the hell is this?" he demanded in a loud voice. "Who the devil are you?"

Galfred fled back to the night nursery in terror.

When my husband awoke next morning he had no memory of the incident in the peachery or his concerns about Cresswell's schooling.

We were hosting a dinner that evening and had invited the Misses Anstey, spinster sisters who live at The Brake, Reverend Harris and his wife and Mr and Mrs Phillips from Wellswood. Most unusually, Mr

Robert Cary had agreed to attend and was to bring his mother. The Carys like to keep themselves to themselves and generally stay walled up in Torre Abbey, and so this occasion had particular significance for us. Society life in Torquay is no easy matter, believe me.

I had ordered roast fowl with watercress and breast of veal, stuffed and rolled. I had place cards made up in town with the names printed on silk, and showed the servants how to fold the napkins into the shape of palm leaves. William led Mrs Cary into the dining room while I took Mr Cary's arm and showed him to the seat next to myself. Page served the soup and each guest turned to his neighbour and murmured politely; perhaps an observation on the weather, or the roads, or arrivals in Torquay this week for the season. We were all well informed about this as lists were printed in the Torquay Times, but many of the fine visitors leased villas from Mr Cary himself, and he was quietly describing his latest tenants to the elder Miss Anstey. I could hear my husband addressing Mrs Cary in a very loud voice, talking about his father's industrial achievements. We have never previously drawn our acquaintances' attention to this period of our heritage, preferring to emphasize the gentry aspect of the Tayleur family and their seat at Buntingsdale Hall in Market Drayton, but William was now describing his father's work at the foundry in Warrington.

"Our locomotives go all over the world – every dark, inaccessible, forgotten corner! We have just shipped three to the Great Indian Peninsular Railway and two for East India. In fact, my father made locomotives for Russia – for the Tsar himself. My father's engine pulled the royal train – probably still does, unless those damned insurgents have succeeded in blowing it up of course. But we would have heard wouldn't we?

It would have been in the newspaper if they'd blown up the Russian royal train?" He looked enquiringly around the table, where the guests seemed uneasy and were staring at their soup, crumbling bread, tracing the lace of the tablecloth with ungloved fingers.

"The Romanovs intend to build in Torquay," Mr Phillips said, making some attempt to dissipate the awkward silence. "They have purchased land up on the headland at Daddyhole."

"What a marvellous thing for our town," exclaimed the younger Miss Anstey. "Imagine meeting the Empress in a tea shop!"

"She may order clothes here – we could request the same patterns," said Mrs Phillips.

"And who will they bring with them?" my husband demanded loudly, slamming his fist on the table. "Damned rebels and assassinators – you will no longer believe they are marvellous for Torquay, madam, when bombs are exploding under our carriages and murderers are leaping out of crowds and firing pistols in every direction."

"My dear Mr Tayleur," Reverend Harris interrupted, "You are alarming the ladies. All this is a gross exaggeration and could never happen in Torquay."

My husband ignored him. "Russian peasants lurking around the Lincombes, waiting for them to emerge from their lair, blowing up our trains if they take a trip to Exeter..." He wheeled his arms in the air, almost disarraying Mrs Cary's headdress and causing her to utter a small cry. Her son, who had previously been endeavouring to disappear within his cravat, stood up at once and came round to her chair.

"Come Mama, we should leave now. Mrs Tayleur, I am afraid my mother is becoming rather distressed. I hope you will forgive me if I take her home."

But before I could respond my husband veered onto a different subject, seemingly forgetting all about the dangers of a Russian holiday palace on Daddyhole Plain and reverting to his father. His voice had now become very loud indeed. "Did you know that the Tsar himself invited my father for a ride? He requested that my father join him for a trip on the royal train, as he had built it! A jaunt around mighty Russia, steaming across the steppe, watching bubbling samovars, knocking back vodka while Cossacks were dancing. Damned peculiar buildings there though – why do they make them such ridiculous shapes?" He glared round the table and waited for an answer.

"My dear," I interrupted gently, "Your soup is getting cold."

My husband stared at me malevolently from the opposite end of the table. His face was flushed and his nostrils were flaring. "Are you telling me to be quiet, madam? To hell with the soup and to hell with you as well. If I want to entertain my own guests at my own table in my own house, who are you to gainsay me? You argue with me woman and I will put you away just as I did the last one. Pack you off back to your family, damn you. Though I grant she had never interrupted me at table. No – her sins were of quite a different nature, believe me..."

Several more guests had risen from their chairs and were murmuring about leaving. I rang the bell for Page, my hands shaking uncontrollably and a feeling of horrified fear and anger rising unbidden into my throat. I could not believe William had mentioned his first wife and hinted at their scandalous divorce. And the barbarous way he had spoken to me was not to be borne – how could I look our neighbours in the face again? His scurrilous swearing and oafish behaviour were so unlike his true self that I felt bewildered and amazed by the turn of events. Meanwhile William was staring around at his guests, his pupils so dilated they looked like black jelly.

Reverend Harris touched my husband's arm. "Perhaps you need to rest, Mr Tayleur," he said. "You must have been under some kind of strain in recent days. A period of quiet recuperation and you will be yourself once again."

"Don't talk such damned nonsense man, there's nothing wrong with me." William propelled the vicar back towards his chair. "Here, sit down and finish your soup. We've only just started." But the ladies were determinedly pulling on their gloves. They looked shocked and very anxious to be gone. Page came into the dining room and seemed perplexed to find the guests on their feet, untouched bowls of soup around the table and his master, red and excited, waving his arms and shouting that they should all sit down.

I murmured to the butler as discreetly as I could, "Page, I think Mr Tayleur is rather unwell. Perhaps you could help him to his room?" But my husband had no intention of leaving quietly and poured more wine into his glass. Then he sat down at his place once more and picked up his soup spoon.

"We must leave you," said Reverend Harris firmly. "I do hope that Mr Tayleur will be feeling much better in the morning." The other guests murmured in agreement and moved towards the door, while stealing glances back at my husband who was spooning soup into his mouth rather noisily and spilling much of it down his waistcoat.

I had absolutely no idea what to say to them. "I am so very sorry," I began in a fluster, following them out into the hall. They were hurriedly taking their cloaks from Page and seemed reluctant to look at me. Only Reverend Harris kindly stepped towards me.

"Do not worry my dear Mrs Tayleur. I am sure your husband will be back to his old self in the morning."

Then they all scuttled away, probably desperate to gossip about the events of this evening with every matron, dowager and dandy they could find in Torquay. They must have thought that my husband had drunk too much wine, but I knew that was not the case at all. So what could possibly explain his wild, excitable behaviour and the terrible things he had said? What could be wrong with him?

I went slowly back into the dining room to find William ripping up all the slices of bread he could find and throwing the pieces at the candles, perhaps in a vain attempt to extinguish them.

"Where the hell is the veal you ordered?" he demanded.

"The veal will not be served," I replied testily, "Because all the guests have left."

"Where have they gone?" He seemed to be genuinely puzzled about their departure.

"They have gone home William; they actually fled from here because you ruined our dinner party. How could you behave the way you did – shouting and swearing and making preposterous claims? How dare you speak to me the way you did? I have never been spoken to in that manner in the entire course of my life. And in public! Have you no idea what effect this will have on our standing in society? And Mr Robert Cary had accepted an invitation to dine with us at last and you behaved like a drunkard. No-one will ever dine with us again! What will they think of us now?"

"Hold your tongue woman! I will not be berated like a servant. I am the master of this house and you are a shrew. Two wives – one a shrew and the other a whore – good God, how can one man be so unfortunate?"

"William, do not say such terrible things..."

But my husband had stood up, sending his chair crashing to the floor, and was lurching towards the door. He turned once to look at me and muttered, "I will see you in hell." I sank down onto a chair and put my head in my hands. What was happening? What illness had struck my husband and caused him to behave in this manner? How could we ever redeem ourselves in the eyes of society? These tortuous questions kept me awake throughout the entire night.

It was with trepidation that I awaited my husband the following morning, but he came in to breakfast as if none of the events of the previous evening had ever happened.

"Good morning my dear," he said, going over to the sideboard and heaping veal croquettes and grilled cutlets onto his plate. "I must say I'm devilish hungry this morning. What a bright, crisp day it is – have you observed the weather as yet? I wondered if you would like a ride out in the phaeton?"

Now a ride in the phaeton was a particular treat. It was such a high wheeled carriage that you could bowl along and have excellent views of all around you. And it was built for speed, although I never liked William to drive fast. That is probably why I was rarely invited to join him, and heaven knows how fast he drove when alone. But if he was restored to himself once more and prepared to make peace with a carriage ride, then I could do nothing but agree to go.

I was hoping we would drive down through Wellswood and along Victoria Parade, always the place to be seen at this time of year when Torquay was bursting with the royal, the famous and the rich, but instead William turned in the other direction as we emerged from our drive, and trotted down towards

Torre. It was cold but sunny and my spirits lifted a little as we sped along. My husband is an excellent driver and made a fine picture as he controlled the great horse easily, and waved his carriage whip cheerfully at the common people of St Marychurch. He was calm and content and quite a different person from the terrifying being of the previous evening, who seemed to have lost every sense of propriety and decency. He said nothing, but frequently took out his pocket watch and looked at the time. I could only attribute his behaviour during dinner to have been the result of a temporary fever; a passing illness which had now left him.

We were heading towards Lawes Bridge, a place where the railway line runs parallel and close to the road. William slowed the horse to a walk and checked his watch once again, while looking searchingly up the line where the train would be coming from Newton Abbot. Sure enough, we soon heard the puffing and whistling that announced the train was approaching. As the cloud of grey smoke billowed up above the trees, my husband brought the whip down smartly on the horse's back. "Get up there!" he shouted, then set his face grimly forwards as the horse set off at a gallop and the phaeton lurched and swayed alarmingly.

"My dear," I gasped, trying to clutch at my hat and hold onto the low side of the carriage at the same time, "Please make the horse slow down." But he made no sign that he had even heard me, and continued to whip the horse and smack the reins down repeatedly. The trees on the far side of the railway line, their winter branches reaching out like cold fingers, blurred into a towering shroud of thorns as we pounded past them, and the train tore up behind us, screaming and belching out acrid smoke. I could hear the wheels scraping on the metal rails and the fireman's shovel feeding the flaming furnace. William kept looking over his shoulder to judge the speed with which the train was gaining on us. He was standing, crouched forward over the reins jockey-style, flecks of foam around his mouth. I glanced downwards. The road was racing by sickeningly and the carriage was jolting so much that my bones seemed to have become disengaged, one from the other, until I felt it was only my corset that held my shaken body in one sorry piece. I tried to grasp at my husband's arm but the violent movement of the carriage rendered this impossible.

As the train drew closer William suddenly veered the carriage off the road and onto the scrubland next to the rails. My terror reached even greater heights – did he have some diabolical plan to drive us between the wheels of the engine? The gasping and screaming of the locomotive was ear-splitting and we were enveloped in a hot, grimy fog. The engine pounded rhythmically in a hideous dance of death. The wheels were roaring along the line, just inches from our carriage. And at that moment, unbelievably, my husband stood upright and placed one foot on the seat. Keeping his balance with difficulty he tossed the reins into my lap and then launched himself towards the footplate of the engine. I gave a strangled scream and reached towards him uselessly. It seemed he would plummet between the galloping carriage and the speeding train, but the fireman had flung himself towards the edge of the footplate and managed to grab his coat and drag him on board.

The carriage was bolting on relentlessly, the horse driven by the terror of the screaming monster beside him. I forced myself to look ahead and saw that the station was terrifyingly close, with several people on the platform all crowding to the edge and staring at my full tilt approach. I had no idea how to stop our horse crashing into the stone edge of the platform and killing me and a number of bystanders as well. The train was steaming and whistling into the station and I could hear women's screams, some of which must have been my own. The horse showed no sign whatsoever of slowing down or even noticing that obstacles were looming dangerously in his path. I must have closed my eyes because with great suddenness two gentlemen from the platform and several workers in railway uniform appeared and were grasping the horse's harness and the carriage and exerting all their strength to bring them to a stop. The horse reared and cried and one of the gentlemen was knocked to the ground and had to roll out from under the flailing hooves, but somehow this succeeded in bringing my ordeal to an end and the carriage stopped. Hands reached up to help me free myself while others held the horse and disentangled it from the carriage trappings. I found it impossible to stand unaided – my legs were shaking uncontrollably and I felt faint and sick. As I was helped towards the ladies' waiting room I caught a glimpse of my husband, waving and smiling from the footplate of the engine as if he was greatly pleased with what he had done.

I sent for the doctor as soon as we got home. He remained closeted with William for a long time, but when Page brought him to me in the drawing room he did not have very much to say.

"I think Mr Tayleur badly needs to rest," he suggested. "He should take a spoonful of this tonic with every meal and I will visit him tomorrow. Do not hesitate to send for me in the meantime if you are at all worried." And he bowed over my hand and left. I looked at the medicine bottle and the sticky green liquid it contained and felt, in my heart of hearts, that this would not help my husband to recover his health.

This bottle was by no means the only medicine the doctor had given my husband during the past few weeks. For some time I had been aware that William used a mercury salve to alleviate painful sores on his leg. The mercury did afford him some relief, and Dr Toogood recommended that it would therefore be even more beneficial to take doses of Van Swieten's Liquor, a form of mercuric chloride, the Viennese treatment for ailments William did not discuss with me. He had been only too glad to try it.

The following morning Page came to tell me that my husband was suffering from a severe headache. I hurried to his room and found him standing by the window in his night shirt and smashing his head against the wall repeatedly. I ran over to him and pulled him away. "What are you doing to yourself?" I asked, while persuading him to sit on the bed.

He turned his face towards me and I was shocked by his expression. He looked tormented and terrified and his eyes wore a haunted look the like of which I have never encountered before or since. "My mind, Mary Ellen – my mind is torturing me. It has no mercy; no compassion."

I was at a loss as to what to say. I patted his arm and suggested he got dressed and came down to breakfast. "You will feel better when you have had something to eat and a hot drink," I ventured.

He pulled his arm away impatiently. "Does your memory ever play tricks? My mind is calling up all the very worst memories I have – every sin I have committed, every cruelty or unkindness, every shame and wrong doing – they are floating to the surface like detritus from the depths of my soul. The Day of Judgement is upon us and I will be judged on these..."

He let out a howling cry and jumped up, resuming his place by the window and hitting his head violently against the glass. The pane broke with a crack like a pistol shot and a deep red wound appeared in his forehead. Blood started to leak down his face. I ran out of his bedroom door and across the landing, leaning over the banisters and calling for Page.

"Go and fetch Dr Toogood this instant," I shouted down to the butler in the hall below, "And send the maid up here with warm water and a bandage."

When I ran back into the bedroom William was struggling into his breeches. "You must sit quietly for a while my dear," I said placatingly. "Dr Toogood will be here in a moment to see to your wound."

"To hell with Dr Toogood," my husband replied in a very bellicose manner. "I have no time for the Toogoods of this world; I must see Kitson this morning. I have urgent business to conduct with him."

"William, how can you possibly visit the solicitor's offices with blood pouring out of your head? You will be mistaken for a ruffian and sent away."

The maid came in with a bowl and some soft cloths.

"You have been bedevilling me for months, madam, about making a new will to favour your children. I am, this very morning, in the right frame of mind to comply with your vexatious demands. Do not prevent me from leaving the house Mrs Tayleur, or I may well change my mind and leave the will as it stands!"

I managed to take his shirt out of his hands and lay it down where it could not be besmirched with blood. "My dear, we would never prevent you from going about your business, but please allow us to clean up the wound before you go. What will Mr Kitson think if you arrive looking like a pirate? He is used to clients from the best circles. You cannot measure up to the likes of Sir Lawrence Palk if you have blood all over your shirt, can you?"

This seemed to make sense to him, and he allowed us to manoeuvre him onto a cane chair, bathe his face and tie a bandage around his head.

He was charging down the stairs just as Dr Toogood was shown through into the hall.

"There you are Doctor!" William exclaimed heartily. "You said that you would bleed me on your next visit, but as you can see I have bled myself! That will save money on your account!" And he grabbed up his hat and stick and whirled out of the front door.

The doctor looked amazed. "Where is he going?" he asked.

"He is going to see Mr Kitson in order to conduct some legal business," I replied.

Dr Toogood looked very troubled on hearing this. "I do not believe that Mr Tayleur is in any fit state to be conducting legal business at present," he said.

Charles Kitson
The Terrace, Torquay – 1858

The following contains my affidavit concerning the events of January 1858 and the mental state of my client Mr William Houlbrooke Tayleur. Even though several weeks have passed I remember the proceedings clearly, and reiterate my firm belief that Mr Tayleur was of sound mind and perfectly capable of composing a last will and testament that accurately reflected his wishes.

Mr Tayleur arrived at my chambers during the morning of January 17th 1858. He required my services to execute a new will. I noticed that Mr Tayleur was excitable but I attributed this to his anxiety about correcting mistakes made by his previous solicitor when drawing up the last will. There appeared to be nothing in his demeanour which indicated an unsound mind. At the time I rather suspected a slight indulgence in wine. His condition did not appear to be such as to incapacitate him from transacting business.

He listed the distribution of his assets in a coherent fashion and had firm ideas about exactly how this must be done. I do remember that he was restless and continually paced around the room, but I believed that he did this to aid his thought processes. When we had completed the business to his satisfaction he remarked, "Now the old will is invalid and that will put Lace right." Mr Lace was the solicitor who worked for him before. As he was leaving he asked me if it was possible for us to write a document that would come into force in the event of him losing his mind. I was taken aback by this request and informed him that it was not possible.

Two days after this I was called from church by Mr Tayleur's doctor, who came into the building and walked down the aisle looking for me. I was much surprised by this and embarrassed at leaving while the sermon was being preached. Once outside in the churchyard, Dr Toogood immediately explained that my client was much excited in consequence of something he asserted I had done. Mr Tayleur was in such a wild frame of mind that the doctor despaired of calming him down by any means other than by fetching me. I could not imagine what I had said to cause this excitement, and I must admit to feeling some perturbation on our journey back to Hampton House.

The butler opened the door and showed us into the study. Mr Tayleur rose from his desk and strode over to shake my hand in his usual friendly way. He seemed perfectly cool and reasonable and made no allusion to anything I had said or done. I stayed for between five and ten minutes and then I left.

Dr Isaac Baruch Toogood
St Marychurch – 1858

The following is my affidavit as to the mental condition of Mr William Houlbrooke Tayleur of Hampton House Torquay, on the occasion of him executing a will on January 17th 1858.

My patient possessed a temperament that could be irritable and impatient, but showed no indications of insanity prior to 1858.

On January 16th I was summoned to Hampton House by Mrs Tayleur after an extremely alarming incident at the railway station. She told me that her husband had endangered both his own life and hers, and incidentally that of their carriage horse, by racing the train as it pulled into Torquay Station and then flinging himself onto the footplate of the locomotive. She was left alone in the carriage, and if it had not been for the quick thinking and brute strength of some railway workers and passengers, a hideous and tragic accident would have resulted.

I found him to be restless and rambling when I arrived. He could be reasonable for a moment, and then talked simple nonsense or expressed wild, extravagant ideas. He was incoherent for much of the time, and his mind was wandering. I suggested that I should visit the next morning and submit him to bleeding and purging. I prescribed a tonic to be administered that evening.

I was sent for with some urgency the following morning, and met Mr Tayleur on his way out to town.

He wore a bandage, and Mrs Tayleur explained that he had banged his head against a window pane, which had broken under the onslaught.

Two days later he became excessively agitated while I was examining him and was much excited about something Mr Kitson had said or done. He insisted that the solicitor had insulted him and demanded that he should be made to come to the house and make a full and abject apology. I tried unsuccessfully to calm him. I did persuade him to take a dose of bromide of potassium, but even this did not alleviate his distress. I remember him exclaiming, "These damned lawyers! Think they're above the law. Think it exists for their personal convenience! Kitson may have bigger fish to fry, he may be tied up with Lawrence Palk's doings, but I'll damned well make him face me! What will he charge me for an apology? Eh? I hardly dare greet the man in the street lest it appears on his bloody account sheet! Five shillings for lifting his hat to me... ten if it's a Sunday!"

I realised that the only way to bring my patient's violent temper under control was indeed to fetch Mr Kitson, and persuade him to cobble together some sort of apology that would meet with Mr Tayleur's approval, even if the solicitor could not understand what he had done to offend my patient. Unwilling to leave him alone in his present state, I asked the butler and Mrs Tayleur to stay with him while I went to fetch Mr Kitson.

I rode to his home and knocked on the door, but the maid explained that both Mr and Mrs Kitson were in church. Leaving my horse at his house, I hurried into the church and down the aisle, anxiously scanning faces until I identified where he was sitting. It was no easy matter to attract his attention during the sermon while trying to be discreet, and then persuade him silently that he must come outside with me. He was most surprised to hear my explanation and my mission, and categorically stated that he had done nothing whatsoever to offend Mr Tayleur. I managed to communicate the urgency of his accompanying me back to Hampton House and finally, with some reluctance, he agreed.

We both felt no small trepidation about what our reception would be like. I described my patient's wild mood to Mr Kitson but assured him that the butler would be present if assistance was needed. You can imagine our relief when Mr Tayleur welcomed us into his study in a rational and friendly manner. It could be that Mr Kitson believed I had wasted his time.

I returned during the evening and discovered the patient again in some distress. Mrs Tayleur had persuaded him to take to his bed as he was suffering from a painful headache and shaking with fever. His face was covered with a swollen red rash and he was sweating copiously. He appeared to be labouring under the delusion that a swarm of bees was moving around the room intent on attacking him.

"He asked me to open the windows as he was so very hot," his wife explained. "But as soon as I had pulled down the sash he commenced a terrible screaming and tried to hide under the bed. The servants' rooms are at the end of the corridor and they may be able to hear the noise my husband is making." Mr Tayleur was indeed flapping his arms in front of his face and ducking his head as if to avoid the swarm.

"Stop them!" he started to cry, and his voice was strangely hoarse. "Make them stop that devilish buzzing!" And he pulled the sheet over his head and cowered under the bedclothes.

Mrs Tayleur was clearly at a loss and very afraid of

attracting unwelcome attention from the servants, and so I suggested that she went to her room and got some rest, and I would stay with her husband throughout the night.

I then attempted to examine the patient but this proved to be extremely difficult. He was very restless indeed, and once he judged that the swarm of bees was no longer a danger to him, he kept trying to get out of the bed. He had a rapid pulse, enlarged glands, painful red skin lesions and some abnormalities in his pupil reflexes. I came to the conclusion that he was suffering from erysipelas, but this would by no means explain the disturbed state of his mind. He spoke continuously, much of this being of an incoherent nature, but he did seem to be deeply perturbed about events that had occurred in the past, some of them long ago. I did not know that my patient had been married to a lady before the current Mrs Tayleur, and the circumstances of their parting were clearly still troubling him.

His eyes had been darting about the room, but suddenly they rested on me and he became even more agitated.

"I have made a new will," he told me. "Put right the old wrongs. Put them all in their places. Fetch me the old one – bring it here – quick man, quick..."

He indicated a leather bag in a corner of the room and I brought it over to him. His concentration immediately improved and he sifted through the contents until he found a yellowing vellum document which he flourished at me.

"Take it – here – and put it on the fire. Then it's done with. Go on – burn it, burn it."

I looked at the document he had put in my hand. It was partially torn but still perfectly legible. It was indeed his previous will, with a later codicil attached to the back. I knew at once that I must not destroy it. It was already my firm opinion that Mr Tayleur was not of sound mind and had been incapable of transacting any business for some days. The new will was therefore in all likelihood invalid. If I burned the old will as he wanted me to do, Mr Tayleur would die intestate, which would be disastrous in the case of such a wealthy man. I explained to him that I could not put it on the fire.

At that point he became wild again and climbed out of the bed, attempting to snatch the document out of my hands and throw it into the flames himself, while loudly damning me to hell and cursing me soundly. I was forced to put the document behind my back so it was out of his reach, and dodge around the room as he lunged at me. But the patient was soon overcome with fatigue as a result of his fever and he sank back onto the bed. I proceeded to talk to him calmly and firmly, and persuaded him to take a draught of hydrate of chloral. I explained that, as a medical man, it would be highly irregular for me to destroy such an important legal document, but I assured him that I would hand it to his solicitor first thing in the morning. He seemed to accept this.

A calmer period followed. I sat him up against the pillows and he appeared less agitated; only rocking back and forth and mumbling. Now and then he plucked at the bedclothes, and after a while he said audibly, "I don't know the way back."

"The way back, sir?" I asked. "Where do you want to go? I believe you were born in Liverpool – do you wish to see the city again?"

He made no answer to this, but soon appealed to me again. "My mind – my mind is so..." He grasped his head with both hands and shook it with some violence. "Sometimes it feels as if it will explode into hundreds of pieces. Just be left with pieces."

Those were the last coherent words I heard him utter. The night was very long indeed and Mr Tayleur did not sleep. Occasionally he got out of bed and paced the room, but most of the time he seemed to be struggling violently, jerking his arms and legs and rambling endlessly. I attempted to apply a mustard plaster to afford him some relief, but he pulled away from me and would accept no further ministrations from me whatsoever.

When morning eventually arrived I informed Mrs Tayleur that my intention was to ask a colleague for a second opinion as to her husband's condition. I advised her to have a cage placed over the fire and to keep her husband locked in his bedroom. I then went to visit Mr Kitson in his chambers and handed my patient's old will into his safe keeping. He informed me that, shortly before making the new will, Mr Tayleur had asked the solicitor if he could prepare an instrument that would take effect in the event of my patient losing his sanity. Mr Kitson had replied that this was not possible. Such a remark would demonstrate that Mr Tayleur was already aware that his mind was not fully under his control, and he was not sure of retaining such control for any reasonable length of time.

It is my opinion that by the time Mr Tayleur made the new will he was already in a state of mania. My observations of his behaviour during that week lead me to conclude that he was unable to give rational answers to the most simple of questions, unable to control his conduct, expressed delusional and absurd ideas, and frequently behaved in a violent manner. My colleague agreed with me that the patient had become a lunatic.

Mary Ellen Tayleur
Hampton House - January 1858

He left, after telling me to put a cage in front of the fire and a Bible next to the bed, to try to coax my husband to drink beef tea and to keep the door of his room locked, causing me to enquire as to why the Bible was necessary.

"We are seeking solace for a disordered soul," he replied, "And the good Lord would seem to be a fitting place to begin."

By this time it was not only my husband's soul that was in a disordered state. He was much in need of a shave, though Dr Toogood had forbidden any access to razors, his shirt had lost all contact with his breeches and was hanging open at the neck, his waistcoat was unbuttoned and patched with sweat. Worst of all was his hair, which was standing up in a wild dishevelled mane around his face, and I realised with a shock that this gave him the appearance of a madman.

He was lying back on his pillows with his eyes half closed, clearly exhausted from the endless prowling and ranting of the night before. I was thankful that he was at least quiet; the maids were flitting about on the landing, no doubt avid for any information they could scuttle down the back stairs to convey. But I knew that I must ask for help; I had absolutely no idea how to use a razor, and was terrified lest my husband wrest the blade from me and do damage to both of us.

The fire having died, I felt it would be safe to leave him, and I slipped out of the room and locked the door behind me. I thought it would also be an opportunity for him to make use of his chamber pot in privacy. Then I went down to the drawing room and rang for Page, knowing that I had no choice but to take him into my confidence.

"I know I can rely on your complete discretion," I began, after telling him to shut the door so that we could speak in privacy. "Mr Tayleur is suffering from nervous exhaustion and, although he will soon recover completely, his behaviour is somewhat irrational at present. Dr Toogood is returning shortly, but in the meantime I would appreciate your assistance in helping my husband to wash, shave and change his clothes. Would you please ask Mrs Tozer to prepare beef tea for him, while sharing with her as little as possible regarding Mr Tayleur's affliction. I am sure the servants are already aware that he is indisposed, but I want no gossip Page – do you understand? Not a single word about his illness leaves this house under any circumstances. Any mention of it in the servants' dining room and you must stamp on it straightaway. I will dismiss anyone who shows the slightest curiosity or discusses the subject. Please tell them that."

Page assured me he would do this, then went to the kitchen to order the beef tea and collect towels and hot water. I met him outside my husband's door a short while later, and we unlocked it and entered the room together.

My husband was in the process of climbing out of the window. He had wrenched up the sash and dragged over a chair, and was now crouching with one foot on this while hooking his other leg over the sill. On seeing us his mission became more urgent, and he was about to tumble out when Page and I managed to grasp hold of him and pull him back inside. He growled with fury and fought to escape from our clutches, but Page succeeded in pinning him down on the floor while I pulled down the sash and locked it, then closed the shutters and put the bar across.

It then became clear that my husband had indeed taken advantage of the privacy lately afforded to him and attempted to use the chamber pot. He had been only partially successful, and created a foul-smelling mess on both the chamber cabinet and his breeches, these last having been removed and abandoned on the floor. He had managed to pull up his nether garments but not tie them, and they were now descending as a result of our struggle.

"Do you know what time the doctor plans to return?" Page gasped, still preventing my husband from rising.

"He thought it would be around noon," I answered, kneeling next to William and taking his arm. "For goodness' sake William, you are in a shameful condition. How could you allow yourself to get into this state? Have you no pride? You must get onto the bed so that we can clean you and restore your dignity and your self-respect." I shook him, but he would not look at me or show any sign of having heard me.

"If we take one arm each we could drag him over to the bed," I said to Page, and between us we managed to pull him across the floor. He then became quieter and even climbed onto the bed himself. I closed the bed curtains to afford him some privacy while Page poured the hot water from the can into the ewer, and brought the soap and flannels. By stint of frequently emptying the filthy water into the slop pail and starting again with fresh, we cleaned his face and hands and the soiled parts of his body, and dressed him in clean breeches. He lay quite passively and looked at neither of us, but how he could allow his butler to perform such intimate operations I had no idea. This was no longer the husband I knew, and how he would face Page once he was restored to himself was another unanswerable question.

I suppose he lay quietly just to put us off our guard, because as soon as Page approached him with the razor he leapt up and grabbed the blade from the butler's hand. We both instinctively jumped away from the bed and he followed us, the curtains draping closed again behind him.

"My dear, please give me the razor so that Page can help you to shave," I said. He ignored me and started to move around the room as if searching for something, holding the razor in his hand all the while.

Suddenly he spoke, quite clearly and coherently, wheeling round in my direction. "Where have you hidden him?" he said.

"We have hidden no-one my dear," I replied, trying to make the tone of my voice conciliatory. "To whom are you referring?"

But this seemed to make him very angry. " 'To whom are you referring?' " he repeated, mockingly imitating the inflexion in my voice. " 'To whom are you referring?' For God's sake Emma, you know only too well to whom I am referring. Where is the bloody man? I know you have brought him up here. I know you took him into our own bed. How could you do that? How could you give yourself to that spineless weakling? Was he as much of a man as I am? He certainly didn't look like it with his sandy whiskers and shifty chin..."

Page and I had been listening to this outburst in horror, the shock and surprise rendering us both quite unable to move. Suddenly William turned towards the bed.

"Now I know where the devil is – he's still in there, isn't he? You've left him between the sheets so that you can go back for more of him! Come out here Lennox – come and face me, you coward. Stand in front of me and explain why you helped yourself to my wife. By God, I'll kill you!" And William launched himself at the bed curtains, hacking at them with the blade as if he was attempting to reach someone hiding for his life within.

The razor was not designed for this purpose and very soon my husband's hand was as lacerated as the curtains, and blood was streaming down his arm. The handle of the razor became too slippery to hold and he dropped it, resorting to tearing at the bed curtains with his nails and his teeth. He growled and sobbed and repeated the name Lennox several times. I dashed over to retrieve the razor while Page attempted to reason with my husband.

"Mr Tayleur, there is no-one hiding behind the bed curtains," he insisted, pulling them open to prove his point.

William immediately dropped to the floor and commenced searching under the bed, still panting with fury and determination.

"There is no visitor in the house at all, sir, and certainly no gentleman by the name of Lennox. I meet every visitor at the door, and I always know exactly who is in the house. There is no-one here sir, I assure you."

William climbed out from under the bed but remained kneeling by it, as if to trap any person who started to emerge from there. "He comes late at night, man. You wouldn't see him. Creeps up to my wife's bed."

"Never William!" I was horrified. "How can you say such wicked things about me? This is a Christian household! He does not know what he is saying Page, I assure you. Has he been reading novels?"

"I think you should get back into bed, sir," Page tried to reason with him. "We need to bandage the cuts on your hand and you should be resting."

"Resting?" William snorted with contempt. "If some greasy libertine breached your home and tupped your wife, would you REST? He deserves what's coming to him – leave me alone and let me deal with this."

"William, none of this is true. You are imagining things my dear and you are ill. Please let us put you into bed."

He looked at me with fury. "Imagining things am I? You know better than anyone, madam, that this is true indeed."

My strength left me then and I sank into a chair and started to cry. To be spoken of in such dreadful terms in front of a servant was more than I could bear. It was at that moment that Dr Toogood came into the room, along with his colleague Dr Nankwell. The maid who showed them in stood open-mouthed in the doorway until Page waved her firmly away.

"Good God! What is occurring here?" Toogood exclaimed. Page explained the events of the morning while the two doctors picked up my husband, manhandled him onto the bed and proceeded to dress his wounds. He continued with his terrible accusations all the time, until Dr Toogood suggested that I went downstairs to have something to eat and left them to see to my husband.

Eating would have sickened me, but I went straight to the kitchen and caught the maid in mid-sentence, regaling everything she had seen and heard to the assembled gaping servants. I would have dismissed her there and then, but I knew she would leave the house and spread her malicious tittle tattle along the length and breadth of St. Marychurch if I did, so I swallowed down my fury and gave all of them a talking to. I told them that I demanded total loyalty and that their master's illness must be a completely private affair, even after he had recovered. I forbade any of them mentioning it within the house or outside it, and threatened dismissal without references for any servant who did. I then took myself to the drawing room and faced alone my fears and the horrors that had arrived in my life so suddenly. I did recognise that I could not deal with this situation without help, and I opened my desk and wrote a blunt note to my brother-in-law at Shevington – "William is very ill. Come to me at Hampton immediately." I folded and sealed it and wrote the direction with a shaking hand, then rang for a maid. "Run to the post office with this. It must be sent without any delay." As soon as she had closed the door I cast myself upon the crimson sofa and put my head in my hands.

It was several hours before the doctors were shown in. "We have administered a sleeping draught," Dr Nankwell explained. "And Mr Tayleur is resting now. For his safety we have had the windows nailed shut and removed all the furniture from the room. Your butler found a simple slump bed which will be far less dangerous than the four-poster. He has also put a cage over the fire."

"And have you procured a Bible for him?" I asked with some sarcasm.

"Indeed," the doctor replied.

"I must assure you gentlemen, that every word my husband has uttered this morning has been a terrible lie. It has been extremely painful for me to have my honour and respectability questioned, and I have been made to listen to things no wife should be forced to hear."

"Have no fear Mrs Tayleur, the patient's ravings mean nothing and are the result of his illness," Dr Nankwell assured me.

"How long am I to suffer from these outrageous outpourings? When will my husband be cured? I would be heartily grateful if you could employ every remedy within your means to effect his complete recovery as soon as possible."

The two doctors looked at each other. Then Dr Toogood asked if they may sit down. I was somewhat alarmed when they sat next to me, and Dr Toogood leaned towards me as if he was about to impart information of a confidential nature. I backed away from him.

"Mrs Tayleur," he said. "I am afraid we can give you no assurance that there is a cure for your husband's condition. I cannot even offer hope that it may improve. I brought my colleague here today to elicit his opinion of your husband's case, and he agrees wholeheartedly with my diagnosis. It is with great sorrow that I must tell you we believe Mr Tayleur has completely lost his sanity."

I stared at them. "But that is impossible," I said. "My husband is a gentleman from a good family. He is a clever man with many responsibilities. You are wrong. Surely he is suffering from a brain fever and he will get better."

"There is a chance that he could recover, but in the meantime we have to make arrangements for him to have the best possible care. In order to do that, Dr Nankwell and I must certify him as insane."

I was horrified. "No! You cannot do that to him! What will people say? We will be discussed over every dinner table in Torquay." I covered my eyes with both hands and groaned.

"Mrs Tayleur, we are bound by the law in this

matter. It is for your husband's safety that the Lunacy Commission must be made aware of his circumstances and the care we are going to provide for him. In a few months an inquisition will be held and if your husband has recovered and can prove his sanity, then the matter will be dropped."

A horrible idea then entered my head. "Must he go to an asylum to be cared for?" Every sane person alive must harbour a dread of these places, and carry in their memory tales of the way they treated the old king, pictures of wretches in Bedlam, and stories of titled ladies visiting asylums for sport. "This is the stuff of penny dreadfuls," I said.

"You have a fine home here," the doctor replied. "Surely there are sufficient rooms for Mr Tayleur to be cared for in this house. You would need to employ a personal valet for him, who would actually be a person experienced in the care of lunatics, and we would visit regularly to administer whatever medicines he required."

I was horrified by the very idea. "Look after him here?" I exclaimed. "But that is impossible! I have three small children, and they have already been alarmed by the comings and goings and the strange noises. I have a house full of servants, greedy for gossip and salacious details, and it would be impossible to hide this for five minutes from Torquay society. No, if he is so badly afflicted he must be taken away. He must go quickly before any more damage is done. He must go today."

"My dear Mrs Tayleur," Dr Toogood interrupted. "It is not as easy as that. If you will not have him here then we must secure a place where he can be cared for in safety. There are new laws that protect the insane from harm and his future must be considered very carefully by all of us."

I stared hard at both of them. "Just get him out of here!" I said, and my voice sounded strangled and high.

One of the doctors rang the bell and sent the maid for hot tea. They gave me a sleeping draught to drink later and assured me that they had given Page full instructions regarding my husband's care for the remainder of the day. They said they would return in the morning with suggestions as to the best care for my husband. I didn't go near William again that day.

I slept fitfully, despite the sleeping draught, and was conscious of muffled noises coming from my husband's room. On several occasions I thought something was being bumped or dragged on the floor, a deep groaning noise woke me once, and I could hear laughter and even screams. Our rooms are only separated by the upstairs drawing room, which lies between, and it was some comfort to know that the servants and the children all slept in another wing of the house, well out of earshot.

I was reluctant to open his door in the morning, and breakfasted first. The servants were subdued, and it was strange to see the maid bringing the dishes to the sideboard instead of Page.

When I did go to my husband, it was Page I noticed first. He looked haggard and unshaven and his eyes were bloodshot with exhaustion. He had brought one of the gardeners upstairs to help him and the two of them had stayed with William throughout the night. The room was fetid and stale, even though they had been punctilious about emptying the chamber pot and keeping my husband clean, and all the shutters were still closed. William was sitting on the floor in the corner, his back against the wall, staring at nothing.

"He has been there most of the night, madam," Page said. "We managed to get him into bed a few times, but he insisted on climbing out again and going back to the corner."

"Why are you sitting on the floor William?" I asked him in a no-nonsense tone of voice. "Let's get you back to bed where you can be comfortable." I walked over to him and offered him my hand to help him up, but he behaved as if I had not spoken at all, and continued to stare ahead blindly.

I turned to the two servants. "He must snap out of this; he is just making himself ridiculous. Page, in the morning you always fetch the newspaper for Mr Tayleur. Please do so now, and perhaps if I read it to him it will focus his mind and we can all get back to normal."

Page duly brought the newspaper up and handed it to me, and then I told them both to get some rest as the doctors would be arriving shortly. As William would not move from the floor I sat on his bed and started to read aloud. It was soon clear that he was listening to me, and the vacant look left his eyes. Suddenly he said, "What is the date today?"

"The date?" I asked.

"Yes woman – it will be on the front of the newspaper."

"It is the twenty-first of January," I told him.

He was immediately transformed and pulled himself up. "The twenty-first of January!" he exclaimed. "Fetch my coat woman, I have to go out."

"You cannot go out William," I remonstrated, but he was opening the chamber cabinet despite my presence, and relieving himself. I averted my eyes in embarrassment. Having rearranged his breeches he looked around the room impatiently.

"Where are my damned boots? Where is Page? I need a necktie and I need my damned hat. Don't just stand there looking like an imbecile, ring the bell and get some staff up here."

"Where do you have to go my dear?" I asked, hoping to stall for time to give the doctors a chance to arrive.

"It is the twenty-first of January! What do you mean – where do I have to go? It is the day they start the work on the new line into Torquay and Sir Lawrence Palk is lifting the first sod. If that old sod is lifting sods then I have to be there to see it. Although why they have chosen him to perform this weighty task is quite beyond me. What has Palk got to do with railways? Race horses and French dancing girls are much more his line, whereas my father built most of the locomotives in operation today! They should have asked me!" He was getting angrier by the minute, and dribbles of foam were appearing at the sides of his mouth. Unable to locate his boots in the bare room, he wrenched open the door and charged onto the landing, and I realised with horror that I had omitted to lock his door.

I raced after him, but he was already galloping down the stairs and bellowing for Page, and both the maids and the cook herself were running out of the kitchen corridor to find the cause of the commotion.

"I need the carriage!" he barked at them. "Have it sent round now. And fetch my damned boots!"

I reached the bottom of the stairs and took his arm. "Let us wait in the study for the carriage to come round," I suggested calmly. "And that will give Page time to finish brushing your boots and bring them to you."

He seemed to accept this and allowed me to take him into the study. I was able to look out of the study window to see if there was any sign of the doctors, and ring the bell to summon Page. The poor butler looked even worse than he had earlier in the morning; perhaps he had actually fallen asleep after I had sent him off. He was certainly alarmed to find my husband downstairs and insisting on leaving the house. William had been pulling papers out of the drawers of his desk and throwing them on the floor, but he looked up when Page came into the room.

"Good God man, what a state you are in. Have you had a shave this morning? I need my boots – it is the twenty-first of January. Quick man, I cannot be late."

Page looked at me enquiringly and I shook my head. I was presuming that William would not leave the house in his stockinged feet.

"I will fetch them at once sir," he said, and left the room.

William then started to pace with impatience, stopping at the window every few minutes to check for the arrival of the carriage. But it was Dr Toogood's horse he saw first, closely followed by that of Dr Nankwell. I sagged with relief.

"What is that damned doctor doing here?" William exclaimed. "And his bloody side-kick! What will that do to my account eh, having two of the wretches in attendance?"

Page brought them into the study, but my husband tried to push past them and get through the door. Dr Toogood managed to head him off and shut the door smartly, standing with his back against it and his hand on the doorknob.

"Get out of my way man! I have to get to the station at Torre. It is the twenty-first of January, the day they start the work. I must get to the ceremony in time!"

"We have no intention of holding you up Mr Tayleur," Dr Nankwell said soothingly. "We simply wish to carry out a swift examination to ascertain whether the fever you were suffering from lately has now abated. As soon as we have done that, and made sure your temperature is of a safe level, then you can ride over to the ceremony. There is plenty of time."

"Damn my temperature! I don't care whether it's a safe level or not. I have to be at the railway. I tell you, I must be there."

"Of course you must be there sir," Dr Toogood said. "Our examination will take just a few minutes, as long as you co-operate with us and don't cause any difficulties."

Before my husband could answer, both doctors had seized his arms and were propelling him up the stairs and back to his bedroom. We heard him screaming in protest, then the door slammed and the key turned in the lock.

"He cannot stay here," I said to Page, then sent the butler to seize the opportunity of a little more rest.

The doctors spent some hours with my husband, bleeding him and applying purgatives and administering whatever draughts they thought may quieten him. Dr Toogood was then shown into the drawing room and sat down near to me without being invited to do so.

"I hope you have made arrangements to take my husband away immediately," I said.

"That is exactly the matter we need to discuss, Mrs Tayleur," he replied, clearing his throat and shuffling forward on the chair. "You need have no fears about any possibility of incarcerating him within an asylum. These institutions are primarily for the poor, and the County Asylum at Exminster has no provision for private patients. A family with any means is expected to make their own arrangements for their afflicted relation. You are unfortunate in that Devon is greatly lacking in private madhouses. There is one such place in Plympton, but I have obtained the latest Lunacy Commission report and it makes very grim reading indeed. Your husband would find neither solace nor safety under that roof."

"So you are telling me that there is nowhere in the whole of the county where my husband can be cared for with compassion? Can money not purchase civility? He is a very wealthy man; surely it is not impossible to find a way of caring for him honourably."

"Some families seek appropriate accommodation further afield and look to London, where there are many more such institutions, some regarded favourably by the Lunacy Commission Inspectors. However, my colleague and I have been investigating other possibilities and I can recommend a course of action which I believe to be the very best solution to the problem."

"Please continue, Dr Toogood."

"I previously stated that you were unfortunate to live in this county as private madhouses are few and of dubious quality. However, the superintendent of the Exminster Asylum is one Dr John Charles Bucknill, one of the leading alienists in the country today."

"I do not know what an alienist might be."

"It is simply the term for doctors who specialize in the treatment of the insane. Dr Bucknill is very forward thinking, and believes every lunatic should be treated with kindness and respect. He refuses to use any form of restraint; strait-jackets, straps and shackling are totally forbidden. His patients are encouraged to walk in the fresh air, enjoy beautiful views and occupy their time with gardening, painting and other pleasant pursuits. Exminster is regarded approvingly by the Commission."

"This is all very commendable Dr Toogood, but you have already explained that my husband cannot be treated in the asylum."

"That is so Mrs Tayleur, but he can be treated by Dr Bucknill himself as a private patient. My recommendation would be that you take a small house within the village of Exminster itself and employ an attendant who will care for your husband throughout the days and nights. The attendant would be associated with the asylum and appropriately trained. Dr Bucknill would personally supervise Mr Tayleur's treatment and visit him daily. In this way, you would be providing the best care available for your husband."

"And will this man be able to cure him?"

"Dr Bucknill does believe that insanity is a brain disease that is treatable with medication. A cure would, however, depend on the cause of your husband's condition. Sometimes patients lose their sanity and never have any hope of recovering it."

"Why has my husband gone mad, Dr Toogood? Can you offer any explanation at all for this terrible state of affairs?"

Dr Toogood was silent for a few moments before he offered an answer. "It is my belief Mrs Tayleur, that your husband has been suffering from a disease for some time. During this last week the disease has reached his brain, with these devastating consequences. In my experience, patients suffering from this disease do not recover, and die within a fairly short time."

My head was aching painfully as I listened to the doctor, who seemed to be delivering savage blows one after the other. I felt an overwhelming need to leave the house entirely, leave the lunatic in his bedroom with the tattling staff to care for him as best they could, and forget that any of this nightmare had ever happened.

"In the meantime," the doctor went on, "It is

imperative that a nurse is employed to care for your husband until we can make arrangements for his move to Exminster. It is wholly unsuitable for your butler and gardener to be attempting to look after his needs and calm him during his violent phases. I will procure a suitably experienced attendant today."

As it was I could not bear to see my husband again. He had become a monster in my mind. I trusted Page to deal with him until the nurse arrived and instructed the nursemaid to take the children for walks around St. Marychurch. She was much surprised by this, as I usually insist that she restricts the children's exercise to the grounds of the mansion and avoids all contact with the local people, but I wanted them well away. Then I waited for my brother-in-law to arrive.

He came towards late afternoon on the following day, churning up the gravel in a hired fly from the station. I met him at the front door myself.

"Good God Mary Ellen, what is the matter?"

It was then that I cried; reaching out to him while great sobs tore up from my chest and an uncontrollable shaking assailed me. He took my arm and led me quickly through the hall and into the library, sat me on a chair and rang the bell. "Not the servants..." I managed to gasp out, and he went to the door to meet the maid and ask her to bring a glass of brandy and water.

He stood over me while I sipped it and watched as I applied a handkerchief to my face, and then asked, "What on earth ails my brother? He must be seriously ill to occasion this distress? For God's sake tell me what has happened."

"William has lost his wits," I replied.

"Lost his wits? Is it his damned temper again? Has he suffered a seizure?"

"No, he has gone mad."

"Mary Ellen, I do not understand what you mean. Does he have violent headaches? Fever? What are the doctors doing to cure him?"

"He is insane. He is a lunatic."

John Tayleur sank into a chair next to me as if his legs had suddenly lost their strength. He stared at me with round, horrified eyes. The dreadful truth hung in the room around us like a hideous pall, and for a moment we were both suffocated by its meaning.

"Surely there is some hope for him?" John said after a few long minutes.

"The doctors fear not. They have explained to me that they believe he was suffering for some time past from a disease which has now reached his brain. It happened with great suddenness – all within the course of a week."

John's face seemed to lose all its colour. "There but for the grace of God..." he muttered.

"You should see him," I said. "He is upstairs in his room. But John – he has to leave this house. He cannot stay here another day. The servants are prattling and I am fearful that this will get out. First the villagers, then the great and the good of Torquay. We will be the talk of every dinner table from the huts and hovels of Pimlico to the fine villas of Osborne Crescent. We have to be rid of him. And quickly."

"I doubt whether the people of Pimlico have dinner tables to sit round at all. But I do understand your need for discretion – surely the children are becoming aware of what is happening? Are they distressed by these events?"

"I am trying to keep the children in the nurseries or out in the village. But children have short memories; once William has gone I'm sure they will no longer think of him or what they have witnessed."

John looked at me with an expression I could not quite read. "I do not believe children ever forget parents from whom they have been parted, even if they were quite young at the time. Losing a mother or father through bereavement, or some other circumstance, will always cause lasting pain and suffering of some measure."

I was sufficiently exasperated to shrug off a little of my despair and emit a snort. "John Tayleur – you enjoyed the company and comfort of both your parents until you were well into middle age! What do you know of the feelings of parentless children?"

My brother-in-law seemed to be suppressing anger at this, but I had no idea what could have irritated him. "This is not the time Mary Ellen. I need to see my brother; will you accompany me? It may afford him some comfort to be with both of us."

I stood up reluctantly and led the way out of the library and up the stairs. We stopped outside my husband's door and listened. There was no sound except that of water being emptied into a slop pail. I knocked quietly so that the nurse could unlock the door, and we both went in.

William was sitting in a chair by the window, looking out into the garden. He was dressed in clean clothes and had been freshly shaved. His hair had been combed but not washed, and lay in rather greasy lengths over his collar. The attendant, a thick-set man presumably from the asylum, was tidying some items of the chamber service on the wash stand which had been returned to the room at his request.

John went straight over to his brother. "William, dear old soul, what has been happening?"

William continued to look out of the window at the garden, without even a blink to show he had heard John's voice. It had started to rain – that grey pitiless drizzle of January – and a low mist was spreading from the sea. The garden appeared like a dead thing; the trees reaching out with skeletal arms, the shrubs brown and withered, the flower beds empty and cold. I shivered. John touched William's arm and leaned over him. William slowly turned to look at him, without any recognition whatsoever, and shrank away from his touch.

"William – do you not know your own brother? It is I, John, come all the way from Shevington to visit you."

William made no reply and gave no sign that he had heard. He turned back to stare at the garden through the rain covered panes.

John straightened up and addressed the nurse. "Has my brother been given drugs this day?"

"He has had a draught to quieten him, sir. It will do him no harm and allows his mind some respite from the torment."

"What torment do you mean? Explain yourself."

"The patient is very much troubled by events from his past," the attendant replied. "It appears that his affliction has caused painful and long-buried memories to surface, some of which make him enraged and some render him grief-stricken. He now has little control over his feelings or the manner in which he expresses them, and a preparation which calms his mind can provide relief from the turmoil of his thoughts."

"I suppose this is better than a strait jacket," my brother-in-law observed.

"Dr Bucknill's approach does not involve the use of restraints, sir. You can be sure he will receive the best possible care from that gentleman. He is the best in the business."

John nodded at this, then turned to my husband

once again. He spoke loudly, slowly and clearly. "We will take good care of you William, have no fear. We will do everything in our power to ensure you go to a quiet, comfortable home so that you can rest."

I saw William frown at this, and then he muttered, "Not going."

"William, you have got to go," I said firmly. "We will find a nice little house for you where you will have everything you need. And when you are better you can come home again."

He jerked round in his chair and, without any warning, grabbed my arm so viciously that I cried out in pain. "Witch! You damned witch! What are you doing? What vile scheme are you hatching? You will be rid of me will you? Well it is I who will be rid of you! Get out of my house! I never want to set eyes on you again. Damn you to hell you hag!"

"William!" John exclaimed, clearly shocked. "Whatever are you saying? How can you talk to Mary Ellen in that manner? Let her arm go; you are injuring her." He was attempting to remove William's fingers from around my arm as he spoke, but this simply had the effect of making my husband cling on all the tighter and dig his nails into my skin.

"Let me handle this, sir," intervened the attendant. He gestured for John to stand aside and positioned himself directly in front of William. "You are hurting the lady Mr Tayleur. You don't want to hurt her so let go of her arm now. Let her loose Mr Tayleur." Then he gently took hold of William's arm and waited. I felt my husband's grip slacken and then he slumped forward in his chair. "I think you had better leave now," the attendant said to us.

John and I walked quickly over to the door. I was nursing my arm and feeling it gingerly with the fingers of my other hand. John stopped and looked back at his brother, then we left the room and the key turned in the lock behind us. We descended the stairs without a word, mindful of prying servants, and almost fell into the drawing room, closing the door behind us.

"God help us," John said, sinking onto the couch, "What are we to do with him? He is a danger to himself and to the rest of us. He is lost, dear God he is lost." He started to cry. While he fumbled in his pockets for a handkerchief and attempted to pull himself together, I undid the button on the cuff of my blouse and examined the damage to my arm. A vivid bruise had appeared already and the area was painfully swollen. A pattern of red crescents marked where William's nails had pressed into my flesh. I certainly did not want to ask for assistance from the maid, and so I quietly went up to my own room and swabbed my arm with arnica. This made it sting, but I straightened my sleeve and fastened the button, then attended to my hair which had become disarranged in the struggle. I waited for a moment in front of the looking glass, making sure that I was sufficiently collected to return to the drawing room and face my brother-in-law.

"I will send for tea," I said firmly, tugging the bell pull as soon as I entered the room. John was standing in front of the fire and holding his hands out to the warmth. He was shaking.

"How is your arm?" he asked.

"It will mend soon enough," I replied, "Unlike the wicked remarks my husband flings at me, in front of visitors and servants, with no regard whatsoever for my feelings or my reputation. I have suffered enough John; he must be taken away. I cannot bear any more."

"What are the doctors' recommendations?"

"He will be moved to a house near to the asylum at Exminster, and put in the care of Dr Bucknill, the superintendent himself. But this will take time, and he must be removed from here immediately. He cannot stay another hour."

We stopped our conversation while the maid brought in the tea tray and placed it on the table. John had his hand on the mantelpiece and his head was lowered towards the fire.

"I believe a local solicitor sees to William's affairs?" he said.

"That is Mr Kitson in Torquay," I replied.

"I will drive down to see him immediately. William has property in Dawlish. If Kitson can remove the tenants we can have my brother taken there until a house in Exminster can be procured." He swigged his tea, then left to arrange the carriage. I walked to the bottom of the staircase and listened. I could hear the noise of movement coming from my husband's bedroom. It sounded as if he was running backwards and forwards and bumping into the walls. I could also hear a low sobbing. I returned to the drawing room to wait.

They took him that night, after dark. Both Dr Toogood and Dr Nankwell were here, and together with the attendant they walked my husband down the stairs. The doctors held his arms firmly, one on either side of him, and the attendant preceded them. Page followed, carrying a portmanteau and a leather satchel. They moved as quickly as possible, almost bundling William along between them, so that he would not realise that they were taking him away from his home and into an unknown future. But once in the hallway he lifted his head and started to struggle. I was standing in the door of the drawing room and he saw me.

He looked at me with eyes that were focused and clear and full of understanding, then called out, "Mary Ellen, for God's sake don't let them do this to me!" I did not reply or make any movement towards him. When they reached the dark, wooden partition between the inner and outer hall he managed somehow to grasp the edge of the door frame and hung onto it, curling his body into it and clinging on desperately. The attendant tried to loosen his fingers, but as soon as one hand was free and he started on the other, William grasped the wood again. He started to cry then, a sobbing howl that echoed around the hall and up the stairs to the atrium.

"Stop him making that noise!" I demanded. "The children and the servants must not be party to this!" But already footsteps were scurrying in rooms above, and the kitchen door was opening. "Page, you must keep the servants in the kitchen wing. Do not allow them through that door!" The butler dropped my husband's bags and ushered the goggle-eyed maids back into their corridor. He then disappeared, presumably up the back stairs to deal with the nursery maid and the children.

It happened quickly after that. William's fingers were prized from the door frame and he was dragged through the outer hall and the front door. I followed them, waiting in the shelter of the porch as it was still raining. John was already outside with a hired carriage – imperative so that no-one would recognise our own – the door of which was open. It was dark, but I could make out the struggle that ensued. William was desperate not to be put inside the carriage and he fought like an animal, biting, growling and clawing. Even when the carriage door was finally shut, and all four men were inside, he managed to get the door open again and was crawling out. The carriage was drawing away by this time, and he was hauled back inside, but one of his legs was still hanging out of the carriage as it rumbled down the drive.

I was left alone by the front door, shaken and dazed with horror. What a terrible journey it would be, jolting along the high, rocky coast road to Dawlish in a dark carriage with the blinds down and rain pelting against the windows, trying to keep my husband from reaching the doors and flinging himself out. Would he be forced to stay on the floor between their feet like a dog, or would they manage to heave him onto the seat and afford him some comfort? I went back inside. Page must have kept the servants firmly in the back for the house was completely silent, except for the ticking of the hall clock and the thrumming of raindrops on the atrium above me. My husband's bags still lay where Page had dropped them; the squire of St Marychurch, son of a famous, wealthy industrialist, member of an ancient gentry family, had left the mansion with nothing at all. I leaned on the curve of the banister and looked hopelessly around me. Hampton seemed to weigh down onto my back and my shoulders. It was a heavy weight indeed.

Charles William Tayleur
Trinity College Cambridge – March 1858

I was horrified when I received the letter from my uncle John Tayleur. It was not a long letter, just a concise statement informing me of the recent events at Hampton House. My father, he explained, had suddenly descended into lunacy as a result of a disease from which he had been suffering for some years. There was little hope of any recovery, but an inquisition would be held towards the end of the year to ascertain the progress of his mental condition. He had been removed from Hampton and was now residing in a small house in the village of Exminster, very near to the Devon County Lunatic Asylum. He was being cared for by an experienced attendant, and visited regularly by Dr Bucknill, the superintendent of the asylum. As a result, my uncle had left Shevington Hall and was staying at Hampton House. There was much to be done about my father's financial affairs, and my stepmother was most distressed and in need of his support, as were her children. He assured me that he would keep me informed about the situation and would see both my brothers and myself at Shevington for the Easter holiday.

The letter had me both enraged and confused. My first thought was that my stepmother had contrived to have my father put away so that she could control his estate and ensure that it passed to her own children. Wrongful incarceration has always been a subject of dread in all quarters of society, kept alive by terrifying tales in both the press and popular novels. I knew that this had become more difficult since new laws were meant to protect innocent people from their unscrupulous and greedy relatives, but cases still appeared in the newspapers. Mary Ellen would have had to persuade two doctors of my father's insanity, and they would have signed two separate certificates of lunacy. I had every faith in her capacity to manage this; in my mind she had the cunning of a witch. But what of my uncle? John Tayleur had long been the supporter and sanctuary of my brothers and myself. He had provided a home for us when my father showed no inclination to do so, and offered a listening ear when my stepmother rendered it impossible for me to remain at Hampton several years before. He had clothed us and cared for us, with no thought of any remuneration. How could he possibly be party to this scheme of Mary Ellen's?

Then my father came into my mind. I remembered him as tall and powerful, issuing orders and commands and always in control of any situation. What had happened to him, and what had he suffered?

There was only one thing I could do. I would have to visit my father and discover the truth for myself. I pulled a bag out of the cupboard and started to pack.

The journey from Cambridge was arduous and afforded me too much time to think. I walked to the imposing railway station, a fine contrast to the ramshackle outfit in Torquay, and travelled into London on the train. After crossing the city to Paddington on an omnibus I then caught the train to Exeter. This was a painful stage; sitting on Brunel's Western Railway, possibly drawn along by a locomotive built by my own grandfather's company, caused me to wonder at the sorry mess our family was in, despite all the wealth and advantages at our disposal. From the window I watched the frost covered fields whip by, and bare trees seemed to reach out their bony arms in despair. But I was fired up with the need to rescue my father. If only I could have sent him a message to tell him I was on my way and would soon be tearing him from the clutches of his captors. I worked out my plans as the train steamed on. If it proved difficult to get him out of the house I would appeal to local magistrates. They would see at once that he was totally sane and that a terrible injustice was being perpetrated. The thought of racing to my father's aid was uplifting. He would be grateful. The rift between us would be mended. He would be a father to myself and my brothers again. It was possible to wait for a train which would take me to Exminster, but by this time I was seething with impatience to get to the end of the interminable journey. I hired a conveyance at Exeter station to take me the last three miles.

By this time the day was on the wane and the winter sun was very low. I saw the asylum before we even reached the village; it loomed up suddenly out of the dusk as we rounded a corner, glowering forbiddingly from the top of the hill. I uttered an exclamation, which encouraged the driver to provide me with conversation.

"I have never driven a single soul round that corner who hasn't gasped at the sight of the madhouse," he said with some relish.

"I had not expected it to be so big," I answered.

"If you've got the time I can drive you up to the gates for a better view," he suggested, no doubt to increase the fare, but I was willing to take the opportunity.

As we entered the village street he pulled the horse round to the right, and stopped at a large gateway. A man appeared from the lodge and unlocked the gates. My driver slipped some coins into his hand and we drove into a long, wide driveway, planted with young lime trees. The gate was locked behind us. It appeared that my driver had some sort of arrangement with the lodge keeper and was at liberty to bring his passengers for a scenic tour of the asylum grounds, much as the gentry visited Bedlam in less enlightened times. Making use of human misery to provide entertainment seemed a low pastime indeed at that moment, yet here I was, sitting in the back of a trap and gazing about me in fascination.

The drive wound through extensive parklands with neatly cut lawns, well-tended flower beds and bordered pathways. I presumed there was no shortage of labour to maintain the grounds. Straight ahead of us was a handsome four storey house with an imposing clock tower, but linked to it on either side were lower and more forbidding buildings.

"That's the Doctors' Place," my driver explained. He pointed to the buildings on either side. "That there is the entrance for men, and the women go in on the other side." Behind this frontage sinister, grey buildings curved in a vast semi-circle, and I could see that other wings radiated out behind these. It reminded me of engravings I had seen of Pentonville Prison.

The driver pointed at a block on the right. "They keep the worst ones in there," he said. I couldn't help peering up at the windows, searching for shapes and shadows inside. We can all summon up images of insanity, formed from newspapers and lurid prints. The beings lodged within those stone walls must have long, dishevelled hair, faces pulled into wild grimaces and nails like talons, and spend their time running frantically backwards and forwards and laughing at nothing. Perhaps this was what I most feared for my father, and by straining to see what was behind those windows I was preparing myself for what I would discover inside the cottage tomorrow. But I could hear no sound at all from where I was sitting and the windows gave up no secrets, although a servant was clearly lighting the gas lamps in the doctors' house.

"Are you wondering what it's like inside?" the driver prompted, perhaps disappointed by my seeming lack of curiosity.

"You have a source of information about the interior?" I asked.

"I do indeed sir, as my cousin's wife comes up regular to work in the laundry here. She tells tales that would make your hair curl, though I see your hair has curled enough already. She says some of them are cunning, and will say anything to get out through the doors. They sound absolutely rational and sane as you and me, but once they escaped down into the village their violent side would come out, and they'd be a danger to one and all. She says the warders are mighty strange too, and often she can't tell the difference between the patients and those on the pay roll. It's a rum do all round, and the asylum changed the village for ever."

It was rapidly getting darker by now, and I explained to the driver that it was time to return to the high street so that I could fix up accommodation for the night.

"My advice would be to head down to the other end of the village and put up at The Royal Oak," he replied. "The Stowey Arms is right outside the gates of the asylum, but that's too close for comfort if you ask me. If one of those violent types got out he'd head straight for The Stowey Arms, you mark my words. And I wouldn't like to be in there when he arrived!"

I told him that I would follow his advice, and he drove down to the gates, which were unlocked for us silently once again, then along the high street and past the church. It took some minutes to drive through the village, but at length he pulled up in front of an inn with warm yellow light glowing in the windows. I alighted from the trap and paid the driver for my ride from the station and the added jaunt up to the asylum, then I stepped inside and asked for a room.

By the time I had eaten it was dark and I had no fancy to brave the cold night and walk towards the asylum in search of my father's residence. Strange imaginings occupied me, prompted by the trap driver's chattering – did inmates make their way outside under cover of darkness and wander the streets of this village, peering into cottage windows with their wild, staring eyes and longing for the comfort of a family hearth? If I stepped outside would I be assaulted by a demented creature wearing shroud-like clothes and screaming without control? Would mad hands grasp at me from around a dark corner and drag me towards a murderous end? These thoughts played with me throughout the night, in and out of frenzied dreams, and I woke in the morning in a depressed and fearful state.

I could eat little breakfast, although the room downstairs was clean and the food well cooked. I was full of fear when I stepped outside onto the high street and looked once more towards the asylum on the hill. Cold seeped into my boots as soon as I started to walk and the sky had that heavy grey look that often signifies an imminent snow fall. The village women were weaving in and out of the few shops, shawls drawn tightly around them and baskets looped over their arms. There seemed to be a strange silence hanging over the street, but perhaps this was simply due to the lack of carts and waggons at that moment. I told myself that the ominous quiet would be dispelled as soon as a horse clopped along the road. But no horse appeared, and I made my way towards the asylum, and the row of cottages in its shadow.

I knew from the description in my uncle's letter exactly which cottage had been taken for my father, and found it without difficulty. It was a fair size, the paint was smart and recently done, a small garden at the front was tidy and even rather pretty. The shutters were all closed but smoke was creeping from the chimney. Summoning all my courage I walked up the narrow path and rapped the knocker twice. I thought I then heard a voice but no-one came to the door. I waited a few minutes, my throat tight with fear and my empty stomach churning, and then knocked again. Now I heard bolts being drawn back and the key turning in the lock. The door creaked open just far enough to allow a maid to put her head around. She did not speak.

"I have come to see Mr William Houlbrooke Tayleur," I told her. "I have had a long journey and I would be grateful if you would let me in and inform him that I am here."

The maid looked behind her, into the house, then turned to me again. "I have instructions not to admit any visitors," she said. She was about to shut the door, but I put my hand against it to prevent her doing so.

"I am Mr Tayleur's eldest son; my name is Charles William Tayleur. Would you please extend me the courtesy of telling your master that I have come to see him? I am not accustomed to being sent away by a maid." I took my hand away, expecting her to invite me in.

"Please wait a minute," she replied, and shut the door.

It is difficult to describe the turmoil I felt after this encounter. I was already wracked with nerves, but now I felt sick and bewildered. How could I gain entry to the house and see my father? Should I go immediately to the magistrates and attempt to bring them here to force entry? I had just decided to try banging on all the windows and shouting for my father so that he would know I was outside, when the door opened and a large man, who was clearly a servant, gestured for me to come in. He showed me into a small, neat room which was presumably a parlour, and invited me to sit down. I took off my hat and held it awkwardly, not sure what to do with it, but he made no move to take it from me, and the maid was nowhere to be seen. He remained in the room, standing between me and the door.

"Would you please tell my father that I am here?" I asked. My voice sounded high and slightly tremulous, and I cleared my throat in an attempt to control it.

"Your father is very ill sir, and we do not advise that he sees visitors in case they unsettle him. I hope you understand, sir."

I am not usually quick to anger, but the habit of servants in this establishment giving orders to a gentleman was angering and offending me. "May I enquire as to whom I am speaking?"

"I am John Shepherd sir, your father's valet."

"Well John Shepherd, I wish to be taken to my father immediately, despite your advice. I wish to see for myself just how ill he is. Where is his room?"

The valet raised his eyebrows, but showed no sign of moving. He stood like a sturdy post in that small room, his wiry hair brushing against the low beamed ceiling.

"If you do not take me to him I will bring the magistrates to this house and you will be forced to show him to us. It is my belief that he is being held here against his will!"

At that, John Shepherd opened the door and made a sign that I should follow him. I left my hat on the chair. We went down the narrow cottage hall and I noticed a high shelf with a row of patterned plates, and a half open door behind which there was much clattering of pots and dishes. The house was not cold, but neither could it in any sense be called cosy.

My father was sitting in a room at the back, propped upright in a straight backed chair. I was overwhelmed with relief to see him. "Father! Thank God!" I exclaimed, and hurried over to him. He did not look at me, but seemed to be staring at a yellow cup and saucer on the table next to him. I recognised it as part of a tea service used at Hampton. Shepherd called for the maid, and asked her to bring another chair into the room, there being only the one, and it was placed next to where my father was sitting. I sank onto it with some relief.

"Father – it's me – Charles. I have come all the way from Cambridge to see you and find out how you are." My father made no sign that he had heard me, and went on staring at his cup with a blank expression. I took a moment to examine his appearance. He looked much the same as I remembered, though rather pale and suffering from some angry looking sores around his mouth. His waistcoat and jacket were clean, his hair well-cut and washed, and he had clearly been shaved that morning.

"Are you well Father?" I asked. At that moment a thick trail of drool started to make its way from the side of his mouth and down his chin. Shepherd came over at once with a handkerchief and wiped it away.

My father showed no sign of noticing. "I have come to help you," I went on. "If you are being kept here against your will I can take you away. Perhaps we could go to Uncle Edward in Warrington. I will help you to claim your rights and your property once again." I reached over and touched his hand. Then he looked at me, and I was shocked by the expression in his eyes. They looked hard and cold, yet somehow vacant, but they fixed on my face. He scowled. Then he shook away my hand, picked up his cup and hurled it across the room. It smashed against the wall, clattering to the floor in fragments and a small pool of cold tea.

John Shepherd came to stand in front of him. "Now Mr Tayleur, we can't have you breaking the good china. That's spoilt the set. There are only five cups left. What will Mrs Tayleur say? She will be disappointed that you have broken that cup."

My father's answer was to grab the saucer quickly and throw that as well. It hit the fireplace and broke in two.

"Dr Bucknill is coming to see you this morning," Shepherd said, his voice even and patient, rather as you would speak to a child. "I am going to tell him that you've been smashing the pretty china. He'll say you have to have the common white crockery like the servants. You won't like that, will you?"

My father was still looking at me in a bellicose manner, and suddenly he spoke. His voice was just as I remembered. "Where is your mother?" he asked.

I was so surprised that I did not think carefully about my reply. "Mother is dead," I said. "She died many years ago." An expression of bewilderment crossed his face and he started to rock backwards and forwards in his chair and make a strange, low wailing noise. More dribble was escaping from his mouth and

Shepherd stepped forward and wiped it away. Then he took hold of my father's shoulders and held him still. My father commenced staring at me once more, and as soon as Shepherd had loosed his grip he jumped up and lunged at me, grasped the lapels of my coat, and shook me so violently that my breath caught in my throat.

"Damn your eyes!" he rasped into my face, and his sour spittle landed on my cheek and felt cold. I tried to push him away, but Shepherd was already wrestling him back into his chair and holding his arms firmly.

"Stand behind me if you please, sir," he said to me, and I obeyed at once. I took out my handkerchief and wiped my face. Meanwhile he was keeping my father firmly in the chair. "You are going to hurt your son if you do that to him," he explained, speaking each word slowly and calmly. "You don't want to injure him Mr Tayleur. We don't shake people; it is wrong."

It was clear that my father responded to his authority and I could not help feeling admiration for the valet, even though my shock and horror were great indeed.

"What is wrong with him?" I asked. "What did I do to anger him?"

Shepherd waited until my father was sitting still and had resumed his vacant expression, then he stood up and turned to me. "What's wrong with him, sir? He is mad, that's what is wrong with him. He's got no wits, no reason and no mind. Lunatics take on suddenly without any warning, there's usually no explaining what has spooked them."

"Will he always be like this?" I asked, with a feeling of dread as to what the answer would be.

"You must talk to the doctor about that," Shepherd replied.

As Dr Bucknill's visit was expected shortly,

Shepherd showed me back into the parlour and rang for the maid so that I could be offered refreshment. The maid who arrived was the one I had encountered at the front door. I was accustomed to maids being young girls, but this was a mature woman perhaps about forty years of age. I requested a cup of tea and she left silently. My hat was still on the chair where I had left it, although I had expected she would have removed it to a hat stand while I was occupied with my father.

That half hour in the small parlour was harrowing indeed. I found that both my hands and my knees were shaking, and I paced the length of the room and back to try to quieten them. It was now too horribly clear that my father really was insane, and my stepmother and uncle were innocent of any traitorous conspiracy. I would not be leaving the cottage with him that morning and effecting a victorious rescue. I felt utter bewilderment about how this terrible thing could have happened, and my mind began to race with questions.

I was soon able to put these to Dr Bucknill as he was shown into the parlour before he went to my father. He hurried into the room, a surprisingly small man exuding enormous energy, and shook my hand warmly. I noticed that the maid had relieved him of his hat and coat.

"I hear that you have had a long journey?" he said.

"I came from Cambridge yesterday," I replied.

"Not exactly the best weather for travelling, but I can understand that you wished to see your father." He sat down and gestured for me to resume my seat also. "You have seen my patient and I am sure you have matters you would like to discuss. I have not got long." He spoke as if his time was limited; his words tumbling over themselves.

"Will my father recover?" I asked.

"I cannot answer with any absolute certainty, but it is unlikely. We are doing our best to help him to reconnect with his memories and to stimulate his mind, and to ensure that his life here is pleasant."

"The man Shepherd handles him very well. I was impressed by his calm manner and his patience."

"Shepherd is one of my most experienced and skilled attendants. We do not treat the lunatics with any harsh methods or cruelty as they did in the past. I run the asylum on certain sound principles. The patients are given occupations such as gardening, painting and basket making. They are taken out into the fresh air as often as possible, and there are fine views for them to enjoy from the windows. The basic tenet of my approach is respect. These wretched people were once parents, wives, husbands. They had occupations and talents. We remember this whenever we speak to them and we are respectful. They will then treat others will respect. These are the methods we are employing to care for your father. I often take him walking with me in the grounds of the asylum so that he can enjoy the beauty of the young trees and the views over the countryside."

Relief flooded through me. I had been tormented for days by dreadful Hogarthian images of inhumane tortures.

"In fact Mr Tayleur," Bucknill continued. "I believe you could prove useful to me. If you would accompany me to your father's room again we could ascertain to what extent he remembers you."

This request made me apprehensive, but my trust in Bucknill and his assistant was complete, and I followed him to the back of the house again.

He shook my father's hand warmly on entering the room, and stood directly in front of him just as

Shepherd had done. The valet was present, standing in the corner unobtrusively.

"How are you today William?" the doctor asked.

I was taken aback. "You address my father by his Christian name?" I asked.

"I am attempting to help your father to remember who he is. William is the name by which he knows himself, and so it is vital that he hears it repeatedly. If we all stand on ceremony and call him Mr Tayleur, his own name will be something else he has lost." He turned back to my father. "You have your son visiting you today William. Are you pleased to see him? He has come a long way. Look, here is Charles. Have you greeted him?"

My father grunted in response to the doctor's questions, but he did look at me when the doctor used my name.

Bucknill then spoke to me. "Mr Tayleur, could you address your father directly and remind him of some incident from the past? Perhaps you have a pleasant memory that he could share? If you awaken the memory for him it would be extremely beneficial. Stand in front of him as I do and look into his face as you speak."

I wracked my brains for such a memory. My father was often away from home and did not spare much time for us when he returned. My memories of childhood focused on the happy, playful, loving presence of my mother. But then I remembered riding on his shoulders, bouncing as he strode down the lawn, his great voice booming across the garden and his rich laugh rolling and rumbling. His hair must have been quite long then; I remembered holding onto his black curls and the smears of hair oil they left on my fingers. I would lie in bed later, sniffing their foreign, spicy smell.

I stood in front of him as instructed and looked into his eyes, but he slid his gaze away at once. "Father, do you remember carrying me on your back in the garden? I was very small then. We used to gallop up and down and I would imagine you were my fine horse. Sometimes you made bark boats for us, like Chinese junks, and we would launch them onto the pond and see whose boat took the longest to sink. Do you remember the terrible geese at the end of the lane? You used to call them Napoleon's damned varmints."

My father frowned and it did look as if he was trying to remember.

"Horse," he said.

"Yes, we pretended you were my horse."

"My horse," he repeated, and his voice was louder. "Fetch my horse, fetch my horse!"

He then tried to rise from his chair and Bucknill moved into my place, took hold of my father's arms and firmly sat him down.

"You do not need your horse today William," he explained. "Charles has been telling you about riding on your shoulders in the garden. Do you remember that? Do you remember the geese? It sounds as if your children were frightened of them."

My father commenced his rocking movements again, and Bucknill held his shoulders to steady him. His mouth slackened and more saliva escaped, glistening on his chin and throat. Bucknill took a linen cloth from the table and wiped it.

"Charles has had a long journey in this cold, winter weather. What have you got to say to him William? Is there anything you want to talk to him about?" The doctor gestured for me to move in front of my father once more.

"This is a very pleasant cottage," I said. "Are you

happy here Father? Your window opens directly onto the garden – what a treat that will be when the spring arrives."

"Indeed," said Bucknill. "We will be planting shrubs and flowers so that he has a view to enjoy." He turned to my father. "We will plant them together William. Shepherd will help. Gardening is excellent therapy and I am hoping the weather will be warm enough for you to spend much of your time out there. Do you enjoy gardening William?"

My father made no sign that he had heard.

"We always had gardeners to do that," I explained.

"What were your father's particular interests?" the doctor asked.

"He loved to ride, and carriage driving." I realised that I actually knew little about his favourite pursuits; I had hardly spent any time with him during the last few years.

"Did he ever paint?"

"Good heavens! I cannot imagine that he ever did. That does not sound like him at all. He loved to be outdoors and never relished sitting still for very long."

"We encourage all our patients to paint. It can be a valuable way of expressing themselves when other faculties have become limited. I would appreciate your comments on your father's paintings; you could perhaps explain the symbolism and associations."

Shepherd opened a drawer in the sideboard and took out several large pieces of paper, each one thickly coated in paint. He laid them on the table. My father sat impassively as I left him and started to examine his paintings. They were child-like but dark. He had used mostly black and heavy blue colours, sometimes filling in spaces marked out by pencil first. I soon realised that several of them showed stormy seas with glowering, laden skies, and when I squinted closely I could make out struggling ships tilting so badly that they lay sideways on the waves, their masts broken and their sails shredded. In one picture he had used his own fingerprints to depict the bodies in the water.

"He is painting shipwrecks," I said. "A ship built by my grandfather's company sank off Lambay Island with great loss of life. The shock killed my grandfather. It seems that is much on my father's mind."

There was one painting of a house. It was the house a child would draw, with a simple front door and two windows on either side; none of the pillars and castellations of his own homes. Dark shadows were all around the house with sinister figures lurking inside them, and black clouds filled the sky above. In one of the windows was a woman with her hair down, looking out as if she was watching for someone. Had he painted my mother?

"This does not look like any of the houses we ever lived in," I said. I lifted the painting up and showed it to my father. "Where is this house?" I asked him. "It isn't fine enough to be Lavender Hill or Hampton. When did you live here?"

He did not look at me or the painting, and made no answer. I returned to stand in front of his chair. "I must go back to Cambridge, Father. Do you have any messages to send to Cresswell and Edward?"

He started to rock again and a look of pain crossed his face. "Where is Emma?" he muttered. "Running around with that imbecile...fetch her back! Bring her inside!" He looked at me then, as if appealing to me for help. "Go and get her. Bring her back." Tears started to run down his cheeks. I had never seen my father cry and it shocked me. "I want my horse, fetch my horse, I'll go. My boots! Where are my riding boots? Where is the horse?"

Bucknill took my place and sat down with my father. Shepherd came over and wiped my father's face. They both spoke soothingly and calmed him, then the doctor said, "I think your father is tired, Mr Tayleur. Perhaps that is enough for this visit. You would be welcome to visit again in a few weeks."

I went over to the door and looked at my father again. "Papa?" I said. He glanced at me and this time his eyes were full of sadness.

I found my own way back to the parlour, picked up my hat and pulled on my coat. There was no sign of the sepulchral maid so I let myself out of the cottage. I realised that, in every real sense, I was now an orphan.

Charles William Tayleur
Trinity College Cambridge - May 1858

As soon as I returned here I wrote a letter to my uncle John Tayleur, this time addressed to Hampton House. I described my father's wretched condition, but emphasised the skill and patience of Dr Bucknill and his attendant. I repeated the essence of Bucknill's conversation with me, praising his modern approach to treatment both in the asylum and in my father's cottage. I reassured my uncle that the decisions he had taken for my father's care had been well chosen, and we could all be certain that my father was receiving the best possible care.

His reply shocked me. His letter was brought to my rooms just as I was hurrying to a lecture, but I sat down in my armchair and broke the seal hurriedly. "I have been in correspondence with your uncle Edward Tayleur in Warrington," he wrote, "and we are both in agreement that you should be told the whereabouts of your brother Albert Gresley Heathcote. Your father gave us strict instructions that you must never be given any information about him whatsoever. Our consciences have always been extremely uneasy about this, but we were bound by your father's wishes. As your father is no longer capable of rational thought, and I have been appointed as the guardian of his estate, we have come to the conclusion that you should be told. I am only sorry that the facts have been withheld from you for so long."

The black, spidery handwriting seemed to blur and shake before my eyes, and I lifted the letter nearer to my face and peered at each word with great care.

"After your mother's death, Albert was taken in by her brother Charles Heathcote and his wife. This seemed an ideal solution to the problem as your uncle Charles had no children of his own. However, Albert had only been in his household for a year or so when your uncle died. For reasons that are not clear to us, Charles Heathcote's wife did not want Albert in her home any longer, and the Heathcote family appealed to your uncle Edward Tayleur. Edward agreed to meet your mother's family to discuss the situation. Perhaps he was planning to offer financial assistance, but when he arrived at the designated meeting place they had brought the child with them. Edward took Albert back to Warrington in his carriage that very day, and he has remained there ever since. I can now assure you my dear Charles, that you would be very welcome to visit your brother there if you wished to do so."

With great impatience I dashed off four letters – one to my uncle John thanking him for telling me at last, one to my uncle Edward to alert him that I would be arriving shortly, and one each to Cresswell and Ned to let them know that our brother was found. Then I pulled out my portmanteau once again and set out on the journey to Lancashire.

I was born in Liverpool but rarely think of the town. We moved south when I was very young and lived in more picturesque places, but somehow I felt pleased to see the dark buildings of the north again, with their soot blackened stones, and the many windows of the looming mills and factories winking dustily in the sunshine. My uncle's home in Warrington was by no means as grand as Hampton, but it had an imposing drive leading to a handsome frontage. My aunt and uncle were welcoming and most sympathetic in their manner towards me. I had not seen them since I was a small boy and they commented on how like my father I was, and looked at each other as they did so.

They asked after him. I told them about my recent visit to Exminster and the expert care provided by Dr Bucknill. But it was also necessary to describe my poor father's confusion and volatile disposition.

"He was always prone to sudden rages," my uncle said. "Could this be a temporary brain fever from which he will recover in time?"

"The doctors do not think so," I replied. "Insanity overtook him with great suddenness and ferocity and there seems little hope that he will regain his mind. He does not know where he is or what has happened to him."

"Did he recognise you?" my aunt enquired.

"I think he did. He became very angry and shook me, and shouted 'Damn your eyes!' which was the expression he used when we annoyed him as children."

"Hah!" my uncle exclaimed. "Those were words he often used when we were young together - I remember it well! So certain aspects of the past remain in his memory?"

"An important element of Bucknill's treatment involves regaining memories, and he questions my father about things he remembers. The doctor thought my visit could be helpful in this respect, but it seemed to have the opposite effect."

"Will he be receiving other visitors?" my aunt asked. "Will your stepmother go often?"

"I do not know," I replied.

"So there are still difficulties between you and Mrs Tayleur?" said my uncle. When I nodded he went on, "Charles, you must rectify this. Your father's financial and business affairs are considerable, and must now be managed by somebody. My brother John will be taking some responsibility, but he will not be able to make decisions without Mary Ellen's permission. She will have control over what happens in the future. It seems that several executors will be appointed, and she will be one of them. In order to protect your own interests you must communicate with her Charles, and you must communicate with her in an amicable manner."

"I do not understand Uncle. Why would I need to ingratiate myself into her good books?"

"Because she will have a say in any requests made on your father's estate. You wish your allowance to continue so that you can take your degree and perhaps study further? Both Cresswell and Edward will require the same. In time you may need these allowances to increase, and you will have to gain her approval. Any financial matters previously dealt with by your father will now be under her control."

I groaned. She had made it clear many years before that she did not think we should be relying on my father for financial support. My ambition to become a barrister looked set to be hard won.

"What of Albert?" I asked. "How is he? May I see him?"

"Of course," my uncle said. "I am sure you have a great deal to talk to him about, but try not to upset him. He is a sickly child who falls ill easily."

"You have not yet sent him away to school?"

"Both your aunt and I are unwilling to do so, although it would now perhaps be possible to apply to your father's estate for a contribution towards the fees. A tutor comes here on three mornings each week, but Albert tires quickly and we believe boarding school would be too much for him." My aunt rang the bell and asked the maid to bring Master Albert down to the drawing room. I found myself to be on the verge of tears. I was excited about meeting him at last, and deeply moved to be doing so.

I don't know what I expected. Perhaps, somewhere inside me, I imagined Albert would have thin, sandy hair and a weak sloping chin, much as Edward had described Arthur Lennox. Perhaps I was dreading that this would be his appearance. But I could not have been more wrong; the nine year old boy who came into the room was the image of my father. He had the same thick, curly dark hair and slightly staring brown eyes, but he clearly lacked my father's robust constitution and looked thin and pale. He came over to our uncle and stood uncertainly, gazing at me with some confusion.

"Allow me to introduce you," my uncle said. "Albert Gresley Heathcote, this is your brother Charles William Tayleur." We shook hands. "It is high time you met. Now your aunt and I will leave you to get to know each other."

"But first I will order some tea and cakes," my aunt said. "The cook has been baking huge quantities of buns for this very occasion; boys and buns go so very well together." My uncle and aunt both laughed, but Albert and I were occupied in staring at each other. We were left alone.

After a few minutes of awkward silence, Albert asked, "Are you my papa?"

I had to smile. "Goodness, no; I am not old enough to be your papa. We are brothers. I am only a few years older than you are. We have two other brothers, Cresswell and Edward. There are four of us altogether."

"Where is Papa? Is he also coming to visit me?"

"Papa is very ill at present and cannot leave his home. But you will see Cresswell and Edward as soon as we can arrange it. They are greatly looking forward to seeing you. We have always wanted to find you again."

Albert was still searching my face. "You look just like me," he said.

At that moment the maid came in, carrying a tray with a tea pot and a large plate of currant buns.

"Would you be kind enough to bring a looking glass?" I asked her.

"Yes sir," she bobbed and hurried out.

While we were waiting for her to return I got Albert seated and poured a cup of tea for him. Then I handed him a plate with two buns on it.

"I say, these look very good indeed," I said. If I want buns like these I have to go to an extremely expensive tea shop in Cambridge. Mind you, when I was at Eton there was a good one in Windsor."

"That's where the Queen lives. I am named after the Queen's husband."

"Indeed you are. Albert is an excellent name. In fact all your names are prestigious. The Gresley family is very grand indeed. Our great-grandmother was Anne

Gresley. One of our ancestors was knighted at the coronation of Anne Boleyn."

"Oh I have heard about her!" Albert exclaimed. "She had her head cut off."

"That's right, and our ancestor was fortunate that his knighthood was not stripped away because he was associated with her."

The maid came in with the looking glass and I gave it to Albert. "Look at yourself and then look at me. What do you notice?"

He obediently studied his reflection with serious concentration and turned to me. Then he grinned widely.

"Look!" he said, handing me the glass. "We have the same hair. Your nose is the same as mine and so are your eyes. You've got my face!"

And I started to laugh, touched by his delight in discovering our similarities. I tucked into the buns with enthusiasm and persuaded Albert to nibble at one, and I have to say that they were greatly superior to anything one could buy in Windsor.

"If you are my brother," Albert asked with his mouth full, "why do we have different names?"

I thought quickly before answering. I had no wish to give Albert any notion of my father's rejection or the unhappy beginning of his life. "You went to live with our mother's family – the Heathcotes – and so I suppose they wanted you to have their name. They are a wealthy family and own many ironworks and collieries."

"Uncle Edward is wealthy too, and he owns the Vulcan Foundry and the shipyard at Bank Quay. He took me to watch the big ship being launched down the river."

I was amazed. "Did he? You were actually there when they launched the Tayleur?" He nodded. "You must have been only three or four years old. Do you remember it?"

"I remember that there were lots and lots of people on the bridge and down the river bank. When the ship went into the water they all got splashed and some of them got really wet. Everyone was cheering and shouting and there were flags and bunting. We went inside for sandwiches and there were speeches. Then it rained and all the bunting got wet."

"You were really lucky to be there Albert. I wish I had seen it."

"Tell me about the Gresleys," he said.

I wracked my brains to remember some of my mother's stories. She had been very proud of belonging to such an ancient family, and often told us about them.

"There is a town called Castle-Gresley in Derbyshire. Our family had a castle there and that's how it got its name. There is another town near to it called Church-Gresley and our family owned both places at one time. They have a splendid manor house called Drakelow Hall and a huge chest of treasure is hidden there. Sir Thomas Gresley and his wife were misers and wouldn't spend any money at all; instead they saved it all up and used to enjoy counting the coins. They put the treasure somewhere very safe and no-one has ever been able to find it."

"Can we go and look for it?"

"The family are not allowed to live at Drakelow so we would not be able to go there. When Sir Roger Gresley died, sometime in the 1830s, his widow was allowed to stay on in the house. She has married someone else now but she still won't leave. Her name is Lady Sophia. Our mother felt angry about her hanging onto the house."

"What was our mother like? She died and I don't

remember her."

"You were three when she died, do you have no memory of her at all?"

"Sometimes I think I do. Sometimes I hear a voice singing, very close, and imagine that she must have rocked me while she sang, but that is all. Tell me about her."

How could I begin to tell this boy about the mother he had never known? "She was pretty," I said, "and good at playing games. She was always laughing and she liked to dance. She used to read to us and take us for walks."

"Do we look like her?"

I thought about the portrait of my father that hangs in the drawing room at Hampton. His hair is long enough to curl over the wing collar of his evening shirt but recedes high on his forehead. His mouth is on the edge of smiling, although his eyes seem heavy with sadness. I looked at that portrait often when we stayed in Torquay, and wondered what he was thinking of when he was sitting for the artist. There is no portrait of my mother. "No, you and I look like our father. Ned and Cresswell are more like her. It won't be long before you can meet them, and you will meet our uncle John at the same time."

"I have met Uncle John; he has come here a few times to see me."

"Has he?" I said in surprise.

"I don't really want uncles – we seem to have a large number of them, and aunts as well. I want to belong to a proper family. It will be nice to have brothers."

"Well actually, there are some more."

"Some more? What do you mean?"

"Our father married another wife after Mama died, so we have a stepmother."

"Like Snow White and Cinderella?"

"Yes – exactly like Snow White and Cinderella. She has three children, so we have two half-brothers and a half-sister called Galfred, Eveline and William. William is still a baby."

Albert was silent while he took all this in. Then he said, "I don't want a stepmother."

"No, neither do I," I agreed without hesitation, "but don't worry about her. You won't have to see her."

"What does she look like?" he asked.

"Like a bad-tempered King Charles spaniel," I replied, and we both laughed heartily.

After we had made fine work of consuming some of the buns, Albert took me upstairs to see his room. It was a large apartment at the front of the house, with views over the small park and the countryside beyond. On the carpet was a large tinplate train, and Albert showed me how he could pull it round the room as the wheels turned smoothly. Waiting for the train to arrive at the washstand was a group of rather scruffy lead soldiers, presumably from Uncle Edward's boyhood, and carved wooden animals of various sizes were grazing on the rug by the bed to afford a picturesque outlook for the passengers. I was amused to see an elephant and a stalking tiger amongst the cows, sheep and horses.

Much more splendid was a smaller train, set on a table near the window. The locomotive was a shiny green colour, with a tall gold chimney, a separate green tender and two red coaches. Attached to the engine was a wire arm about a foot long. At the other end of the arm was a rounded red box, shaped like a clover leaf, containing a clockwork mechanism. When Albert placed the key in the top of this and wound it, the arm pulled the train around in a circle. I had never seen such a toy, and expressed enormous admiration. Albert allowed me to take a turn at winding it, and showed me how the train would keep going for longer if the coaches were removed.

"It is a Rotary Railway Express," he explained. "Uncle Edward heard about it and was determined to obtain one for me. It came in a long wooden box."

I was conscious then of feeling greatly relieved. It was clear that Albert was loved and had a happy life. I decided not to return to university as the term was nearly over anyway, but to accompany Albert immediately to Shevington Hall, just a twelve mile journey from Warrington, and wait for my brothers and Uncle John to arrive there for Easter. Uncle Edward was in agreement, and Albert excitedly packed a box and prepared to meet his brothers at last.

There followed one of the happiest holidays I have ever had. Cresswell and Edward could see the resemblance between Albert and myself immediately, and if they had doubted at any time that he was really our brother, those fears were quickly dispelled. However, they were concerned about his frail appearance, and questioned me about his health on our first evening together, after he had gone to bed.

"Uncle Edward told me that he tires easily, and that is why he is not to be sent away to school."

"He is so pale and thin," Cresswell observed. "Has he suffered recently from some illness or infection?"

"None has been mentioned to me," I replied.

But we did our best to liven him up during our three weeks together. He was not used to riding so our uncle procured a trap for our use, and we took him for rides around the park and down into town to visit the sweet shops. We set up stumps on the smooth lawn in front of the house and played endless games of cricket. My uncle went up into the attics to find a model sailing ship that he used to play with when he was a boy, and we mended the rigging and sailed it on the lake. Cresswell was much taken with a book that had recently been published called "Tom Brown's Schooldays". This featured Cresswell's own school, and he would spend hours reading it to us, adding his own comments about the realism and accuracy with which Rugby was portrayed. I think Albert was heartily glad that he would not be going away to school after listening open-mouthed to all the lurid accounts of torture and bullying.

One afternoon we built a bonfire together, after solicitously obtaining permission from the gardener and being shown to a corner of the vegetable garden. Even my Aunt Eliza took an interest in this project, and brought potatoes for us to bake in the embers, and chestnuts to roast. As soon as it was dark my brothers and my small cousin gathered around excitedly while I set the small, dry sticks at the bottom of the heap alight. Uncle John helped me to manage the fire, knowing exactly how many branches to add at any one time without smothering the flames. The boys danced and whooped around it for a time, pretending to be savages. They sat down when the cook brought out a large jug of hot chocolate and poured steaming cupfuls for all of us, and we listened to the spitting and crackling of the fire and sang songs we remembered from childhood. My uncle and I fished the blackened potatoes out with sticks and laid them on a stone to cool and Cresswell helpfully brought fire irons from the drawing room so that we could retrieve the chestnuts more efficiently.

By this time the fierceness had gone out of the fire, and it glowed a warm deep red by our feet. Edward made a start on one of the potatoes, tossing it from hand to hand for a while, then breaking it open and exposing the clean white inside. Albert followed his lead and they both picked the potato from the black skins with their teeth. The maid had brought out a bowl of salt in which to dip the chestnuts, and dishes of nuts and fruit to supplement our supper. I watched my brothers as they peeled chestnuts and laughed together, and I looked up at the stars in the clear sky and wondered if our mother could somehow see us and know that we were a family at long last.

There were darker moments that had to be dealt with. I took Cresswell and Edward for a walk one evening and described our father's illness to them. They were aghast at the suddenness with which he had lost his sanity, and horrified to hear of his condition. If I had not been able to tell them that I had seen him with my own eyes, they would have found it all impossible to believe. They wanted to know about the future: would Papa die? Would they be able to remain at school and go on to take degrees at a university? Would our stepmother remain at Hampton? These were questions to which I had no answers and as soon as I could I requested some of my uncle's time, and sat with him alone in his study.

"The doctors think that your father will only live a matter of weeks," Uncle John explained. "It will be a mercy for him to leave this life, for they see no hope of him ever regaining his sanity. Now that the disease has reached his brain it will soon kill him."

A matter which had been weighing heavily on my mind for years now came into sharp focus. "When my father married my stepmother," I said, "Mary Ellen told me that she would do everything within her power to ensure her son would be the heir to his estates and I would be disinherited. Can you tell me if she succeeded? Has my father made a new will in Galfred's favour?"

My uncle shifted uncomfortably in his leather chair and my heart sank within my chest. The future suddenly seemed terribly uncertain.

"There is a problem with your father's will," my uncle said.

"A problem?" I asked, my hands shaking.

"Your father made a will in 1854. However, in January this year he went to his solicitor in Torquay and insisted on making a new will, which is very different from the first."

"Does the new will make Galfred the heir to Hampton?"

"No Charles, it does not. You are the heir to Hampton and you will become the tenant for life immediately on your father's death. I have a copy of each will because I am now responsible for administering his estates. The problem is not the actual contents of the wills, which I will show you in a moment, but which of them will be legal and valid. The new will was written just days before your father was certified insane. It was written during the very week when his behaviour became violent and unreasonable. It can therefore be argued that he was in no fit state to make decisions and it could be overthrown in favour of the first. But this will mean a court case Charles, with Mary Ellen fighting us on behalf of her children."

He took two documents out of the drawer in his desk and handed them to me. On the front sheet of both was a red stamp with the words "In Lunacy".

"Good God!" I exclaimed. "What does this mean?"

"Your father's papers have mostly been removed to the Lunacy Commission. Some may be returned after the inquisition in September. In the meantime the commissioners are protecting your father's interests. In all correspondence they refer to him as The

Lunatic. He is no longer capable of administering his estates himself."

Images of my father flickered across my mind – playing with us in the garden at Lavender Hill, picking Cresswell up and swinging him onto his shoulders and galloping up and down the lawn; throwing me through the door of his study when his face had taken on a dark hue of fury; slumped in a chair in the cottage at Exminster with drool down his chin. How could this strong, powerful man become merely The Lunatic? My throat burned and I was horrified to feel tears pricking at my eyelids. I put my hand over my face.

My uncle was unfolding one of the documents in front of me. "This is the will from 1854," he began. "It is dated September 4th and you will see there is a codicil dated one year later. We are fortunate to have this in our possession. Your father tried to destroy it in his bedroom fire during the onset of his illness. The original is torn and scorched, but still legible. I think you will find the opening statement quite surprising."

I blinked the moisture away from my eyes and took up the document. After the usual brief preamble the will stated, "I give and bequeath to my trustees and executors to be paid immediately on my decease the sum of two thousand pounds to hold in trust for the child known by the name of Albert Heathcote now under the care of Charles Heathcote of Warrington and I direct the said trustees for the time being to apply so much as they or he shall think fit of the income and annual produce of the said sum of two thousand pounds towards the maintenance and education of the said child during his minority."

I was astounded. "Albert!" I exclaimed. "What does this mean? Such a sum! Two thousand pounds!"

"It is indeed a generous sum Charles," my uncle

replied. "He could live as a gentleman, albeit a modest one, if he was always cautious with the capital. The will states that your stepmother would receive only half that sum on your father's death, although provision is also made for her income."

"But he has never acknowledged Albert! He would not allow his name to be mentioned by any of us, and made sure we never even knew where he was living! Why did he leave such a legacy for him?"

"I have always believed your father, my brother, to be a good man with a conscience and this will proves that I am right in my judgement. It had clearly always troubled him that he could have been mistaken about Albert's parentage, and he took this opportunity to make some sort of amends."

"Thank God!" I said. "Now Albert has a secure, independent future…"

"Do not be too hasty Charles," my uncle interrupted. "The second will makes no mention of Albert whatsoever. He is completely disinherited, as if he simply does not exist."

"Why? What caused my father to change his mind so radically? If he has a conscience as you claim, how could he act with such injustice?"

"One answer to that Charles, is that he was no longer in control of his mind when he gave instructions for the second will, although the solicitor Kitson is sure that he was. Also, you must note the change in his circumstances. The first will was written after his marriage to Mary Ellen but before the birth of their children. When the second will was written he was anxious to make better provision for his second family."

I felt the familiar sick lurch of apprehension and dread assail my stomach. I started to speak, but my uncle held up his hand to stop me. "You must also consider the influence of your stepmother upon your father. She was bitterly opposed to any acknowledgement of Albert and utterly refuted the idea that he could possibly be your father's son. Whatever William's own feelings, once she had provided him with three children he must have felt it was his duty to placate her. You know her character, do you not agree with me?"

I nodded, for I knew he was right. I pictured her bustling around Hampton, following my father from room to room and poisoning him against all my mother's children.

"Please explain the other ways in which the two wills are different," I said somewhat wearily, for I could well imagine the answer.

"In order to help you understand, I must tell you a little about my father - your grandfather. He was an astute and brilliant businessman but he always attributed his great success to his own grandfather. Charles Tayleur was the youngest son in the family and his eldest brother inherited the whole of the estate. However, his grandfather left each of the three grandsons the sum of ten thousand pounds. Charles used this to start trading as a merchant and began to build his fortune. At one point he bought the entire contents of a ship and sold them at huge profit. As you know, he invested in the Liverpool to Manchester railway and that is how he became involved with the Stephensons. By the time he died he was a very rich man indeed. But he never forgot the kindness and generosity of his grandfather, and he was determined to do the same for his own grandchildren. Accordingly, he left the sum of thirty thousand pounds to each of his children, to be put in trust for their children. Except for your aunt Jane; she was not left thirty thousand pounds."

I was surprised and bewildered by this. "But Grandfather was especially fond of Aunt Jane. I remember she visited him often and they were particularly close."

"They were indeed particularly close. She was his eldest daughter and his favourite from the moment she was born. He did not leave her thirty thousand pounds, but one hundred thousand pounds, to be divided amongst her children after her death. Heaven knows she had no need of all that money – the Phibbs family is rich enough."

"One hundred thousand pounds?" I could barely imagine such riches. My eyes must have been as round as jam jar lids, for my uncle laughed at my expression.

"Well, that is their affair. But the thirty thousand pounds left to your father for his children is the main issue in the second will. I have to tell you Charles, that it was never your grandfather's intention that you should have a share of this sum. As the eldest son of Charles Tayleur's eldest son, you will inherit most of the properties, of which there are many."

I waved my hand and shook my head. I fully understood this. It was the welfare of my brothers that was concerning me by now.

"In the second will," my uncle continued, "the thirty thousand pounds will be divided between Mary Ellen's children only. There is other provision made for them under their parents' marriage settlement, and they will therefore receive further sums from the estate in addition to this. Your father also gave instructions for several of the properties to be sold, and the proceeds divided between his three children by Mary Ellen, as well as Cresswell and Edward. But this will undoubtedly favours his second family to the detriment of the first."

"What will happen?" I asked.

"While I was staying at Hampton after the removal of your father, I took the precaution of speaking to the solicitor Kitson, and the two doctors who attended your father and issued the certificates declaring him to be insane. I asked all of them to provide me with written statements about the events that occurred during the days in which your father was ill. They all did this, and I have these documents in my safe here at Shevington. I also carried out a detailed inventory of the furniture and effects in both Hampton House and the rented cottage in Exminster. All these are clearly bequeathed to you in both wills, and I have explained to Mary Ellen that she may make use of them during what remains of her husband's life, but you will take possession immediately on his death."

"Thank you Uncle," I said, with real gratitude.

"I would imagine that probate will not be granted on either of the wills after your father dies, and we will have to wait upon the decision of a court of law. Meanwhile, I am one of the trustees looking after the administration of your father's estate, along with Mary Ellen and a solicitor, and rest assured that I will do everything in my power to protect your interests and those of your brothers."

I thanked him again, then folded the will carefully and replaced it on his desk. The red ink jumped out at me again – "In Lunacy". I wondered how long it would be before my father's terrible life was brought to a close, and the Battle of Wills could begin.

In Lunacy

William. William. Damned doctor making free with my name. My mother, sisters, brothers call me William. Then women. Often in bed. A bed name. Too intimate for doctors. We walk in the gardens he and I, the doctor and the squire, when the others are all inside. We won't be disturbed he says. But they watch us, lined up like grubby kitchen plates at the windows. Staring out. Do you remember he always asks. Do you remember this and that? What do I remember? Difficult to say. The sea – there was always the sea – dark and oily in Liverpool, glittering in Torquay. Glittering as if all the lost, wrecked treasure underneath was calling out to be found. Women. Well one was no more than a girl, working in the usual place by the docks. Took me to a garret smelling of rats, rancid meat, dirty clothes. The bed was grey and soiled but I barely noticed. Her face was painted, even though she was young and her skin was smooth. I often wondered if she was the one who caused all my problems. She had circles of rouge on her cheeks like a doll.

One of them had a doll with a wax face, a present at Christmas when she was a child. She told me the tale at length, despite me having no interest in hearing it, no interest in her childhood, no real interest in her by that time. How the doll was beautiful and she was thrilled, delighted to own it. How she took it to bed with her and slept with it pressed against her cheek. How the warmth had melted it and she woke in the morning to find it hideous, grotesque, deformed. I knew how she felt.

Horses were easier than women: loyal, straightforward beasts. Those were my happy times, galloping against the wind on a fine morning, my head clearing with every hoof beat, the power and spirit of the horse cleansing the irritations of the day. I find myself thinking about the horse, wondering where it is. I ask for it to be brought to the door, saddled and ready, but they never do. It has gone.

It has all gone, except the damned tea set. The rooms are cramped and low and the windows small. I remember Hampton, but with some pain. I remember Lavender Hill, but with much more pain. I know Emma went from there and sometimes I see her face, unpainted, but just as much a whore's face as the women by the docks. I see his face too – a weak chin, gingery whiskers, thin balding hair. I wonder what she suffered after she left. Whether his wife forgave him, or even knew what he had done.

I think about the child. Sometimes a doubt creeps into my mind – could he have been mine? Did I send my own son away and abandon him to such an uncertain fate? I never saw him again, and can remember nothing of what he looked like in those first days of life. But I believed he was the spawn of Lennox. I did what I had to do.

The children merge together; I cannot find their faces. Some of them upset my wife. Charles was damnably defiant, not gentlemanly, a disgrace she said. It was best he stayed away then. But I missed him. Never dared say that, but there you are. Missed those times when they were all small and we charged about in the garden. I'll say that for Emma – she was always laughing; she knew how to be happy and how to create happy times. The other one had no idea. We had some good years, Emma and I. She had real beauty. I have a memory of her with her hair down, but I cannot go there. As it says in the play: that way madness lies, no more of that.

Mary Ellen Tayleur
Hampton House - September 1861

The events of that dreadful week remain fresh in my memory, as I am sure they always will. After my husband had been driven away from our home forever, my brother-in-law led me back into the drawing room and rang for hot, sweet tea. He sat with me for a while and then repaired to the study, despite the lateness of the hour. I sat staring into the fire, praying that all the horrors of those last awful days were unreal, a fantasy, a nightmare from which I would wake. I slowly became aware of a clamour ringing in my head – a conglomeration of screams, cries, thumps and shouts, and I was uncertain whether they were jangling just within my ears or throughout the whole house. It would prove to be weeks before this stopped, weeks before I could once again stand on the landing and hear only the muted sounds of the children playing in the nurseries at the far end of the corridor, and the muffled rattle of plates and pans in the depths of the house.

The following day the Torquay Times carried a report about the ceremony celebrating the building of the new railway line to Paignton. Sir Lawrence Palk had stepped forward amidst great applause to cut the first sod and announce the commencement of the works. But his attempt was thwarted by the icy ground which was frozen as hard as rock. Despite much pressing on the spade with his aristocratic foot (although William always insisted he was no more an aristocrat than our dog), Palk was quite unable to make any inroad in the turf whatsoever. The implement was passed to Charles Seale-Hayne, whose muscly frame perhaps showed more promise of success. He thrust the spade into the soil with great determination, only to find the handle splintering in two within his grasp. The crowd roared with delight, and my face broke into a stiff smile as I read. How William would have loved that story; if only he could have been there to witness Palk's discomfiture. I pictured him throwing his head back and roaring with laughter, and wished from the bottom of my heart that he was sitting here at Hampton with me and we could laugh together. And then I remembered the scandalous accusations he had cruelly shouted at me, in front of my servants, my relatives and two doctors, and my heart hardened.

During the mournful days that followed I spent much time standing in front of my husband's portrait which hangs above the fireplace in the main drawing room. It is a handsome piece, and captures the likeness extremely well. William gazes out of the frame with a slight smile about his lips, and the most striking aspect of the painting is the serenity of his expression. Once I found myself reaching up and touching his hand, which rests on the back of a chair, and feeling just the glossy oil paint under my fingertips. I often looked into his face and wondered about the man I had known for those eight short years. I remembered the charming playfulness of our courtship which changed once we were married, although between his bursts of temper he was always tender and gentlemanly until that last terrible week. His face rarely looked so peaceful in life, but I knew that he revelled in being squire and was entirely happy when he was riding out with his dogs or ensconced in his study with his steward. I missed him. I missed the man he had been, and regretted the monster he had become.

John Tayleur soon became concerned for my welfare and made it his business to join me in the drawing room whenever he could, although his time was much taken up with my husband's business affairs.

"I am so very afraid," I told him one afternoon, as we took tea together. "I am fearful that the servants will find it impossible to be discreet and will tattle about William's misfortunes until they are bandied throughout Torquay."

"I suggest that we let it be known that William has had to travel to Warrington," John said thoughtfully. "Our brother Edward has recently been experiencing some financial difficulties with the foundries, and is looking into the possibility of closing down both Bank Quay and Vulcan. It would be entirely plausible that William is needed there to advise his brother and support him, and he would need to stay in Lancashire for a considerable time."

I sighed with relief. This would indeed give us some time to manufacture other reasons for his permanent absence from Torquay. John looked at me. Perhaps he felt troubled by the strain and suffering he could see in my face. I have had little time for my looking glass lately, but I am well aware that these few weeks have added years to my appearance.

"You are too much alone," he said. "You need something to occupy your time and prevent you brooding over recent events."

"And what would you suggest?" I asked, at a loss as to what I could do.

"I think you should teach Eveline to sew," John replied unexpectedly.

"Eveline is barely three years old!" I exclaimed. "What on earth do you know about teaching young females about sewing? Would it not be dangerous to put a needle in the hands of such a young child?"

"I admit that I know nothing of such matters. But I do clearly remember my mother sitting for hours with my sisters and showing them how to make stitches. Jane was older, but Sarah was very small and I'm sure Mother gave her a thicker sort of needle. Does such a thing exist?"

I thought about this. "Well she could have been using a darning needle I suppose. And if she had a loosely woven cloth she would be able to put the needle through quite easily."

"My mother believed that a girl could not start too early to learn needlecraft. Both my sisters were accomplished needlewomen when they were quite young, and I believe they still derive much enjoyment from their skill."

"Why yes," I said. "I do remember your sister Jane embroidered beautifully. We used to sew together quite often and my work did not compare favourably with hers. She delighted in making pretty dresses for Henrietta and Isabella."

"There you are," said John. "I think it would do you

good to spend time with Eveline, and you may well provide her with skills, interests and pleasures that will last her whole life and for which she will always be grateful."

I took his advice, and the following morning I asked the nursery maid to bring Eveline to my upstairs sitting room. The maid was a little startled by this as I generally saw the children for an hour before dressing for dinner and rarely at other times, and she brought Eveline to me with a quizzical expression on her face. I gestured that she should leave and shut the door behind her. I had prepared an embroidery hoop with a length of dish cloth material, and threaded red wool onto a darning needle. We sat together in my window and I showed my small daughter how to pull the wool through the cloth. She mastered this without too much difficulty, but found it hard to know where to insert the needle in the back so she could draw the wool through to the front once more. I patiently made lines on the cloth with a pencil, and she followed these with enormous care. She was soon making running stitches from one side of the ring to the other. They were far from even or straight, but that did not prevent either of us from feeling great pride in this achievement.

Over the next few days we started to work on a simple sampler, with running stitches of different sizes and in several colours and even a few cross stitches. What a dear little girl my daughter is. My tormented, grief-stricken mind started to heal while I sat in the window with Eveline, and the sewing lessons became a daily pleasure for us both.

Meanwhile John Tayleur had been organising the establishment in Exminster where my husband would be cared for, and as soon as William was settled there the two of us went to visit him. I cannot describe my feelings as the carriage took us closer. I was praying for a miracle, hoping that he would already be cured by this remarkable Bucknill and would burst into the room to greet us, totally restored to his own self. And I was dreading the meeting, writhing with discomfort at the thought of him repeating any of his vile claims about my conduct. Not to mention my confusion, for it appeared I was married to two totally different men; one rather impatient and even subject to rages, but kindly and unmistakably a gentleman; and the other a hopeless lunatic. Which man was waiting for me in Exminster? Or would there be yet a third?

I felt sick, and the jolting of the carriage exacerbated this unbearably.

At last we turned off the main Exeter road and John pointed to the asylum at the top of the hill. I shuddered and turned away. The village was strung out along the main street between two public houses, and consisted of low cob cottages and several shops. The homespun inhabitants turned to stare at our conveyance and I hid my face from their gaze. We turned off the main road into a small lane, and stopped after just a few yards. "I considered it wise not to take a house on the high street," John was explaining. "This one affords William a little privacy, although the villagers can see him being taken up to the asylum. The doctor sends a covered carriage but they still know what is going on. I believe they are more than used to such arrangements here." This produced an image in my mind of a place cluttered with madmen, of lunatics careening through the lanes in covered carriages and forming a line of conveyances up the drive to the asylum like those delivering merrymakers to a ball. I shook my head and looked out of the window.

The cottage where my husband was now living was

small, and only a tiny strip of garden separated it from the road in front. John had ensured that it was painted and well cleaned before we took on the lease, but the windows were small with tiny panes and judging by the number of these, there could not be many rooms inside. A track led along the side of the house to a larger garden behind. We alighted and walked through the little gate to stand under the porch. It was clear, even in the wintry weather, that there were many rose bushes at the front of the house, and in the summer months they would produce a profusion of flowers. Of course, each coloured rose has a different meaning. I thought fleetingly about these – red lovers' roses, white roses for innocence and purity, orange for desire and pink roses for gentility – how totally unsuitable for the house with its present purpose. We need flowers for hopelessness and loss, for pain and despair. But perhaps the thorns will do well for now.

The door was opening and a maid showed us into the tiny, low-beamed parlour. When she had disappeared with our hats and cloaks I asked my brother-in-law how many servants I was employing in the house. "There are three – John Shepherd is the valet, but he is also an experienced nurse from the asylum. Then there is a housekeeper and the maid. A girl from the village comes in when necessary to help prepare meals."

The valet entered the room then, and we enquired after my husband.

"Having a quiet day today, madam. I have told him you are visiting and he is looking forward to seeing you."

When we went through to the back room my husband was pacing backwards and forwards, glancing out of the window each time he passed it. He was limping slightly, presumably because the ulcers on his legs were still troubling him, and I could see weeping, red sores around his mouth. Otherwise he appeared to be clean and neatly dressed, though somewhat thinner than before. As soon as we entered the room he came up to my brother-in-law and grasped the sleeve of his coat.

"John," he said, in a low, rasping voice.

"William – old chap!" John replied. "How are you?"

"I want to go home now," William said, his eyes fixed on John's coat sleeve.

"When you are better we will take you home immediately," John said, but that was clearly not what my husband wanted to hear. He started to make a wailing noise, almost like a dog baying at the moon, and at once the valet stepped over to him and took hold of his arms.

"Now Mr Tayleur, we don't need that noise. Mrs Tayleur has come to see you and you haven't greeted her yet. Say 'how do you do' to your wife instead of making that disagreeable sound."

But William took no notice of me. He pulled his arms from the valet's grasp and recommenced his prowling by the window.

"You are limping William," John observed. "Is your leg giving you a great deal of pain? Does the doctor give you medication for it?"

"Leg, leg, lost my leg sir," William answered, looking down at his leg as he did so.

"We clean the ulcerated areas each day, and apply fresh dressings," the valet said, "But Mr Tayleur is no longer being treated with mercury."

"He was being given mercury?" John exclaimed in surprise. "I had no knowledge of that. By God, small wonder he is in this state."

William seemed to realise then that we had not

come to take him back to Torquay, and he slumped onto a hard chair in the corner of the room, his head sagging over his chest. He did not acknowledge me in any way.

It has been like that on most of the occasions I have gone, but one terrible day he seemed to be under the impression that I was his first wife, and he became extremely agitated and abusive, demanding to know why I had treated him so badly and trying to touch me. Shepherd quickly came to my aid, but I am reluctant to visit now. I have had several discussions with Bucknill, and he sees no real hope of improvement. The whole establishment – servants, food, coal and medical fees – costs nearly five hundred pounds each year. I have to pay this out of my yearly allowance of one thousand pounds.

My stepson however, receives an allowance not far short of this, and does not have any of my onerous responsibilities. He was admitted to Lincoln's Inn in March this year and commenced the legal training he has always demanded. Both he and his brothers remain a drain on the estate.

London - September 1868

My dear Mrs Tayleur,

I am writing to inform you that I will shortly be leaving the country for a prolonged period, probably many years, as you once advised me to do. I have been told by several colleagues, most far more experienced and highly esteemed than myself, that setting up chambers as a barrister will be more rewarding in Brussels than in London. The climate will be healthier for my wife and children, and the general ambience of that beautiful city will be more pleasing to all of us.

I will write to you again as soon as we have taken a house and have a permanent address, and I would greatly appreciate news of my father whenever you have any to convey. As I am sure you are aware, I have visited my father as often as I could within the restraints upon my time. I have been much relieved to find that the departure of John Charles Bucknill for the Lord Chancellor's Department in 1862 has had no detrimental effect on my father's treatment, and that his successor Dr Symes Saunders continues to minister to him personally along the lines of Dr Bucknill's philosophy. I knew when I took my leave of him recently that this would, in all probability, be the last time I would see him. I pray that he will soon find peace and relief from his sufferings, which have been far more prolonged than the doctors predicted.

Meanwhile, I would be grateful if you could pass my warmest fraternal greetings to Galfred and William, and give Eveline a kiss from my wife and myself.

With warm wishes for your continued good health,
Charles William Tayleur.

For I had at last met my stepbrothers and stepsister. Cresswell and Edward had spent some part of each school holiday at Hampton, following the advice of my uncle, and knew Mary Ellen's children quite well. But I had never been back, and I had not seen my stepmother since I left the mansion in late summer 1854, just a few months after my father's marriage and the devastating loss of the ship. I was still a schoolboy at Eton then, raw with anger and grief at losing my mother and full of anxiety about the uncertain future for myself and all my brothers. Those were dark years. Looking back I recognise now that I was very afraid of Mary Ellen. I was fearful of the power she had to turn my father against us, and when you have lost one parent the prospect of losing the other is terrifying. I was afraid of her ability to have me disinherited and to throw the future into uncertainty and chaos. And I knew that her implacable opposition to Albert meant that my father would never be reconciled to him, and he would never be given a proper place within our family. In fact, "our family" had been undermined by her; rubbed away as if it had never really been there.

But Fortune's Wheel had started to turn, and Mary Ellen and I had been moved to different positions. After three years as a law student at Lincoln's Inn I was called to the Bar there, in the Great Hall, and fulfilled my dream of becoming a barrister. Just two months earlier I had been married to Mary Jane Preston, and found a happiness that had been missing from my life for many years.

In the meantime, on January 15th 1864 Lord Arthur Lennox died. I read his obituary with distaste. He was the youngest son of the Duke of Richmond, Member of Parliament for Chichester then Great Yarmouth, a Junior Lord of the Treasury, Lieutenant – Colonel in the Light Infantry battalion of the Sussex Militia; in fact he had amassed a string of fine sounding titles which did not include seducer of my mother. I wondered if he had ever thought of her while he was socialising in his lordly circles. How had he felt when he heard of her disgrace? If I believed that for some moment he had experienced guilt, longing, sorrow or regret I would not have felt such contempt for him on his death. But he walked away from her after shattering the foundations of her life. I was glad he was dead.

As part of my training I spent some time at Tudor College in Malvern. Without any doubt, this is the most beautiful place I have ever lived. The warm, red building was situated right by the Malvern Hills, and I could be through the wicket gate and up the narrow, winding path within minutes. It did not take long to climb to the top of the hill, where breathtaking views of three counties were laid out in front of me. I spent many hours walking there, sometimes even late at night when studying had made my eyes burn with tiredness and I badly needed the sweet fresh air and the owl-filled quiet. I loved to patrol the length of the hills, imagining the ancient soldiers anxiously watching for the dreaded Romans, before trudging wearily back to the British Camp at the end of their shift.

It was during one of my rambles that I met a young lady from Manchester. She was with her sister, and they were impressively kitted out with maps, binoculars and leather drinking bottles. I came across them trying to identify local landmarks, but having some difficulty controlling their map and their hats at the same time in the strong breeze.

"Can I be of any assistance?" I enquired.

The younger lady looked at me gratefully. "Do you live near here?" she asked.

"I am living at Tudor College at present," I replied. "I am a law student. But I am quite familiar with the hills and the places that can be seen from here."

I proceeded to point out the most interesting of these, and helped them to roll up their map and stow it in the large canvas bag they had brought with them. I was amused to see that they were well furnished with packets of sandwiches, a fruit cake, sketching equipment and a whistle.

"We were told to bring a whistle in case a fog descended suddenly," the elder sister explained.

"How very sensible," I said, and they both took note of the fact that I was strolling on the hills in light clothing and carrying no equipment whatsoever. "Do you have bars of mint cake in case you are stranded for days and need to survive on just your wits? The wherewithal to make a fire, and tools to build a shelter could also be useful."

They both smiled, and the younger sister said, "May we know your name Mr Law Student? As you are feeling free to laugh at us, perhaps we should be properly introduced?"

So I learned that Mary Jane Preston and her elder sister were staying in Malvern to take the waters, as Miss Susannah Preston had not been in good health. I was not at all surprised that they believed the Malvern Hills would be an improvement on the grim, smoky skies of Manchester. However, I did explain that I had been born in Liverpool and that my grandfather had been much involved in the building of the railway between that town and their own.

"Am I correct in assuming that you spell your name

T-a-y-l-e-u-r and not the more usual way?" Miss Susannah Preston asked.

"You are indeed, Miss Preston. My grandfather was called Charles Tayleur and I was named after him."

The elder sister stopped rearranging the contents of the canvas bag and Mary Jane lowered the binoculars. They both looked at me with some concentration. "In fact," I continued, "There is a family story that the gardener, on hearing that my grandfather had just purchased the house in Torquay, turned to the dog and said, 'I suppose we will have to call you Growleur from now on.'" They laughed, but then assumed much more serious expressions.

"Then your grandfather's company built the iron ship – the Tayleur," Miss Preston said. "It was a terrible tragedy; we followed it in the newspapers. How many years ago was the ship wrecked?"

"It was nine years ago," I replied. "My grandfather never recovered from the shock of losing the ship. He died a few weeks later."

"That is very sad," the younger sister said, reaching out and touching my arm in sympathy. "It must have been a harrowing time for your family; I am sorry."

I nodded my thanks, thinking to myself that it was far from being the only difficult time the family had endured.

I suggested that we continue our conversation down in the town, where the wind wasn't whipping the words out of our mouths and the ladies could feel more secure about their hats. We went into the tea shop on Belle Vue Terrace and I was able to ask the ladies about their family. Their father had died, but they now lived comfortably with their mother in North Meols near Southport. During their father's lifetime the family estate was situated in Ardwick and they had been neighbours of the famous Mrs Gaskell, who had died three years before. They explained that the famous authoress often called upon their mother, but the families had never dined together. "My aunt Jane would be most interested to hear that you were acquaintances of Mrs Gaskell," I remarked. "She enjoys reading novels and I know she is familiar with Mrs Gaskell's work. I will write to her and tell her about our meeting."

"And we will write to our mother and tell her that we have made the acquaintance of Charles Tayleur's grandson," Susannah Preston replied.

I found them to be lively company; they both held spirited opinions on current affairs and seemed to view life with a mixture of compassion and humour. They appeared to enjoy my company as well, and we met regularly at the Assembly Rooms for tea dances and concerts and walked often on the hills. My studies certainly suffered during this time, but my soul did not. In fact I lived in a daze of happiness, counting the hours between my meetings with the sisters and finding the world in general to be a brighter, kinder place.

I soon discovered they were up for adventure. I had been regaling stories about my fellow students at the Law College, and I was describing their tradition of climbing the hills before dawn had broken and watching the sunrise from the top.

"Oh we must do that!" Mary Jane exclaimed. "I have never seen a true sunrise! Mr Tayleur – I beg you to assist us in this enterprise; will you act as our guide and take us onto the hills to see dawn breaking?"

"We would have to start our walk when it was still quite dark," I said. "I am not sure it would be quite proper for you to be climbing about the hills with me at night."

"Stuff and nonsense!" Miss Susannah Preston

replied testily. "We are not in Manchester now. There are no prim dowagers pursing their lips or disapproving gentlemen raising their eyebrows. If the students at your college can watch the sun rise from the hills, why can't we?"

"If we were in Manchester we would not be able to see the sun rise at all," her sister said. "It would be completely hidden behind the black smoke belching out of the factory chimneys and the grey murk from thousands of coal fires. If you deny us this opportunity Mr Tayleur, we may never have the chance again." I laughed for there was no arguing with them, and we made arrangements to meet outside their hotel on the next night when I calculated there would be sufficient moonlight to negotiate the path safely.

I do not believe I will ever forget that dawn walk. We stole through the streets together, delighting in the adventure and looking at the drawn curtains and locked shutters where the people of Malvern were all still sleeping. Not a soul knew we were there. Once on the hills it was necessary for me to help the sisters up the path by taking their hands on occasion and guiding them over the rougher areas. We arrived at the top just as a peep of colour was showing on the horizon, and as we stood there awe-struck, streaks of orange and red began to creep up until they were streaming across the sky like banners announcing the main part of the procession. When the sun followed, blazing gold and rising quickly, Mary Jane gasped and took hold of my arm. She gripped it tightly and crept close against me as we watched the light pour over us and listened to the birds everywhere begin to call. I knew at that moment that I loved her, and I looked down at her sweet face and longed to kiss her.

A few days later she met me alone when I called at

the Great Malvern Hotel to accompany the sisters on another walk. Susannah was very unwell that morning she explained, and she hoped I would not object to having just her for company. I assured her that I certainly had no objections whatsoever, but I did enquire with some concern about Miss Preston's health. Apparently she had a weak chest, and although the good, clear air of Malvern was proving very beneficial, she still had difficult days.

Mary Jane tucked her hand round my arm as we walked along, and looked up at me with a warm, trusting expression that clutched at my heart.

"Miss Preston," I said, "I am deeply worried about the impropriety of you walking along the open street with me in this manner, completely unchaperoned."

She laughed. "I can think of no solution to this problem Mr Tayleur, what do you think we should do?"

"We could of course ask the next passer-by to walk along with us," I suggested, "and then your respectability would not be compromised further."

The next passer-by proved to be a rather unsavoury old sailor who spat streams of tobacco onto the pavement, and we both burst into peals of laughter.

"I have a better idea," I said, stopping and turning towards her. "Would you agree to marry me? If we were formally engaged, there could be no objection to us walking alone together."

Her little, pointed face lit up with happiness. "Mr Tayleur – Charles – I would agree to marry you. I would like that very much."

"So would I," I said, and bent down to kiss her mouth. Her lips were very soft and a delighted blush spread over her cheeks.

That same morning I opened the whole sorry box of secrets and told her about my family. It would have been grossly unfair to encourage her into a marriage where so many horrors were waiting to be discovered. We sat on the grass of the hillside and I held her hands, and described the scandalous divorce of my parents, the wrongful stain of illegitimacy on my innocent brother, the unpleasantness of my stepmother and the hopeless, horrifying insanity of my father. I was terrified that she would withdraw her hands in terror and announce that she could never become part of such a family, but instead her face creased with pity.

"You no longer have to carry this burden all alone," she said. "Now you will always have me to support you."

"My brothers and I have lived like gypsies since we lost our mother," I told her. "We have no family home. During term times we have always had school or university, but the holidays are a problem for all of us. We stay with the families of our friends or with our uncle John, but we are always aware of trespassing too long on their kindness."

Mary Jane took my face in her hands. I had received no such tender touch since I last saw my mother, and tears swam over my eyes and down my face. "We will make a real home for you and your brothers," she said. "There will be no need for any of you to wander anymore." Then we flung our arms around each other and clung together, and I shut my eyes in sheer disbelief that such good fortune had come my way at last.

We were married in Manchester on April 12th 1864 with Mary Jane's family and all my brothers present to wish us well, but spent our honeymoon in Malvern where we had already been so happy and I had yet to finish my studies. I was called to the Bar just two months later and joined a law firm in London, and my wife and I took the lease of a small house. The Wheel of Fortune had carried me to the top of the circle; now I was a king indeed.

Over the next few years we were blessed with three children – Alexander, Ada Susannah and Elizabeth – and I have regained the happy family life that was so cruelly snatched away from me when I was a boy. As we are soon leaving England to start a new life in Brussels we made a journey north to visit Mary Jane's sisters, her mother having recently died, and my aunt and uncle at Shevington.

My uncle greeted us warmly as soon as we stepped down from the carriage, and had Alec up on his shoulders before we had reached the front door. Aunt Eliza took Elizabeth from the nurse's arms and proceeded to stroke her cheek and entice her to smile.

"We have other guests staying with us this week," my uncle said, ushering us all into the hall, "And they will be very pleased to make your acquaintance at last."

"I cannot think who that might be," I replied, rather puzzled.

"Your brothers and sister are paying us a visit," my uncle explained. "Galfred, Eveline and William arrived from Torquay a few days ago."

I stopped in my tracks and turned to him in horror. "Is their mother here also?" I asked.

"No Charles, she is not. It is high time you all met and started to overcome the sad rift that exists in the family. They are pleasant children, and you all share the same father."

Mary Ellen came over to stand firm at my side and took my hand in hers. "I am longing to meet them," she said. "Our little ones are their nieces and nephew and it is only right that they should become friends."

"We will all take tea together when you have settled

into your rooms," my aunt said. "Bring the children down with you, and I will send for Galfred, Eveline and William."

They were already in the drawing room when we descended, bringing the nurse with us as both Alec and Ada are of an age to roam around and touch precious ornaments if unchecked. The three of them were standing together near the fireplace and seemed to have been watching for us rather nervously. Galfred stepped forwards and shook my hand as my uncle said, "Your brother Charles." I looked at him intently. Here was Mary Ellen's son; the boy I had once feared would rob me of my rightful inheritance. But he looked nothing like her – in fact none of them showed any sign of her angry spaniel face or red hair. I could see my grandfather in his looks, and he clearly possessed a wiry, restless energy that reminded me of how my father had once been.

"Galfred is preparing to start at Harrow at the end of the summer," Uncle John was saying. "We were hoping you could offer him some advice Charles."

I felt an instant stab of pity for him; of course there was no-one at Hampton who had any clue how to prepare for public school. Galfred had no father to make arrangements for him, and Mary Ellen would have no idea beyond the advice sent by the school itself.

"Well first of all you must on no account believe Cresswell if he tells you to read 'Tom Brown's Schooldays'," I said, and everybody laughed. "We will have a good talk about it," I assured him, "And I will make sure you know the best cricket bat to buy and what dimensions your tuck box should be."

Galfred grinned and then turned to his brother and sister. "This is Eveline," he said. "And this is William."

I shook William's hand and kissed Eveline on the

cheek. They had open, friendly faces and appeared to be genuinely pleased and excited to meet me. I wondered what their mother had told them about me – had she made me out to be a rude oaf? The black sheep of the family? But before many more minutes had passed, Ada and Alec had been lifted up and paraded round the room by their new uncles, who also fed them sugar biscuits from the tea tray and showed them the shiny clocks and ornaments and the views from the windows. My wife and Eveline had struck up a friendship which was to last until death parted them, and Eveline was soon fetching her needlework and sitting close to Mary Jane on the sofa. I smiled to see their heads touching over the embroidery and to hear their animated chatter.

After a short while Galfred sought me out and we went into the gardens to escape the rumpus inside. "I wish you would come to Marychurch," he said unexpectedly. "It's dull as a dungeon there, and we have no-one to talk to unless Cresswell and Edward come down. We have all wanted to meet you for so long and we used to talk about how we imagined you would be."

"Surely the grounds are excellent for riding," I said, "And you have your own cliff path to the beach. My brothers and I found plenty to occupy ourselves during the summer we spent at Hampton together. I seem to remember we were desperate to find the old smugglers' tunnel that came out into the cellar."

"The beach is public so we have rarely been allowed to go there, and the cellar is out of bounds. I believe Mother had the tunnel bricked up when we were small. She did tell us that smugglers were still occasionally bringing goods into Marychurch when she was first married, and our father used to have kegs of brandy brought to the house through the tunnel, just as the occupants of the house did in the old days."

"The old devil!" I exclaimed. "I never knew that! Does she talk about him often?"

"We always know when she is going to visit him, and she generally returns looking melancholy. She has never taken us with her. She has described him as a fine gentleman, an excellent rider and a kind husband. William and Eveline have no memory of him at all, but I remember running down the nursery corridor because I could hear shouting on the landing. He was coming out of his bedroom and when he saw me he asked who I was. He did not recognise me and seemed furious that I was in the house. It is a fearful thing, to have a father living in that way."

I nodded, for it was indeed. "He is very ill Galfred," I said. "This situation cannot go on for much longer." And I felt suddenly saddened, for I fully expect that news of his death will reach me while I am in Brussels.

Charles William Tayleur
Shevington Hall 1871

It is three short years since I was last here in my uncle's house. I think back to the carefree days we spent with Galfred, Eveline and William before setting out on what we believed would be a prosperous future abroad, and I shudder at what lay in wait for us. My brother William is dead, as is my own youngest child, and the news of both these tragedies reached me when I was far away from my family and my wife was alone. My father, however, is still alive and remains hopelessly insane, with the consequence that his estate is beyond our reach and held in a stranglehold by the trustees. Alec is dangerously ill, and we have brought him back to England to be treated by English doctors, English medicines and English food so that we have some small chance of saving him. Our daughters are being cared for in Brussels by their nurse and the other servants. When my uncle came down the steps to welcome us yesterday, I have to admit to falling into his arms and weeping.

For the first few months all went well. Mary Jane found Brussels vastly superior to London, and was soon visiting and being visited by an elegant group of worthy matrons. There was much need for my skills and advice amongst the property owners of the city, but I was also able to carry on the work I had started in England, and stand in court in support of women who would otherwise have no chance of justice. The divorce laws had changed several years before, and now there was no need to obtain an Act of Parliament to divorce your wife many more women were subjected to this harrowing and humiliating experience. The situation was much the same in Brussels. The women were by no means always innocent of the adultery charged against them, but I thought of the children who would be taken from them and estranged, and fought with all my wits to prevent the divorces being granted and the women put aside. Perhaps I inherited my ability from my father, who at one time could stand at the hustings and make impassioned speeches, but somehow I had the power to move judges and juries and consequently succeeded in keeping many mothers and their children from being torn apart. We seemed to lead a perfect life, and our daughter Katherine was born into a contented household.

This charming edifice crumbled one morning when I was crossing the city to deliver some property deeds. It was usually possible for me to walk from my chambers to most appointments, the places of business being largely clustered together in one quarter, but on this occasion it was foggy and the distance was somewhat further than comfortable. I took a cab. The fog became denser as we trotted down less familiar streets, and on one corner grumbling traders were taking down a market for want of customers. My hat and gloves were soon damp with beads of moisture, and I pushed the leather wallet of documents under my coat in an attempt to keep it dry. The sounds around me became more and more muffled, even the clattering of traffic on the busy road, but I could still make out the calls of people on the pavements searching for their companions or warning others of their approach. Meanwhile my driver had been experiencing some difficulty seeing his way forward as the flares he carried were hopelessly inadequate. He had been reining the horse in tightly so as to proceed slowly and cautiously, but suddenly it became spooked by the sooty air and inexplicable blindness, and started to run away with the reins in a most alarming fashion. I heard the driver shouting but it was to no avail, for the cab started to veer across the road in a terrifying manner. I held onto the apron desperately for the hansom shook until my teeth rattled, and it was now hurtling along at a terrible speed. I could hear screaming – bystanders, horses, the driver or myself, and then a deafening crash as another conveyance met ours headlong.

I remember a great cracking and snapping, then I was jolted from my seat and thrown violently into the air. Something huge and black collided with me, and then I smashed onto the ground into a maelstrom. I could smell human urine and the filth from both dogs and horses, and tried desperately to lift my head away from them, but I was trapped by pounding hooves and the cab wheels. I thought fleetingly of Fortune's Wheel – it seemed to be grinding my skull into the cobbled road at that moment – then there was a stinging sensation in my nose and a feeling of terrible sickness and I knew nothing else at all.

I awoke in my own bed. My eyes burned as I tried to move them and the pain in my head was almost beyond human endurance. I groaned. Mary Jane was instantly near to me, wiping my face gently with a cool flannel and then holding a cup to my lips. It was impossible for me to lift my head, so she proceeded to spoon the water into my mouth.

She spoke to me in a low, quiet voice. "Charles – can you see me?"

I made a huge effort to open my eyelids, then closed

them in horror as the bright light assaulted my beleaguered head. I tried to move away from it. Mary Jane seemed to understand, and I was aware of her standing up and crossing the room on slippered feet to close both the blinds and the curtains. With some trepidation I opened my eyes once more and could make out the form of my wife next to the bed. "Yes," I muttered, then closed my eyes again.

"The doctors feared for your sight," she said. I felt her take my hand, then raise it to her lips and kiss it. "We all feared for your life." She was crying then, for tears were falling on my hand and my face. I opened my eyes again and looked at her, noticing with some surprise that she had not put up her hair. In fact she had not even combed it.

"What time is it?" I asked, and my voice sounded strangely high and cracked.

"It is two o'clock in the afternoon," she answered, stroking my cheek with her light fingers.

"You have not done your hair," I said.

That made her smile. "I have not left you since they carried you up here three days ago," she said. "I did not know if you would ever wake again." She started to cry again.

I tried to reach into my mind for a memory that would explain this state of affairs. Why was I lying in agony in a dark room with my wife weeping at my bedside? Why had the doctors feared for my sight? But my head was achingly blank, and the very act of thinking was too painful to be pursued.

"What has happened?" I asked.

"There was an accident," she explained. "The cab that was carrying you ran into a carriage in the fog."

"Was anyone else hurt?"

Mary Jane was quiet for a moment and looked down at the quilt. "The cab driver was killed," she said, "And two ladies who had been walking on the pavement. The driver of the carriage was badly injured. We must just thank God that He has spared you."

Horrible memories began to emerge out of foggy darkness as I listened to her, and I made an attempt to shut them out again. "I have written to your uncle John and to your brothers to tell them," she went on. "I expect to hear from them soon."

Both Edward and Cresswell set off for Brussels as soon as they received my wife's letters, and we were both heartily glad to have their support. Albert, much to my surprise, had decided to join the Merchant Navy, and was away at sea on his first voyage. Galfred wrote from Harrow, assuring me that he would much rather be by my bedside than stuck in lessons, and his sympathetic letter did me more good than any number of medicine bottles.

But my recovery was painfully slow and dogged by dark feelings of hopelessness from which I could not escape. Much as I loved my family, the baby's crying tore through my afflicted head like a knife, and I found the constant chatter of the older children unbearable. Despite my success in helping wronged wives and their families I felt without value, and believed my career to have been a pointless sham. My stepmother's words echoed endlessly in my mind – I was spineless, a coward, a worthless parasite. I was constantly beset with shaking, and often Mary Jane would put her calming hands on my knees and attempt to still their restless quaking.

"I believe the best remedy for your malaise would be a sea voyage," the doctor suggested.

"That would be the worst possible action I could undertake," I remonstrated with horror. "Ships hold a real terror for me, and even the crossing from Dover to France is a torment. The ship built by my grandfather was wrecked in 1854, and the poor souls on board suffered grievously. I will never be able to feel safe at sea, and the dreadful images from that tragedy will always remain with me vividly."

"Then allow me to suggest a European tour," he replied. "I can assure you that this would fill your mind with classical architecture, beautiful paintings and fresh vistas and effect a total cure."

I objected to this suggestion quite as much as to his last. "I cannot possibly abandon my wife and young children for the length of time necessary for such a tour."

But Mary Jane was anxious to have me restored to my old self and sanctioned the plan willingly. I felt this was particularly generous of her as we had lately discovered that she was expecting another child, but she insisted that I must go and so I agreed.

Meanwhile Albert had returned from his naval employment with his health wrecked. To his credit he had carried out his duties diligently and earned the certificate of competency, but his doctor was alarmed and absolutely forbade another tour of duty. He must now have, the doctor said, "absolute mental quiet". I decided that European travel would fit the bill admirably and enlisted him as my companion. I must admit that I was shocked when he stepped down from the railway carriage. He was even thinner than I remembered, his skin was pale and he was still plagued with sores near his mouth and eyes. I could only hope and pray that the warm sunshine and hearty food of France would help him to achieve the kind of health that he had never yet possessed. We left in the autumn, careful to travel before the roads became difficult with the onset of winter, and headed for Paris.

I had always wanted to see this beautiful city but

we found it to be turbulent and unsettled. There was much building work, particularly railway lines, and growing dissatisfaction with the Second Empire. We took rooms in Montmartre and spent hours on the tiny iron balcony, leaning over the railing and watching the crowds in the street below. It was all so much more daring than Brussels – more daring even than London. The ladies wore brighter colours and showed peeps of their ankles as they swished their petticoats above the muddy road. The wine was good, and the more we consumed the more we confided in each other about the furies that raged within us.

"This insanity to which our father has fallen prey," Albert began one evening, "What is the cause? Is it something that could also lurk within ourselves?"

"I do fear that," I replied with honesty. "It is as though a dark beast always hovers behind me. Sometimes it moves closer – it was snapping at my heels in the terrible days after the carriage accident. My head was always full of the sounds from that morning – the screams and explosions. I swear I heard the driver's skull crack open as he smashed into the road. There was no escape from the noises; they tormented me for weeks. I still hear them when I first wake in the morning, but at the time I feared they would send me mad."

"I fear invalidity more than insanity," Albert said, pouring more wine into our glasses. "I have always been sickly and feeble. Another illness could render me incapable of caring for myself. I dread being pushed out in a bath chair with a blanket tucked round my knees."

I laughed. "You must get married little brother! Find a good wife and she will look after you."

"Who would marry me?" he retorted. "I make a poor sort of gentleman, both puny and impecunious. Mary

Ellen keeps my allowance battened down to just fifty pounds a year; I could not support a wife on that amount. I have to find a means of supporting myself but my poor health renders me useless – even my attempt at the Merchant Navy failed pitifully."

"You did not fail," I reminded him. "You gained your certificate of competency as a second mate. It was the doctors who insisted that life at sea would be the death of you."

He sighed and gazed into the distance. "Perhaps that would be best," he muttered.

I shook his shoulder lightly. "That is the wine talking," I said. "When we go home you will meet some sweet girl who will make you feel that life is worth living." He merely snorted in reply.

The turmoil in Europe seemed to match that within ourselves. We left the clamour of Paris, narrowly missing the outbreak of war with Prussia and the siege of the city, and headed for Italy. Here we roamed around, trying to find tranquillity in front of statues, paintings and frescoes, but our demons remained tenaciously within us. I tried to moderate Albert's drinking, but often shared the wine with him until we slurred our way through more confidences and ended by slumping over the table and dozing, sometimes in high class hotels but more often in a back street trattoria.

"Ever since you found me and told me about Cresswell and Edward and the rest, I have felt different from you all," Albert muttered one evening.

"That is understandable," I replied.

"Father never wanted to see me. He never asked the uncles for news of me or cared whether I was alive or dead. How would you feel if he had treated you in that way?"

"Well, once he had married our stepmother his

attitude towards me was much the same." I said.

"But you had many good years with him. I had only a few days and of course I can remember nothing of that time. At least he never refused to acknowledge that you were his son!"

"But he did go a little way to make amends," I began, and then stopped abruptly. I knew it was unwise to tell him about the first will and the bequest. But it was too late; he was all attention and grabbing my arm.

"What do you mean? What did he do?" he demanded.

"He wrote a will shortly after his second marriage," I explained reluctantly, "And left you money…"

"How much money?"

"Two thousand pounds, but…"

"Two thousand pounds? Good God Charles, why did you not tell me this before?" He stood up and threw out his arms like an opera singer taking a curtain call. "I can live a decent life… forget about having to earn a living…"

"For mercy's sake, sit down and listen!" I said, pulling him down onto a chair. "Father wrote a second will, and in that he made no mention of you at all."

Albert's face fell. "So there will be no legacy for me after all," he said in a deflated tone, and put his head in his hands.

"He was already mad when he wrote that second will. There is a good chance it won't stand up, but we won't know until he is dead."

"So there is some hope for me?" Albert said.

"There is some hope," I agreed, but I was already regretting what I had told him. Somehow I knew that this would bring out a reckless streak in my brother, and he would start to spend unwisely in the hope that somehow the legacy would be forthcoming.

We crossed the border into Austria and made our way to Vienna – the City of Music. The journey took several weeks and I was becoming anxious for news of home. I knew that Mary Jane was approaching the date of her confinement. She would be well supported by her sisters and she had already given birth to four healthy children without danger, but I would rest easier once I knew for certain that all was well. As soon as we were settled in a hotel I sent to our last permanent address and requested our mail to be forwarded.

When the packet arrived it was much thicker than I expected. I tore it open and a great number of letters tumbled out onto the table in front of me. I was horrified to see that most of them bore a black edge. Albert was with me, and he suggested that I should be sure to read the letters in their correct order so that I could learn the whole story, rather than immediately ripping open the seals of those that must contain bad news.

"It must be Father," he said. I sighed with relief; of course he would be right. Our poor demented father must have passed away at last, just as I expected when I left England nearly three years ago.

"It is not Father," I said, after breaking the seal on the letter from my stepmother. "She writes that our little brother William caught scarlet fever just days after starting his first term at Clifton College. He was only ill for one week. Desperate to avoid the infection spreading through the school, the decision was made to move him to a small house in Clifton and have him nursed there. Mary Ellen sent her maid up to Bristol to bring him home, but he died shortly after she arrived. He has been brought back to St Marychurch and buried in the churchyard there." I was silent with shock and desolation. William was a delightful young man with a merry expression. He had been a huge success with my children, but he had died a long way from home, and with no one he loved to hold his hand at the last. I felt assailed by pity for his mother; however unfeeling she had been towards me it was clear that she had loved her own children. I was upset that I had not been able to attend his funeral and convey the respects of my family. Much as I wanted to write immediately to Mary Ellen and send my condolences, I knew I must read the other letters first.

In her first letter my wife told me that Ada had become ill with measles. The doctor insisted that she was kept away from the other children and put to bed in a dark room for the sake of preserving her eyesight. It had also been necessary to cut off her hair. I felt a lump in my throat when I read this. My beautiful little daughter had long, shiny hair of which she was justifiably proud. I grabbed the next letter quickly, anxious to read of her safe recovery. But the news was worse. The infection had spread to both Alec and Elizabeth, although little Katherine seemed well so far. The doctor was coming to the house daily and my wife was frantic with worry. Her sisters Alice and Susannah had hurried over to Brussels to be with her, but she was feeling tired and unwell after the long night vigils at the children's bedsides. An awful image came into my mind of my poor children with shorn heads, tossing feverishly on their pillows, and Mary Jane moving heavily from one room to another throughout the night.

The next letter was written by my sister-in-law Susannah. She wrote that Mary Jane had now succumbed to measles which, given her condition, was of grave concern. The baby Katherine remained healthy, and a decision had been taken to remove her from the house in order to keep her safe. She was now staying nearby in the household of a friend.

A few days later Susannah wrote again. Mary Jane's pains had started early, presumably because of her illness, and she had suffered a difficult and protracted labour. In the early hours of the morning she had been delivered of a son. The baby was weak and small but the doctors were doing everything they could for both him and his mother. Mary Jane did not want to give my son a name until I could choose it.

I was heartily relieved to see that the next letter had been addressed in my wife's handwriting, although the black border filled me with terror. She had written:

"My dear husband, it is many days since we heard from you, although we know that you must be nearing your destination and not far now from Vienna. I derive so much comfort from imagining you in such beautiful places! You cannot know how often I have thought of you during the dark days and nights, and prayed that your adventures and the kind weather are making you better and that the memories of it all will sustain you through these difficult times.

I am getting better each day. I know that Susannah's letters must have sent you demented with worry, but there is no need to feel anxious on my behalf. Katherine remains well, and we are leaving her in her present lodging for now, rather than run the risk of bringing her home. Ada and Elizabeth are weak but certainly showing signs of making a good recovery. They both manage to eat a little more each day, and their fever has quite gone. But Alec is still gravely ill.

I have worse news, and it is almost more than I can bear to tell you. No wife, my dear Charles, should ever have to break such news to her husband. As you know, we were blessed with a son, and for ten special days I held him in my arms. I did not want to choose a name for him without knowing your wishes, and so we called him Baby. He was fragile at birth but as the days went on he did not thrive, despite all our efforts. One morning my sisters gently told me that he must be baptised, and that I must name him for his own sake. We talked together about it and I decided on Preston, my own family name. He was baptised that afternoon and shortly afterwards he drew his last breath, cradled close against my breast. I am so sorry we lost our precious son and that you never had the chance to know him.

I must put all my strength into saving the son who remains with us.

I pray for your comfort and the return of your health.

Your loving wife,
Mary Jane."

The letters all seemed to be unreal – just black marks on paper – it was surely impossible for these horrors to be happening to those I loved most in the world. My thoughts focused at first on the baby's name. Preston Tayleur would be a prestigious sounding title for a fine gentleman, but for a tiny baby? For he would never become a gentleman, he would always be a baby, existing nowhere but in our hearts. What would I have chosen for him if I had been blessed with the chance? William? I think not, for the name seems cursed with ill fortune. I realised that I was muttering "Preston Tayleur" over and over without realising and Albert had his arm tight around my shoulders, perturbed by the tears pouring down my face. I pushed the final letter over to him, unable to find the strength to break the seal. What hideous tragedy was lurking inside its folds? The fact that the address was written by my sister-in-law boded ill.

Would I now discover that I had lost both my beloved wife and my first born child? Alec came into my mind, pushing his toy boat on the pond, and I put my arms on the table and lowered my head into them. "You read it," I said.

Albert unfolded it with shaking hands. "My dear Charles," he read. "I am writing to assure you that both Mary Jane and Alexander are receiving the best care that we and the doctors are able to give them. They both remain weak. Your son is still suffering from the effects of the measles which have become lodged within his lungs. It is important that you realise just how much danger he is in. It is certainly not my place to tell you what you should do, but Alice and I strongly believe he should be taken back to England to give him a chance of recovering. The burden upon our sister has become unbearable. She is suffering from the aftermath of a measles infection, a difficult confinement and the grievous loss of her child. We would ask that you consider curtailing your travels and returning to Brussels in order to accompany her and Alexander to England. Your family has need of you. Susannah."

We made the arrangements to return immediately.

Mary Ellen Tayleur
Hampton House – 1872

My husband is still alive and still a lunatic, and I am being driven near demented myself by the sons of his first marriage and their constant importuning for money. Even Albert Heathcote, now styling himself Albert Tayleur though by whose authority I know not, has been living on an allowance from the estate for years. I can well imagine what William's response to this would be, but the rest of the family insist that he must be included and supported even though William never acknowledged him as his son and refused to have his name mentioned. This makes me boil with anger on my husband's behalf, but the other trustees of the estate are quite unable to see reason.

Not one of my stepsons follows a profession, despite all Charles's fine talk about providing a voice for wronged females. It is simply not possible for the estate to support four gentlemen, their wives, families and establishments, as well as this house and the care and accommodation for a lunatic. There is also the education of my own children to be paid for, although they appear to rank a poor second in the opinion of the other trustees. It seems to have become the norm for my morning tray to contain petitions for money, and I am often at a loss to know how to answer them.

Cresswell always addresses me as "My dearest Mother..." no doubt believing that this will soften me into agreeing to his requests. He qualified as a solicitor but soon found regular work to be tiresome, and desisted. When he married he applied for an increase in his allowance to eight hundred pounds per annum, but wrote recently describing himself as being "in very embarrassed circumstances financially". I have been informed by my brother-in-law that Cresswell has borrowed money on the surety of his share of the thirty thousand pounds in my husband's first will – a dangerous gamble indeed. When the trustees decided Galfred and Eveline were to be given an extra allowance I received a letter from Cresswell complaining vociferously about this, and enquiring why "Ned and myself are to be left out?"

Edward shows no sign of joining a profession at all, and he has also married and obtained a larger allowance in consequence. He then wrote and asked for a further grant of five hundred pounds for furniture. Five hundred pounds! What establishment is he running – the Palace of Versailles?

A few weeks ago Heathcote wrote to inform the trustees of his failing health, and requested a grant to enable him to travel abroad as his doctor has advised him to do. I happen to know that he has only recently returned from junketing around Europe with Charles and now he is anxious to be off again, while I sit in my drawing room in St Marychurch and grieve for my dead son and my lost husband.

As for the cock and bull story we had from Charles about a misadventure which prevented him pursuing his profession, it reads like a cheap novel. He stated that it was necessary for him to be given one thousand pounds to cover the expenses incurred by the illness of his wife and several of his children, the need for him to travel in order to recuperate from the carriage accident, medical bills from doctors and the wages of two nurses, and the funeral expenses of his baby son.

The death of a baby is far from being an uncommon occurrence, and his father's trustees cannot be expected to fund every twist and turn of his life. I voiced my objections to my fellow trustees. Charles already receives a very generous allowance of one thousand pounds per annum. When it was raised to this sum he assured the trustees that he would make no further requests until his father died. The constant erosion of the estate through grants of such capital sums will greatly disadvantage my children when we are, at last, able to share out the Tayleur family assets.

In order to go some way to meet these constant requests, my brother-in-law suggested that we should sell some property. We had already taken the decision some years ago to liquidate the shares in the Lima Gas Company that my husband had been so very proud of; those same shares that made him realise all those years ago how very limited my geographical knowledge was. He may have been instrumental in bringing light to Darkest Peru, but the dividends were unprofitable and irregular. John Tayleur then proposed that we should sell a farm out at Sandwell, and two houses and a thatched cottage here in St Marychurch. This move occasioned a furious complaint from Charles, who objected to the selling of property and the consequent disintegration of the estate.

All this makes me wish even more that William had died when his illness first struck, so that the estate could have been divided amongst us all in its entirety. Charles, Cresswell and Edward would be responsible for their own livelihoods; I would be free of the constant pressure of their demands and complaints and my poor husband would have been delivered from the agony of the tortured fate that awaited him.

Galfred admires my eldest stepson, and I am at a loss to account for this. He writes to Charles regularly and seeks his advice whenever a matter worries him.

"A more insolent and ill-mannered young man would be a rare specimen indeed," I told Galfred. "During the summer he spent with us at Hampton he caused a vast amount of trouble and ill-feeling, not least between your father and myself. By the time he flung himself out of the house I had no wish ever to see him again."

"My dear Mama," Galfred replied, "Charles was grieving for the loss of his mother at that time and was doubtless not himself." He moved closer to me and took my hand. "If I had just lost you I would certainly not be in control of myself, and would no doubt be capable of rudeness and unreasonable behaviour." This moved me beyond words. My sweet boy. Both Eveline and Galfred are such a comfort to me. I suppose I have some blessings after all.

Charles William Tayleur
Mount Pleasant Inn, Kenton – 1872

I brought my family home from Brussels forever last month. Our visit with my uncle in Shevington was hugely beneficial for all three of us, and both Mary Jane and Alec were restored to good health. My appetite for travel has definitely been assuaged for a long time to come, but Albert is keen to leave English shores again and continue our exploration of Europe. He has applied to my father's trustees for assistance but I have little hope of his success. His financial position worries me greatly. Since I told him of the existence of the first will and the bequest to himself, he has been spending with some recklessness and his debts are increasing at an alarming rate. I am in no position to help him as my own finances are stretched beyond endurance. My petitions for a sum to alleviate the debts I incurred during our misfortunes in Brussels were denied, sabotaged by my stepmother without a doubt. I then appealed for a compromise, and suggested that I might be allowed to take the lease of one of my father's properties at a reduced rent. Uncle John supported my request, and we will be moving our possessions into Abbots Oak near Leicester in a few weeks. It is quite a fine house, larger than the town houses we occupied in London and Brussels, and there are pleasant gardens for the children to play in. They will now have the chance of such a childhood as my brothers and I enjoyed in the house at Lavender Hill.

My family are staying at Shevington until then, and I took the first opportunity to travel into Devon to visit my father once again. As soon as we returned to England my uncle took me aside and described my father's situation in detail.

"After Bucknill's departure from Exminster his assistant took over as superintendent, and much remained the same at first. But the new man lacked Bucknill's authority and conditions within the asylum quickly started to deteriorate. The wards were already overcrowded, but the influx of lunatics increased relentlessly with the result that the staff now have no hope of treating patients with the respect and consideration upon which Bucknill always insisted. I have to tell you Charles, that restraints are now employed continually, therapy and treatment are rare, nurses and attendants leave before they can be trained and the latest inspection by the Lunacy Commissioners was far from satisfactory."

I was appalled. "How has this affected my father's care?" I demanded.

"Saunders has now left Exminster, but we have managed to ensure that the leading alienist at the asylum will visit the lunatic. His visits are not as frequent or as regular as Bucknill's, and his philosophy differs greatly, but at least your father is seen by a man with expertise in the field."

He went on to tell me that my father had been moved to accommodation in Kenton. He was no longer taken to the asylum as part of his treatment and so there was no need for him to be lodged within the village of Exminster itself. My father's care had become too expensive and economies were necessary. My stepmother was told that she should be spending no more than eight hundred pounds a year on his accommodation and medical bills, and the cottage in

Kenton was smaller and cheaper.

I found it easily in the centre of the village adjoining the Mount Pleasant Inn, where I took a room. In Exminster the cottage chosen to shelter my father had been situated discreetly up a side lane, but Mount Pleasant House opened directly onto the busy high street. As soon as I had dispensed with the trappings of travel I left the inn and went next door.

A portly housekeeper let me in, and inquired if I was Mr Tayleur as soon as I entered the hallway. I assured her that I was, and told her I hoped my letter had arrived, advising them of my visit.

"Oh yes sir, we knew you were coming," she replied. She then turned to the staircase and shouted, "Mr Wreford! Your visitor is here!"

The servant who came down the stairs to greet me was of a somewhat ruffianly appearance. He was a thick set, heavy man in shirt sleeves, wearing trousers more suited to a farmyard than a gentleman's home.

"I am Mr William Houlbrooke Tayleur's son," I said.

"You had better come up," he replied without ceremony. I followed him up the creaking stairs into a small bedroom with closed curtains, and saw my father immediately. My last visit had been shortly before I left for Brussels and he had aged considerably since then, but I reflected that the same was probably true of myself. He was sitting in dimpsy light but I noticed immediately that his head had been shaved.

"Why have you cut my father's hair so short?" I asked.

"We've no time for fancy barber work here," Wreford replied. "He doesn't like to be touched overmuch, and he played up when we combed it. Washing it was the very devil of a job, so the easiest way was to get rid of it altogether."

I presumed that shaving my father was also a devil

of a job because there was several days' growth of stubble on his face.

Wreford offered no instructions about how to proceed, so I went close to my father and sat on a stool near to him. His chair was heavy and bolted to the floor, and I saw that his arms were held to it by leather restraints. Similar straps hung ready by his chest and legs. He was looking past me, his mouth hanging slackly open and drool creeping down his chin. He smelt unclean and there were food stains on the front of his shirt. Even worse than this, all his teeth were black and broken.

"What has happened to his teeth?" I asked.

"When he has a bad fit we have to put a strap in his mouth to keep him still and to prevent him from biting through his tongue. He clamps onto it so hard that his teeth crack under the pressure."

"He must be in considerable pain from teeth like these," I said, my voice full of concern.

"I'd like to see a dentist try to get a wrench in his mouth," the servant retorted.

Unlike John Shepherd, for whom I still had great respect, this attendant made no attempt to stand close to my father and talk to him, so I tried to emulate the methods Bucknill had shown to me on my first visit.

"Good morning Father," I said firmly, planting myself squarely in front of him. "It's Charles. I have been travelling in Europe but I have returned, as you can see. I have brought news of your family. You now have four grandchildren – Alec, Ada, Elizabeth and Katherine. Cresswell is married; he married Lucy Maria Stowell three years ago. Edward is also married – young Ned! – to Susan Grace. Your new daughters-in-law are both lovely ladies."

My father gave no sign that he had heard, but he

sat very still. Wreford stood silently in the shadows.

"And I have news of Albert. He is not entirely well but he accompanied me abroad. He spent time in the Merchant Navy but it did not suit him. He is living in London."

My father's eyes started to shift about and he let out a low growl, like a hunting dog. Then he began to thrash in the chair, pulling at the arm restraints and trying to stand up.

"Stop that," Wreford ordered. He came over to my father, brushing me out of the way quite roughly, and whipped the chest strap around him. Then he buckled it tightly. My father kicked his legs violently. Another attendant ran in and grasped the flailing legs, pinioning them to the chair. All my father could do then was shake his head and continue to growl.

"Our job is hard enough without visitors unsettling him," Wreford said in a complaining tone. "You stop that noise, Mr William, or we'll have to give you something to bite on."

My father seemed to shrink with fear at this. He was still breathing heavily but he turned his face away from the valet and became quiet.

"How does my father occupy his time?" I asked. "He was previously encouraged to paint, and Dr Bucknill believed this helped to order his thoughts. He also worked in the garden and went for walks."

Wreford snorted. "He occupies his time by being mad," he replied. "We couldn't let him outside for fear of alarming the public; heaven knows what he would get up to."

"At the very least you could allow him to look out of the window," I persisted. "Why are the curtains drawn across?"

"Because the bright light excites him. We have to keep him calm."

I sat down next to my father again. I was feeling heartily sorry for him by this time. It struck me that he would never have allowed his dogs to live a life such as this.

"How do you feel Papa?" I asked gently.

He turned his head in my direction.

"He used to be quite capable of speaking," I said. "Can he no longer say anything?"

"Sometimes he shouts out when he has one of his rages," Wreford replied.

"What does he say?"

"He calls for his mother. He also asks for Emma – do you know who she is?"

I shook my head. I could not bear to mention her in front of this servant.

I stood up to leave and touched my father's arm. "Goodbye Papa," I said to him. "I will visit you again soon." I was disturbed to see that tears were creeping down his face.

Wreford took me downstairs to show me out. At the door I turned to him and said, "My father is a long time dying."

"It would be better for him to get on with it," the valet replied.

The following morning I made preparations to leave Kenton and return to my family. I waited outside for my bag to be brought down and for the cab to arrive to take me to Exeter, anxious to stretch my legs and get some fresh air before the journey. There was a fine view of the handsome old church, and I was slowly strolling in this direction when a carriage clattered down the high street and drew up at the door of Mount Pleasant House. A footman alighted and opened the carriage door, and my stepmother climbed out.

I felt a clutch of real fear in my throat and my heart

started to beat heavily. She was dressed in black and her hair was still suspiciously red, but the jowls I remembered so vividly had lengthened to such an extent that her wrinkled skin seemed to be falling from her face. She looked up and saw me, and instantly assumed the familiar expression of disapproval and loathing.

I recalled the pity I had felt for her on hearing of the death of her son, and how I had to admit she had been a kind mother to Galfred, Eveline and William. I went over to face her and held out my hand. "Mrs Tayleur, I am pleased to see you after all these years," I said. "I trust you are well?"

She would not give me her hand. "How can I be well?" she asked. "I have lately buried my son and my husband is mad."

"I am indeed sorry for your misfortunes," I replied. "But will you not shake my hand? We have each lost a child; surely there must be some understanding between us?"

"You did not even know your child!" Mary Ellen retorted with much bitterness. "You never set eyes on him! How can that compare with my loss of William – a child I had cared for lovingly for thirteen years!"

The barb of this cruel remark struck me forcibly, but I had no intention of arguing with her in the street.

"I am not to blame for your misfortunes, madam, grievous though they are."

Her eyes narrowed. "The early years of my marriage were difficult and that was because you caused much tension between your father and myself. I had so little time with him, and you cast a shadow over the few years we had together. Even now you plague my life out with your begging letters. I know you are desperate to get your hands on the estate…"

I became genuinely concerned that she was working herself up into a fit. "Madam, please do not get upset, you are making yourself ill. Perhaps you would care to come into the inn and have a drink of water?"

"I would not care!" she said, and motioned angrily to her footman to open the door of the cottage. Then she gathered the folds of her mourning garb into her mittened claws and swept through the gate, disappearing quickly into the house. I felt shaken and sick. I had no idea that she held me responsible for damaging her marriage. I had never returned to Hampton, never attempted to wrest my father's attention away from her, and yet I was to blame for ruining their few years together. I closed my eyes and forced myself to consider this logically. She was a lonely, jealous, embittered old woman who needed to blame someone for the poor hand that destiny had dealt her. I was by far the more fortunate; I had a loving wife, four delightful children and a home full of happiness, affection and laughter. As the train steamed through the countryside I thanked God for the life He had given to me.

In Lunacy

Well my eyes are damned now. I can see little – like peering through a milky fog – but I know where I am. I am in the anteroom to hell. And there are devils here, wielding straps and forcing foul-tasting implements into my mouth, breaking my teeth and grasping me, dragging, hauling – bed, chair, chamber pot. Everyone else has gone, like the cast of a play leaving the theatre when the performance is done. They have left me behind – sitting on the empty stage, tied to a chair. The doctor disappeared long ago. He was a fool with his do you remember William, but he had a soft voice and a kindness about him. Kindness left with him. The demons have harsh voices rough hands and a smell about them.

There is food and I wait for it. It is the only pleasure left. The smell of the meat takes me back to other dinners when the silver shone in the candlelight and the ladies showed their shoulders and there was laughter. I laugh sometimes now, though nothing is funny, and they run to me and stuff my mouth.

They can stop me talking, stop me moving, stop me *leaving* for God's sake, but they can't stop me dreaming. Thoughts are hard to grasp, slip away like a fish you've tried to hold still in a river, but dreams are much as they always were. In dreams I can see light again and people come back. Charles is there, whittling sticks, and Mother bringing a bowl of warm water and a soft cloth to bathe my knee. Emma is washing her hair, wearing only a camisole streaked wet. She flings her head back and showers droplets of water through the sunshine onto our bed. I swirl brandy round the glass and anticipate the taste, draw in the smell of the horse and shift on the polished leather of the saddle, carve the roasted meat until saliva collects in the corner of my mouth. When the fogs clear a little I wonder what I have done. What crime have I committed that I should be treated like this? It has been a long prison sentence and I think of home. Home is where the heart is, no place like home. Homes swim in and out of my mind but I no longer know which I could return to. Lavender Hill - crime and betrayal and that fox in my very bed, Hampton with its dark tunnel to the cliff top. There was a time when a dark tunnel afforded me great sport and pleasure, but not the one in which I am trapped now. Toxteth where my mother will be waiting – that is the home I will go back to.

Mama I have been unhappy. I want to come home now. I will sit on your knee by the fire dear Mama, and you can weave stories of happier times.

Charles William Tayleur
Hampton House - July 1881

But the Wheel of Fortune had not finished with me yet. My beloved wife Mary Jane died while we were living at Abbots Oak in Ashby de la Zouch. Of course we should have been careful; we knew that she was frail after the birth of our little son in Brussels and she never seemed to be completely well after the ravages of measles, but we were so relieved to be united once more that we clung to each other and drew strength from our affection. Shortly after moving into Abbots Oak it was clear that she was once again expecting a child. We were joyful about this, for it is well known that the only way of recovering from the loss of a baby is to have another.

She was ill from the beginning, and became frailer with every passing month. I feared the outcome and tried not to let her see my anxiety, but I believe she knew that we would soon be parted. On the day when the baby was delivered I defied both the doctor and the nurse and went often into my wife's room, and we were able to offer each other comfort during our last hours together. Our little son Noel was born in the early morning. Mary Jane was very still and pale as the baby was lifted to her face, but she smiled at him and then at me, and looked content. I was only too aware of the lifelong pain of being denied the chance to say goodbye to a precious mother, and I sent for our children to come to the room. We all clung together by her bedside, kissed her hands and her cool cheeks, and I told them that she had to leave us and go to be with their other brother in heaven. They said their farewells and she heard them, and when she left us shortly afterwards she knew that she was loved.

I held my new son and feared for him. To lose a mother is the greatest tragedy that can befall a child. To lose a mother without ever having known her is even worse. I thought of Albert and his ceaseless search for a sense of his own value and felt determined that none of my children would ever suffer as he had. Since I was a boy I had felt responsible for the wellbeing of three younger brothers; now I was alone again with five children. I was never able to give my brothers happy lives, but I would dedicate myself to achieving that for the family that Mary Jane had given to me.

While I was grieving pitifully for my wife and organising wet nurses for my motherless newborn, my brother Albert's situation grew ever more precarious. He had always been a cause of grave worry, even as a baby when he was sent away with our mother and we had no idea of his whereabouts. He was now a troubled young man with poor health and little stamina, and he sought refuge in playing cards and drinking heavily. After our return from Vienna his debts grew alarmingly. I did what I could to help him but my own allowance was barely enough. Mary Ellen continued to ensure that funds from the estate were denied to us, and my father lived on interminably, slumped in his dark room in his own living hell. In 1877 Albert married Ellen Pitfield and we all hoped that this would give him a chance to live a more measured and sober life. It was too late for that. One year after his marriage he was declared to be bankrupt, with all the humiliation that such a state entails. I took on the lease of his home in Teddington to prevent the couple being thrown onto the street, but Albert was very ill and sickened rapidly.

"I cannot die before the lunatic," he said to me as I sat by his bed on one of my frequent visits, "If I die before he does I lose all hope of pulling myself out of this mire of debt." I did not feel that I could remind him at that moment of the uncertainty of the wills and the legacies for all of us. The possibility of gaining two thousand pounds seemed to be all that was keeping him alive. He was so thin that his bones almost appeared through his papery skin, and his poor wife fussed helplessly around him with tonics and quack remedies. I found the burden of Albert and his problems almost too much to bear. I missed Mary Jane inconsolably and my misery and loneliness were not lessened in any way by the passing of time. Only my beloved children kept me from following my wife into death.

But then, at last, my poor father died. It was May Day in 1879, when the girls and boys of the village were running past his windows to collect flowers from the hedgerows, the church bells were ringing and the fiddlers were tuning up for the dancing. Not one member of his family was with him as he passed out of the world that had dealt him such a cruel blow – not one of his sisters or brothers, not one of his sons, or his daughter, or his wife. There was just a servant in the room who would certainly not have held his hand, whispered words of reassurance, or prayed at the end. He had lately become completely blind and unable to rise from his chair, and spent the last weeks rambling and mumbling in a low tone. The doctor who signed his death certificate stated that he had died from old age; violent insanity had softened into simple senility. My father had taken twenty long years to die.

But the Battle of Wills could now commence at last, and the solicitors were anxious to resolve matters quickly for Albert's sake. It was abundantly clear to the Lunacy Commission that the will written by my father in January 1858 could not possibly be accepted as a sane, reliable statement of his wishes, and the first will was proved just four months after his death. But matters were not so easily resolved. I received a letter from Mr Kitson, the son of the solicitor in Torquay who felt so sure that my father was sane in that fateful week in 1858. "Unfortunately the settlement of your father's affairs cannot progress any further," he wrote. "Your brother Galfred Tayleur has written to us to advise that he is challenging the will that has been proved. Until a solution has been reached, it will not be possible to have access to any bank holdings, monies or properties whatsoever. May I suggest that a meeting with your brother could be the best way forward and may avoid a court case, which would be costly and cause unwelcome inroads into your father's estate?"

I was appalled, but wrote immediately to Galfred to inform him that I would shortly be travelling to London to meet him.

I took a cab to Galfred's chambers. He was by this time a partner in a successful legal company, and his room was impressively furnished. He was sitting behind a large desk when I was shown in and he rose to greet me, but did not cross the expensive carpet to shake my hand. This was unusual. I sat down on the hard chair on the other side of the desk and smiled at him.

"How is Eveline?" I asked.

"Eveline and Mother are both quite well thank you," he replied. "Although they are, of course, viewing their removal from Torquay with some trepidation."

"Have they made arrangements for accommodation when they leave Hampton?" I said, but hanging in the air between us was the idea that I was driving Eveline and her mother out of their home.

"We will establish a household together here in London," he replied.

"What a marvellous thing for Eveline!" I said, genuinely pleased for her. "The city will afford her many pleasures and the society here can offer her so much more than being holed up in Torquay."

Galfred shuffled some papers on his desk and started to talk without looking at me. "I am disappointed Charles, that we have so far been unable to negotiate a settlement which would render the division of our father's estate fair and just for Eveline and myself. I have been in correspondence with Kitson and our uncle John, as well as yourself, but every letter I receive insists that the estate cannot be divided further. I have noted that a decision has been made to increase Albert's portion to five thousand pounds, yet no increase has been made on my behalf, or Eveline's."

"As executors we have discussed this fully," I said, leaning forward towards him and attempting to catch his gaze, but he was looking steadfastly down at the papers in front of him. "We cannot understand why you consider the apportionments to be unfair. You and Eveline will receive a considerably greater sum than Cresswell and Edward because of arrangements that were made when our father married your mother."

Galfred frowned, and started to finger the ornate inkstand. I looked at his hands. They were a completely different size and shape from my own; smaller and finer - his mother's hands. He seemed to be selecting and measuring his words with great care before he spoke.

"It is not the will itself that Eveline and I consider to be unjust – it is the large amounts of money both you and your brothers extracted from the estate during the long period of time before our father finally died. You have all been supported by the estate for many years now, and received substantial cash payments when you married. Even Albert has had an allowance. All four of you made regular requests for increases in your allowances and the effect on the fortunes of the family was extremely detrimental. You are of course aware that there is considerably less value in the property and investments than was the case in 1858."

I was beginning to feel a rising anger towards Galfred. We had always enjoyed a warm and friendly relationship, but it now appeared that he had long been harbouring a deep resentment. I thought about my dear, much missed wife and the love she had felt for Eveline as a treasured sister, and was overcome by the sensation that I was once more losing something I had held dear.

"But you also received an allowance from the estate," I said.

"I was educated at my father's expense, which any gentleman's son would expect. As soon as my education was complete and I was able to earn my own living, that is what I chose to do. I have not married and made a claim for setting up a household, nor have I ever requested sums for furniture, travel or medical bills." He looked at me then, with a piercing, accusatory expression, and I did not know how to reply. I was back in the billiard room at Hampton and could almost feel the smooth, warm shape of the cue in my hand. My stepmother's words hung in the air; I had always remembered them, they were burned into my soul. She had called me a parasite and demanded that I sought gainful employment. She seemed to be with us in the room and the memory of that difficult time brought a bitter taste to my mouth.

"Eveline received nothing whatsoever," my brother was continuing. "The salary of her governess was paid by my mother as part of the running cost of the mansion. She has made no requests or demands and asked for nothing on the occasion of her coming of age. As the thirty thousand pounds from our grandfather now has to be divided between four of us, Eveline and I will receive little of our father's fortune, and this will provide only a meagre dowry for her. I therefore intend to pursue a statement of claim on the estate, on her behalf and my own."

"It is a matter of some urgency that our father's affairs are now settled quickly," I protested. "Albert's health is precarious. I do not believe he will live long. It is imperative that the money is released soon so that his debts can be discharged."

Galfred gave a sigh of impatience. "Albert was never acknowledged as a son by my father," he said. "I have no doubt whatsoever that he would be receiving nothing at all had my father retained his sanity to the last."

"He has been a much valued member of this family for the last twenty years," I argued. "We have tried to make amends for the cruel circumstances that rendered him cast out and rejected, all through no fault of his own. If you are correct in supposing that our father's hard attitude would never have changed, that would have been a very grave injustice indeed. I beg you not to resent assistance our brother received; he did not possess the advantages that were yours unstintingly from birth."

"I will not compromise my future and that of my sister so that Albert can be rescued from bankruptcy." Galfred replied, scowling. "His misfortunes are of his own making. His poor health has never prevented him indulging in alcohol and spending hour upon hour at the gaming tables. The will must remain unsettled until Eveline and I are treated fairly, and if that is too late for Albert then that is the way it must be."

I was appalled by Galfred's hard heartedness; it was something I had never suspected before. I decided to leave the subject of Albert well alone, and tried a different argument. "In order to provide you and Eveline with a greater share, it will be necessary to sell some of the property belonging to the estate," I said. I was finding it a challenge to frame my sentences in a coherent manner, quite muddled by the hard look on his face and the angry tone of his words. "You must understand Galfred, that I have a desire to pass on to my son as much of the family's assets as possible. I explained this to your mother some years ago, when she was angling to sell Sandwell and various other properties. It is our duty to keep the estate intact for the benefit of future generations."

"This is a spurious argument," Galfred said, pushing his heavy oak chair backwards so it grated on the parquet, and standing up. He strode over to the window and looked down at the street. "To be honest Charles, I have little interest in your children's future inheritance and feel no need whatsoever to protect it. You and your brothers have received thousands of pounds from the estate throughout the last twenty years, and I am claiming an equivalent amount for my sister and myself. If you are not willing to act in a decent, gentlemanly manner and arrange for the requested amount to be obtained for us, I will challenge you in court to settle the matter." He walked back to his desk and picked up a document, which he handed to me. I glanced through the pompous legal wording and came to the amount of his claim. If he succeeded and this was granted to him, I would be left with little property other than Hampton.

I stood up with a heavy heart. I did not know that Galfred had long believed that he and his sister had been so disadvantaged by the rest of us. I reached out to shake his hand, but he pretended not to see my gesture and moved straight to the door to see me out of his room. Our brotherly bond was broken. I knew that we would not meet again once the court case was done.

It was nearly a year before the case came to court. "Tayleur versus Tayleur" – the very worst kind of case – brother against brother, a civil war. With heavy irony it appeared that Galfred and Eveline were also fighting their own mother. Mary Ellen was one of the executors of the will and her name appeared alongside my uncle John's and my own. But both my stepmother and my sister stayed away from the court room and we had only Galfred to face.

The judge accepted that Galfred and Eveline had received far less from my father's fortune than the rest of us, and also that Eveline must have a worthy dowry. However, he also took into consideration the fact that neither had married and therefore had no children, whereas I have a family of five. His ruling left me with several properties and a better income than I had feared, and the will was settled at long last.

With probate finally granted to us, my uncle and I made a point of paying Albert's debts before we did anything else. Albert and Ellen were able to live in comfort for just one year before my poor brother died.

It has taken a further year to have the bankruptcy annulled, but it had to be done to preserve the respectability and honour of his wife. Albert was a casualty of circumstance, his whole life blighted by the misunderstanding of his birth.

Then I wrote to my stepmother to remind her that Hampton was mine and could she therefore vacate it forthwith. As soon as my uncle confirmed that she and Eveline had indeed left, I made the journey to Torquay with my four younger children and as many of our personal possessions as we could fit into the hired carriage and waggons.

The children were wildly excited and chattered throughout the miles about their new home, their own bedrooms and the possibilities for adventure within the grounds. They plied me with constant questions for, never having seen Hampton, they were anxious to ascertain some idea of the delights awaiting them in St Marychurch. I was grateful for their tireless exuberance as it left me with no chance of examining my own feelings, which were torn about indeed.

We passed the crenelated gateposts at last, now pocked and weathered, passed the lodge where the yapping dog no longer bounded out, and rounded the corner where the mansion came into view. At that moment the old sick sinking feeling assailed me, just as it did during the one summer I spent here as a boy, every time our carriage rattled back up this very drive and I knew there would be dark times to be endured. The house seemed smaller somehow; the stucco was greying, the paint on the window frames was peeling and ivy was clutching its way over much of the front façade, but the same crimson damask drapes were smothering the windows, making the house look closed up and withdrawn. The ground by the entrance appeared much disturbed, no doubt by my stepmother's carriage and the conveyances containing her possessions, and also by my uncle's horse. I knew that he had been here before Mary Ellen left in order to check through the inventory in her presence, and ensure that she had been as good as her word and left the mansion exactly as it had been in 1859. When my father was declared to be insane the contents of Hampton were listed in meticulous detail, and my stepmother was required to sign the document and commit herself to handing everything back to the estate, undamaged and intact, on my father's death. They must all have thought that this would not be for long, that he would die within a short time and she would be just a temporary chatelaine. But for nearly twenty-one long years she remained here, a widow who was not a widow, protecting the terrible truth from prying neighbours and preserving the house as if in aspic – from the fine mahogany four posters and marble inlaid tables to the pickle jars, curtain tassels and daisy rakes.

It was only when I stepped through the front door and entered the main hall that I realised exactly what effect that signed inventory had produced on the mansion and Mary Ellen's life. The floor was covered in the same Persian patterned Brussels carpet, but it was faded, and threadbare by each of the doors that led off the hall. I looked up at the high glass atrium, now grimy and hung with dust-laden cobwebs suspended in skeins like the rigging on a ghost ship. The same paintings hung on the walls, many looking foxed and cracked, and the brass stair rods were dark and dull. The house seemed to have been holding its breath since the moment my father had lost his mind.

The flustered maid who had opened the door was much occupied with the children's coats and luggage. I enquired as to the whereabouts of the butler and instructed her to open the curtains in every room and pull up the blinds. She looked startled but scuttled into the drawing room to start the long process of letting light in. I then stood quite still and drew in the air of the house. From my boyhood I remembered the mansion smelling of new paint and plaster, wax polish, roasting meat and sometimes the sickly taint from the gas lights. That taint was there yet, along with the fustiness of old fabrics, neglected, dusty corners and something suggesting boiled senna pods.

The children were ecstatic and had already commenced scampering into every room and endeavouring to examine everything at once. Katherine grasped my hand while I was still waiting for the butler to put in an appearance. "Come Papa – we have discovered your study – let me show you," and she pulled me into that room full of memories. I found myself once again in the presence of my father's oak writing desk with the ebony inkstand, the model of the Alps and the two globes, his Morocco easy chair and rows and rows of his books, no doubt untouched since he last pulled down a volume. It was all completely unchanged since the day he pushed me out of the door with such violence that I smashed into the staircase. The smell in here was certainly the same as it had always been – a mixture of hair oil, leather and musty paper.

I sat rather gingerly at the desk and ran my fingers across it, but my reverie was interrupted by Elizabeth, Ada and Katherine tumbling into the room together, their faces alight with excitement.

"Papa – you must come and look in the kitchen yard..."

"There is the dearest doghouse you ever saw..."

"It is simply the most enormous doghouse! May we have lots of dogs to live in it?"

"Well," I replied, "I present you with a mansion, a farmery and your own cliff and you fall in love with the old doghouse!" I smiled down at them rather sadly. "When I was staying here I was always made to feel that the doghouse was the proper place to take myself off to."

They all stopped and clung round me. Katherine squeezed my hand. "Dearest Dad – who could possibly ever be unkind to you?" and then they were off on their explorations once more, Ada turning back briefly to ask which rooms they may choose as their own.

"You may all choose whichever you wish. I would like you to have good views of the park, and remember Alec – choose a fine room for him for when he is home from school."

"He can have the nursery," Ada giggled, but I winced as I recalled Edward's lonely sojourn there, and our rooms at the end of the servants' corridor.

"We will shut the nurseries for now," I replied. "We can open them up again when you present me with grandchildren." Ada found this highly amusing, and her laughter echoed round the hall as she flew up the dusty stairs.

Once the children were in the bedrooms the house seemed eerily quiet. There was still no sign of the butler; perhaps he had taken himself off to Torquay to replenish the wine stocks. Now and again I could hear shouts and eerie laughs. Were these made by my children? Or in some strange way had my father's screams and ravings been caught in the walls, to seep out forever as a ghastly enactment of the onset of his lunacy? I was looking inside the drawers of the desk when a particularly gruesome screech had me on my feet and climbing the stairs two at a time. It was clear as soon as I reached the landing that all the children were in the bedroom that had belonged to my stepmother, and making quite a commotion.

I had never been in the grandest bedroom before, and the first thing that struck me was the heaviness of the mahogany furniture, of which there seemed to be a large amount. The children had discovered an old crinoline hanging on a stand, and Noel appeared to be impersonating a wild animal imprisoned within its cage-like structure. He was growling and roaring and lunging at the girls' hands as they pretended to offer him food through the frame. They were all enjoying the game enormously, and disturbing a fair amount of dust which was floating in the sunlight. I sat down on the couch to watch them, while they explained that they had captured this fearsome creature in a jungle deep in Africa and brought it home for their private zoo. I enquired as to how they would feed it and they assured me that it liked to eat sardines and coddled egg. Noel was obligingly savage and noisome until he tired of it, and all the children sank onto the couch with me, quite tired out after their exertions.

To my surprise Ada had chosen this bedroom for herself, and I realised that I could not bear the thought of my beautiful daughter making this fetid place her own. I walked round the room and observed at once that no cleaning had been done – presumably my stepmother had taken her maid away with her. Hair grips lay scattered on the dressing table along with grimy glass bottles containing desiccated dregs, the wash stand was covered with stains and hairs and there was a worn-out scrap of soap in a dish. The crimson damask bed curtains were faded and laden with old dust; the bed sheets had not been changed for some time and exuded a damp, musty smell.

Noel had discovered the chamber pot and held it aloft like a trophy. I felt sick with revulsion and took it from him. It was stained and filthy. I grasped the sash window and forced it upwards, then flung the chamber pot out to the garden below. It smashed into several pieces. Katherine, Elizabeth and Noel were delighted by this new game and hung out of the window to see the broken pot, but Ada remonstrated with me. "Papa – the chamber pot is part of a set – look at all these matching pieces. I have never had such a beautiful chamber service."

"I will take you to Exeter and buy you a chamber service with a hundred matching pieces if that is what you want, but I will not have you using that one."

Ada looked thoughtful. "Is that because your stepmother was unkind to you?" she asked.

"I wish for us to make a fresh start in this house and leave the past behind," I said. "This is our home now and I want you to have your own nice things in it and not have to use an old woman's cast-offs."

"Is Mary Ellen coming back Papa? Her clothes are still hanging in the wardrobe."

I wrenched the heavy wardrobe open and saw at once that Ada was right. In fact it looked as if my stepmother had taken very little with her. "Take Noel to the kitchen and ask for sacks," I said. "Flour sacks, potato sacks, anything will do. If they do not have many then go to the farm." They galloped off down the stairs.

Meanwhile I pulled her stale garments out of the wardrobe and discovered more in a chest of drawers. When the children hurried back I stuffed the clothes into the sacks. There was even a hairpiece of greasy red hair which Noel showed signs of coveting, but I did not want anything at all to remain. Then I carried the sacks out onto the landing and heaved them, one at a time, over the banisters. The children were squealing with delight and servants appeared in the hall below, watching with horror as I hurled yet more of their erstwhile mistress's trappings into the void of the stairwell.

The butler had arrived at last, and was hurrying up the back stairs to join us on the landing. "Do you require assistance, sir?" he asked.

"I am afraid I do not know your name," I replied. "As yet no details of the household staff have been given to me."

"My name is Thomas Howe, sir. I will make sure you have a full list of the staff at once. I will carry the remaining bags downstairs for you, sir."

"We would much rather throw them over the banisters," Noel piped up, and he scampered back into the bedroom and proceeded to drag out the rest.

"Howe, please store all these sacks in an outhouse until Mrs Tayleur sends for them."

"In an outhouse, sir?"

"In an outhouse, please Howe." The butler raised his eyebrows and went off towards the back stairs. No doubt he had been used to ruling the roost when only Eveline and my stepmother were living here, but he was in for a shock now.

My stepmother's bedroom still seemed to be entirely unsuitable for Ada. I looked at the huge mahogany four poster bedstead with distaste and knew that I could not allow my daughter to sleep where Mary Ellen and my father had pleasured each other. "We will go to Exeter and buy you a new bed without these ghastly drapes," I told Ada, and I grasped the bed curtains and pulled hard. Some part of the bed was too old to resist and the four poster frame itself broke apart sending poles, canopy, pelmets and drapes crashing onto the mattress and the floor. I pulled the bell and told the maid to clear the mess and clean the room until it shone. Then I brushed the dust from my coat and went out onto the landing.

Noel had chosen the front bedroom so that he could see the high street and watch the great dray horses delivering barrels to The Dolphin. Elizabeth and Katherine were much taken with the upstairs drawing room but felt worried because it was not a bedroom.

"It is meant as a private sanctuary to which the ladies of the house can withdraw, so it is entirely appropriate for the two of you to have it as your own room. We will put the dolls' house in there and buy new, pretty beds. Have you all decided which bedroom I may have?"

They led me into the next room. It was a fine bedroom with views of the garden and the park beyond, but it had been my father's room. Something about the feeling in there had dissuaded them from claiming it, and they didn't stay with me now, but capered off down the corridor to look at the other bedrooms and the nurseries. There was no fine four poster in here but only an iron slump bedstead such as the servants slept in. Had the doctors decreed that bed hangings would be dangerous for a lunatic? My imagination fired up instantly and the image of my father was before me, his hair tousled and wild, his eyes wide and staring, his shaking hands wrapping the bed curtain tightly round his own throat. I shook my head to rid myself of this and walked over to the window. It certainly seemed that all the furniture had been removed from the room. There remained only a mahogany washstand and towel horse. Had he harmed himself as he thrashed around in his ravings and collided with heavy wardrobes and chests?

There was an elegant Regency fireplace in the room, constructed like many in the mansion from fine grey marble. Even though the room had clearly been unused for many years, there were still cinders within the black iron hearth. I walked over and sifted through them. Were these the remains of the very fire in which my father told the doctor to throw his old will? Did these ashes witness my poor mad father sweltering with fever, pacing and rambling around the room and desperately endeavouring to keep a hold on his wits?

I decided to open the window and let in some fresh air. The bottom sash was nailed shut but I was able, with some difficulty, to release the brass clasp and pull down the upper one. It was stiff and jerky and several flakes of yellowing paint came down with it. I noticed at once that the garden had been rather neglected; the grass was badly in need of a mow and weeds were enveloping the flower beds, but I knew the children would be delighted to have such a space in which to play. I could see the ornamental garden with its raised beds and pathways, but the fountain was rusty and dry and the paths were barely discernible under ivy and dandelions. I made a mental note to send for the gardener first thing in the morning.

I wondered if the shutters would pull across easily or whether they required attention before I retired for the night. The small round handles were wobbly but still strong enough to take the weight of each shutter, and the planks on both sides slid into position quite smoothly. As I went to lift the metal bar to secure them I noticed some pencil writing on the wall at the side of the window, previously obscured by the shutter. Bending near I read,

"I the Lord have called thee in righteousness to open the blind eyes, to bring the prisoners from the prison, and them that sit in darkness out of the prison house."

The words were faded and the letters tremulous, but it was unmistakably my father's hand. What on earth had he suffered when this room had been his prison and he had sat here in darkness?

I rang the bell for Howe and explained to him that I had no wish to sleep on an iron slump bed. I told him to have a proper bedstead brought in from one of the bedrooms that the children were not using, and requested a wardrobe, chest of drawers and dressing glass also.

"Shall I bring a couch and easy chairs, sir?"

"I don't think I will be spending much time in this room, Howe. Just collect anything else you think I may need."

"Very good, sir. Shall I serve tea in your study?"

"No thank you – I will have tea in the drawing room with the children. I take all my meals with them, and the younger ones eat in the dining room – no nursery meals here – do you understand?"

"Certainly sir – I will advise the cook."

During tea we all examined the drawing room as keenly as Livingstone on the Zambesi. Elizabeth and Katherine played the rosewood pianoforte while Noel exclaimed over the silver elephants and gold peacocks. "This room is so full of beautiful things," Ada observed, "But I hardly dare breathe in case I knock against one of those stands and send several priceless ornaments tipping onto the carpet."

"I will get some of those household magazines for you," I said. "And you can arrange the room in a modern style."

Elizabeth laughed. "Papa – Exeter will be completely empty when we have finished our shopping trip! When can we go?

"I don't see why we can't go tomorrow," I replied.

"Can we buy the dog first?" asked Noel.

The spell cast by the inventory was already lifting. Howe had rescued a mahogany case of insects and fish from the kitchen passage and brought it for Noel to inspect. I remembered this case from my grandfather's house in Toxteth and I had loved it when I was a boy. The brittle backed beetles were still basking beneath the glass, their spiny legs arranged neatly, and the fish had somehow retained their shine and a fair amount of their colour as their glass eyes stared at us from faces that had flicked in and out of long ago rivers. Noel requested that the case should be hung in the hall so we could all admire it on a regular basis and this was already underway. The maids were replacing the curtains in the best bedroom with chintz, and bringing painted furniture for the children's rooms to replace the heavy mahogany. Noel had discovered a fine rocking horse in one of the nurseries and felt this should be brought into the drawing room, but we managed to persuade him that the library would be a safer option. "If he has to go into the library to ride his horse, he may even pick up a book once in a while," Ada reasoned.

I went into the study after tea and sensed that things had already begun to change. My children had moved through the house like the beaters at a hunt, rooting out sadness, dispelling the dark secrets and horrors of the past and filling the building with their happy spirits. I wished with all my heart that Mary Jane was here with us, turning the neglected mansion into a loving home and taking her rightful place as the squire's wife. She never left my thoughts, and I tried always to be the father she would want me to be.

The children had now found the peachery at the front of the house, right outside the study window, and I watched them clambering through, excitedly examining the shrivelled branches for evidence of a crop for the summer. Many of the glass panes were cracked or broken and I was concerned that they might injure themselves. I tried to push up the sash of the window but realised that it had not been opened for many years. I took the sash pulls in my hand and pulled hard. Perhaps the last person to open this window had been my father, tugging these same sash pulls in his impatient way, probably to remonstrate with the gardener or the man bringing round the carriage. Katherine saw me and came bounding out of the peachery onto the flower bed under the window. I bent down so that her nose was inches from mine.

"Are the peach trees dead Papa? Will they come back for this summer? I thought Torquay was good for hot trees."

"Take care of Noel near the broken glass. We will nurse the peach trees back to health, sweetheart, even if we have to give each one its own warming pan."

Katherine laughed and hurried back to Noel so she could steer him away from the dangers. I decided to investigate the great grey safe behind my father's desk, my uncle having left the key for me. The safe was housed in a cupboard and, as I opened this, the hairs on the back of my neck stood up and I felt suddenly very cold. The safe had an eerie feeling about it but the documents it contained were easily removed and piled on the desk. I knew that many of the papers had been taken away and were in the possession of the Lunacy Commission, but there were documents pertaining to properties no longer owned by the estate, letters regarding repairs to the mansion, correspondence concerning an old court case with a tradesman who had painted the walls before the plaster was dry and a large number of newspapers dating from the years my father lived in the house. He had not kept any of the letters my brothers and I had written to him from boarding school, although it could of course have been my stepmother who discarded them.

And then, as I was flicking through a sheaf of yellowing receipts, I came across a letter with my own name on the front. The seal was unbroken and I recognised the sweet, sloping handwriting immediately. It was a letter from my mother. It must have been kept from me for twenty-seven years.

I sank onto the chair and broke the seal carefully with my father's knife. My hands were shaking and my tears started to fall as soon as I began to read.

"My darling Charlie,

I am rather ill at present. I do not know what the cause could be, except that I have been torn away from my three precious sons and so no longer have any reason left to live.

I think of nothing but you. I worry that you are not being cared for with sufficient love and not having fun like we always did. Do you remember how we danced? I want you to dance often Charlie, and have a life full of joy.

Try not to judge me too harshly for what I did. Consider the punishment that has been inflicted upon me and decide yourself whether it was just. A few weeks of folly and I have lost my name, my home and my beloved children – in fact my whole life. And yet I did not steal another person's property or cause harm to any living being, but the consequences seem to be as harsh as those meted out to murderers. If we were of the Catholic faith I could throw myself onto the floor of a confessional and beg for forgiveness from a priest. And if I did, what could I say to him? That I have loved outside marriage to the point of madness? That is how it all seems Charlie – my sane wits deserted me and I lost all reason.

One does not seek lunacy or ever expect it, but while I was under its influence life was wilder and brighter than I had ever known it. I felt such real happiness whenever I thought about Arthur Lennox, or heard mention of his name, or spent time in his company. He was not handsome, as your father undoubtedly is, but he was playful and closely attentive, and I felt of greater worth because he valued me.

Doubtless you have been told of the infamous occasion when I went to his Club and asked for him to be brought to me. Such behaviour is unheard of, and served to advertise the sinful nature of our relationship, but I was impervious, wrapped in the cloak of my derangement, caring nothing for the stares of strangers or their opinions of me. Arthur and I had arranged to meet that afternoon, but I had waited and waited in growing misery, alarm and despair, and he did not come. I had to hear his reasons for this, and ask him the true meaning of his abandonment of our plans.

The Secretary of the Club was brought to meet me, and he sent a servant to enquire for Arthur. Several gentlemen stood around the hall, their punctilious manners disguising their surprise and curiosity. Arthur attempted to convince them that I had called on an urgent matter of business, but my distress, which only increased as he appeared at the top of the stairs, and the manner in which I clung to his arm as soon as he reached the hall, made the exact nature of our friendship clear to every person present.

But there was no cure for me; we saw each other still. I could not let him stop, and he was happy to leave his wife and children in their fine house and seek pleasure in my company. In the end I had no free will whatsoever; I had lost the right to that. Your father sent me away without a chance to speak, or to swear that I would be different from then on. My whole life simply fell away from me, and the madness with it, and I was left to writhe with regret, shame, grief and longing for my children.

Your prosaic, clear-minded father would never be able to understand how a fever of the brain assailed me and that for those few months I was not myself. I had found a type of love that had always been denied to me, but the cost was high. I swear to you that Albert Gresley is your true brother and he will need you. Do take care of him Charlie; your father refuses to believe the truth about him and I dread to think of him discarded and alone when I am no longer here. I know you will not fail him because you have a deep goodness in your nature and you have always been such a kind boy.

All that – being a wife, a mistress, a lover – was as nothing compared with being a mother. Whatever crime I committed and whatever punishment I deserved, I know that I raised three fine boys who will be admirable men.

I was indeed a fortunate woman to have you, Cresswell and Edward for my sons and the years we spent together were the happiest of my life. I can only wish now for happy lives for the four of you. Above all else I hope and pray that nothing and nobody will ever come between you and your children, and that you will enjoy their love and their company for the whole of your life.

Never doubt the great love I have for you; I can only pray that one day your dear, kind heart will persuade you to forgive me.

Your loving Mama."

Throughout my reading of this letter I had to hold the pages carefully to prevent damage to them from the steady flow of my tears. I folded it and placed it safely on the desk in front of me, and concentrated on the images of my mother that the reading had produced in my mind. I realised that there had never been any need at all for me to forgive her – I had never, for one single minute, felt that she was to blame. In my memory she had always been her sweet, funny, loving self, and it was not she who had wronged us. And then I knew, without any doubt, that there would be no mistress at Hampton until my children were grown, and only then would I look for a kindly soul who could understand that Alec, Ada, Katherine, Elizabeth and Noel would hold my heart forever.

Charles William Tayleur's granddaughter, Katherine Baker, was born at Hampton House in 1891.
He married Louisa Wolfe in 1896, twenty-two years after inheriting the mansion.

The End